Meant for You

Honeybrook Hollow

Nora Everly

Copyright © 2026 by Nora Everly

All rights reserved.

This book is a work of fiction. Any resemblance to actual persons, living or dead or undead, events, or locales is entirely coincidental.

No part of this book may be reproduced in any form or by any electronic or mechanical means, including information storage and retrieval systems, without written permission from the author, except for the use of brief quotations in a book review.

Any use of this publication to "train" generative artificial intelligence (AI) technologies to generate text is expressly prohibited.

Edits: Emerald Edits

Proofreading: Elizabeth Taylor

Cover Design: Yummy Book Covers

Chapter 1
Nate

This was our first morning waking up in Honeybrook Hollow as residents, not visitors.

And for the first time in months, I could try to relax. Even with the moving mess and the settling-in nerves, the morning felt different. Lighter. Filled with possibilities. The house didn't feel lived-in yet—more like it was holding its breath, waiting to see who we'd become within its walls.

Morning light filtered through the lace curtains my grandmother insisted I keep ("They soften a man," she'd said, patting my cheek), casting soft gold shapes across the wood floors. The heater grumbled to life, rattling like it was waiting for retirement. Somewhere in the kitchen, a faucet dripped steadily, a reminder of the thousand small tasks waiting for me.

But the bottom line was, Honeybrook Hollow was where I'd spent the best parts of my childhood—summer weeks with my grandparents, snowball fights on

Sycamore Street with the neighborhood kids during Christmas vacation, afternoons watching my grandfather fix things in the Pennywhistle Pantry's back room and telling me stories while he worked.

The Pennywhistle Pantry was my grandparents' pride, joy, and decades-long labor of love. A true 1950s style diner, all gleaming chrome and red vinyl booths, the kind of place where people had their *usuals* and their favorite stools and a standing appointment with the Friday night special. It wasn't just a business in Honeybrook Hollow; it was a landmark, woven into the town's memory like a familiar melody. Kids grew up there. Couples had first dates there. Folks celebrated birthdays and big moments there. And now it was mine to take care of. Mine to carry forward.

I'd grown up in Portland, an only child with two parents who loved me in the busy, career-focused, we-show-it-in-practical-ways sort of manner. We weren't a call-every-day family, and that was okay. But they both adored my daughter, Matilda—lovingly known as Tilly—with an intensity that softened all the old distance between us. If that were the version of close they could manage, I'd take it.

A year ago, I'd been an attorney downtown, running on caffeine, anxiety, and the constant fear of being five minutes late to daycare pickup. My life had been fast-paced, polished, successful—and absolutely wrong for raising a little girl who deserved more than squeezed-in evenings and exhausted weekends.

My grandparents saw it long before I admitted it.

"You need more time," Grandma had said. "And Honeybrook Hollow has plenty of that."

So when they decided to retire to a quiet senior condo across town, I stepped into their shoes at the Pennywhistle and now we were officially moved into their house. No more endless litigation, no more eighty-hour weeks—just a diner with a soul of its own, a small town that felt like it could be a real home, and a chance to give Tilly a childhood that didn't have to be rushed.

A thud rattled the upstairs floor.

Followed by a triumphant, "DAAADDY! COME LOOK!"

I jogged upstairs. Tilly burst out of her new bedroom wearing a makeshift superhero cape and pajamas covered in cartoon mermaids. Her hair—my favorite strawberry blonde sunburst—stuck up as though she'd slept inside a wind tunnel.

"I decorated my whole room," she announced proudly. "And made a bed for Waffles." She gestured to the corner where her favorite stuffed reindeer was tucked into a toy cradle.

"Already?" Behind her, the closet doors were plastered with bright, cheerful stickers—smiling suns, glittery rainbows, and a parade of cartoon animals, each one stuck at kid-level and slightly askew. Stuffed animals crowded every surface: bears perched on the window ledge, floppy dogs stacked on the bed, and a plush unicorn peeking out from a laundry basket, making the room feel like a cozy miniature zoo.

"I'm fast."

She was because she had needed to be. Because in our old life, everything moved too fast, and she learned to keep up.

But here? She could slow down. Honeybrook Hollow wasn't just charming; it had a slower pace. This town held pieces of my childhood I'd forgotten I missed until I came back here to stay—the maple-lined streets, the snow-dusted rooftops, the way each porch had its own kind of welcome. A town where my grandparents were ten minutes away instead of a two-hour drive. Where people waved when you walked by and asked how you were.

"Can we go get cocoa?" she asked, eyes wide.

"Right now? We have a lot left to do."

"You said we could have cocoa today because we moved."

I frowned. "No, I said we *might*—"

"Daaaaaad."

Lois barked in agreement. Lois had come into my life the same week Tilly and I landed in Honeybrook Hollow —a two-year-old chocolate lab we'd rescued from the shelter while living in a short-term rental, both of us already dreaming about the day she'd finally have a real backyard to tear through like it was hers.

"I'm outnumbered," I sighed. "And I haven't grocery shopped yet. Let's go."

The Coffee Cabin came into view as we walked around the corner into town. Log siding. White trim. Twinkle lights that stayed up year-round because, as far as I could tell, Honeybrook Hollow had a firm policy about sparkling. A wooden porch with a walk-up window and a tiny counter with two stools. The porch was already scattered with early morning footprints pressed into the light dusting of snow.

The giant chalkboard sign out front read:

COCOA OF THE DAY:
HOLIDAY HANGOVER
Chocolate + Peppermint
(post-holiday coping skills cost extra)

Tilly gasped like she'd rediscovered the portal to Narnia and sprinted ahead with Waffles the reindeer tucked tight under one arm.

I caught up just in time for the window to slide open with a soft chime—

And there she was.

Eliza Darlington.

I spotted her instantly. It was hard not to—Eliza had been burned into my memory from the day she became Tilly's favorite Christmas Coffee Elf. That smile, that sass, that spark I'd been thinking about since December, the first time we'd come to the Coffee Cabin and discovered one of the best things about Honeybrook Hollow. I'd asked her out after that, before everything turned upside down. We were into the new year now and standing here, watching her look up at me with that same knowing smirk... yeah. The date we never had suddenly felt like unfinished business.

Honey brown hair tied up in a messy knot, wisps escaping around her face like they couldn't stand to be contained. A fitted black turtleneck sweater under her Coffee Cabin apron. Eyes sharp and assessing—until they flicked to Tilly and softened, then landed on me and did something else entirely. Something electric. Something like a spark jumping between two live wires.

I still remember the first time I met her—a couple of weeks before Christmas, the air cold enough to bite, and the Coffee Cabin glowing like a little lantern in the snow. Tilly had insisted on hot cocoa, and when Eliza leaned out of that walk-up window, wearing a red beanie and the most unimpressed expression I'd ever seen on someone serving festive peppermint lattes, something in my chest shifted. She teased me about ordering a boring drink and charmed Tilly with a mountain of whipped cream and extra marshmallows. I left that day knowing two things: her coffee ruined me for all other coffee, and I was in real, heart-thumping trouble—from the very first sarcastic smile she threw my way.

"Morning," she said, leaning one elbow on the counter. Her voice always had the tiniest rasp, like she laughed more than she let on.

"Morning," I echoed, trying to hide my reaction to being near her. Her smile hit me as hard as it always did. My god, she was gorgeous.

"You're early. And looking surprisingly awake." She eyed me suspiciously and smiled. It was tiny and involuntary, like she wished she could shove it back inside, but it was already too late. "Blink twice if you're being held hostage by adult responsibility."

I blinked theatrically, then grinned. "Twice? Does that mean I'm allowed a rescue cup of coffee?" Tilly giggled—loud and irrepressible—drawing Eliza's gaze back to her, and for a moment, the playful tension in the air felt warmer than the steam rising from the espresso machine. The space between us buzzed with quiet anticipation, like we could sense this morning was a little different from all the others. "I'm fine. Once I figured out where the good coffee lived in this town, survival became possible."

Eliza's lips quirked at the corner. I could feel Tilly's excitement bubbling next to me, her energy somehow magnifying every tiny moment. As Eliza reached for a stack of paper cups, her fingers danced with practiced ease, and for a split second, I wondered how many quiet mornings she'd spent behind that window, watching the town wake up.

This was always the part I wasn't prepared for. The way her gaze lingered a beat too long on mine. The tug in my stomach when she would lift a brow like she was already judging my life choices, and something hilarious was on the tip of her tongue to say about it.

"Well," she said, voice smooth and dry, "I see you've brought the dog who thinks she's entitled to half my tips."

With impeccable timing, nose twitching like she was on a mission from the Bank of Dog. Lois made a beeline for the tip jar, hopping up, front legs on the counter, to sniff it with such theatrical suspicion you'd think she was checking for counterfeit bills. Every time we came here, without fail, she inspected those crumpled dollar bills and handfuls of coins as if searching for the one magical tip that smelled faintly of beef jerky. Eliza just laughed, nudging the jar a little closer so she could complete her financial audit.

Tilly hopped onto a stool and pressed her mittened hands to the counter. "It's our first day in our new house!"

Eliza leaned over, resting her chin briefly in her hand as she considered us. "So, what's the plan for today? Unpacking? Exploring?" Her eyes flicked to Tilly, then back to me, and for a second, it felt like the three of us were in on a secret.

The low hum of the espresso machine filled the silence before Tilly piped up, "Both! We're going to make it the best house ever." I couldn't help but smile—hopeful, a little nervous, and undeniably grateful for this brand-new beginning.

She slid a hot cocoa toward Tilly—extra marshmallows, of course. Eliza always remembered.

"So," she said, filling a to-go cup with practiced ease, "you're officially a Honeybrook Hollow resident now. How's the adjustment? Any signs of culture shock?"

"A few," I admitted. "It's quieter than I'm used to."

She handed me my coffee. "Give it time," she said. "Places warm up once they decide you're not a flight risk. You'll get used to it."

I raised a brow. "That a Coffee Cabin proverb?"

"It is," she deadpanned. "Available in cross-stitch, limited edition."

A laugh punched right out of me. "You're trouble."

She smirked. "And yet you keep coming back."

I laughed. God, she was quick. And guarded. And gorgeous. And I'd been thinking about her way more than was appropriate.

Tilly slurped whipped cream. Lois stared longingly at Eliza.

I took a sip, stupidly pleased that she made my order without asking what I wanted. "You remembered."

"Of course I did," she said. "You're very memorable."

"...Memorable?"

She froze. "I meant your *order* is memorable. Not— you. I'm going to walk into the woods and let the raccoons claim me."

I laughed. "Too late. Damage done. Now I'm wondering which part of me is so memorable."

"Absolutely not," she said, pointing at me with her stir stick. "We are not exploring that sentence. Subject changed. Immediately. So. Um. You like the new place?" she asked, attempting to drive the conversation back to casual, but her eyes flicked up to mine like the answer mattered and gave her away.

"I do," I said. "Still figuring out where everything goes."

"Organization is important. I've been here a little over a year and still can't find my potato peeler."

I smiled. "Maybe it's in the same dimension as all the missing socks."

We stood there a second too long. Not awkward—just acutely aware of each other and the near date we'd never gone on. Of the way our Christmas time flirtation had felt like a beginning we didn't know how to follow up on. The silence stretched between us. Warm. Charged. Dangerously good.

A car pulled into the drive-thru, breaking the spell. Eliza straightened, tucking a loose strand of hair behind her ear like she needed to hide how flustered she suddenly looked.

"Duty calls," she said softly, brushing a stray curl behind her ear. "Go enjoy the snow before it melts."

"We'll be back tomorrow."

Her smile was small but genuine. "Good. I mean… I'll be here anyway."

I tipped my head. "You could admit you like seeing us."

Her eyes narrowed—just enough to hide the shimmer of amusement. "You are awfully sure of yourself for someone who told me he tripped over a moving box yesterday."

I leaned in a little, "I maintain the box launched a coordinated attack."

She snorted, shaking her head, but the corners of her mouth softened in a way that made something warm unfurl in my chest.

She shook her head, biting back another smile. "Goodbye, Nate."

"Bye, Eliza."

"Bye, Eliza!" Tilly yelled.

Eliza's expression softened for Tilly—so visibly it almost knocked the breath out of me. "See you, sweetheart."

As we walked away—Tilly skipping, Lois trotting—I couldn't stop myself from glancing back.

She was leaning on the counter, watching us.

When our eyes met, she flushed and turned to help her customer at the drive-thru.

Something warm and certain settled in my heart.

I had moved here for Tilly. For stability. For a life that felt like home.

I hadn't expected the woman at the coffee window to make Honeybrook Hollow feel like all of that—and something more.

Chapter 2
Eliza

The smell of espresso had soaked into my hair, my clothes, and probably my soul. Currently, I was scrubbing whipped cream residue off the countertop while pretending that the walk-up window hadn't just hosted the most painfully charming father-daughter duo in the entire state of Oregon.

Nate Winters. And his adorable four-year-old accomplice. And let us not forget the cutest chocolate lab in existence, Lois, who had barked exactly once, as if to announce their presence like a canine herald of doom—or romance, depending on how today played out.

I'd given him sass, naturally. That was the only language I spoke fluently. And he'd stood there with that easy grin, watching me with those infuriatingly gorgeous, kind eyes like he actually liked me. Not in a general, polite-customer kind of way—but in a way that made my pulse skitter and my brain short-circuit.

I couldn't quit thinking about him. He might wear

the flannel and jeans now, but there was something else there, something polished right beneath the worn edges. It didn't help that he also wore an expensive dark grey Chesterfield coat over his worn flannel, highlighting the clash of his two worlds. Broad shoulders and solid thighs, all quiet strength and devastating good looks, the kind that made my thoughts go pleasantly fuzzy around the edges. His dark hair had just the faintest hint of grey at the temples, and those sharp brown eyes, steady, intelligent, missing nothing, had lingered on me long enough to feel intentional.

The way he'd listened, really listened, head tipped slightly like he was filing things away. The quick, precise smile he'd used when I teased him, like he knew exactly how to play along and still come out ahead. He didn't fumble his words. Didn't rush. Spoke with the kind of easy confidence that came from knowing how to hold a room even when he was standing at a walk-up coffee window ordering hot chocolate with extra marshmallows for a little girl.

It was subtle, but the sharpness was still there, tucked neatly under the dad uniform and adorable beanie hat, waiting to be noticed. Sweet and sharp. Warm and wary. I shook my head, annoyed with myself, and turned back to the espresso machine, determined to think about literally anything else.

"Don't look at me like that," I muttered to the espresso machine.

It hissed.

"Exactly. I don't need this right now. Complications."

I'd already let this slip through my fingers once. Nate had asked me out not long after he and Tilly arrived in Honeybrook Hollow—nothing flashy, just coffee, maybe dinner. I'd said yes, because I wanted to get to know him better. And then the holidays hit. The Coffee Cabin was nonstop, Nate was moving and learning how to navigate a whole new life, and we both got busy in the quiet, avoidant way that lets time do the hard part for you. The date never happened. We never talked about it. We just kept orbiting each other, pretending the *almost* wasn't still there.

The bell over the door jingled, and I glanced up to see my sister, Cara, striding in with a book in one hand and a bag from Something Sweet, our sister Piper's bakery, in the other.

She breezed in, her energy as unmistakable as ever. Dressed like a sexy nerd—her thick-rimmed glasses perched perfectly on her nose, hair piled up in a messy bun, and underneath her winter coat, a fitted cardigan over a graphic tee—she looked like she'd stepped out of an indie rom-com. We'd always been told we resembled each other: same big eyes, strong brow, and the kind of stubborn chin that made people ask if we were sisters.

"I brought sustenance," she said, holding up the bakery bag. "And distraction." She grinned as she held up a book from her bookshop down the street.

"Is it the new one with the creatively appendaged alien?" I asked hopefully.

"Obviously." She set the book on the counter. "Also,

you looked like you needed backup. I came as soon as I could get away."

"I'm fine."

"Mmhmm, sure you are." Cara slid onto the stool near the window and peered at me. "So. Tilly. Nate. Lois. I saw them walking here earlier. They come here often, don't they? Don't answer that. I already know they do."

"They require caffeine and cocoa, just like the rest of town." I pretended to wipe the same spot for the third time. "What about them?"

"Tilly and Lois are adorable. And Nate is..."

I waved a hand. "Don't say it."

"Nice? Kind? Good-looking in that hot, wholesome single dad way we all love? Everyone is calling him Hot Diner Dad now. You should hear the ladies talking in the store. Suddenly, single dad romance is my number one best seller. I wonder why."

I narrowed my eyes. "Whose side are you on?"

"I didn't realize there were sides." She opened the bakery bag and pulled out one of Piper's special, fancy macarons. "But since you're making me choose, I'm on the side that thinks maybe you deserve something good. And maybe you should talk about your feelings because clearly you have some. I'm here for you. I wish you would talk to me. I was going to suggest—"

I rolled my eyes. "I'm allergic to feelings. Pretty sure I'll break out in a rash if I talk about them."

"Fine, I'll let it go. But if he's interested in you, I say go for it. He's a good guy, a real honest, good man.

Grandma loves him." She left it at that and didn't push. She never did. That was why we were so close.

Growing up, I always knew I had four half-sisters, scattered across different corners of Honeybrook Hollow. Our grandparents were adamant that we wouldn't drift apart just because our family tree included our lying, cheating, snake of a father. They insisted we spend summers together, holiday breaks, random weekends, and the monthly Darlington Family Weenie Roast, determined that we would be true sisters—not strangers—no matter what. To them, having granddaughters who weren't close like a real family was simply unacceptable, and their stubborn love stitched us together in ways none of us could have managed on our own.

However, even though I knew they loved me, I couldn't help but feel I was the odd one out. Our father was still married to my mom, and they hadn't let me spend as much time with my grandparents as the others did. Plus, they had all grown up in Honeybrook Hollow, while I had grown up in Portland. And don't get me started on our age differences. Paige was forty, and Piper wasn't too far behind. Lucy and Cara were thirty-two, and then there was me, the baby, at twenty-five.

My oldest two sisters, Piper and Paige, were unmistakable with their bright blond hair, while Lucy, Cara, and I had honey brown locks that caught the light in a softer, golden way. Still, no matter the shade, it was clear we were all cut from the same cloth—each of us bore our father's sharp cheekbones, wide-set eyes, and the kind of smile that could charm its way through a dozen family reunions. Sometimes, looking at my sisters felt like staring into a mirror that held pieces of a man we'd all inherited nothing but our looks from. Needless to say, none of us were in touch with him anymore.

I watched Cara nibble on one of the macarons, sunlight catching in her hair and reflecting off the window. For a moment, I allowed myself to imagine what it would be like if I could just say the things swelling in my chest—if I could trust the world with the chaos inside my head. But old habits die hard, and vulnerability still felt like a language I couldn't quite speak. So I simply smiled, hoping she couldn't see through it. No matter how much time I spent here, I still felt like a guest in their memories. They grew up here— together. I didn't; that fact haunted me, maybe it always would.

"Anyway, Nate isn't the only possibility in town. Did you hear there's a new restaurant opening up across from the library? A guy Lucy and I went to school with is a chef. Graham Barton. He's coming back to town."

"Graham?" I repeated, blood draining from my face. "Barton?"

Cara looked up from her macaron. "Yeah, have you met him? I don't remember. Everyone is talking about it. I'm surprised you haven't heard."

"Yeah," I said slowly. "Okay, umm. Yeah."

Graham was my ex. And it was a secret.

At one point in my life, I had wanted to be a chef. I even attended culinary school. But that ended when my relationship with Graham did. Then I moved to Honeybrook Hollow and took up the Coffee Cabin owning, barista life.

I opened my mouth to tell Cara—felt the words rise, press against my teeth, ready to spill out now that they were finally acknowledged even inside my own head. *He wasn't just someone I dated. He was someone who mattered. He was someone who hurt me.* But the explanation snagged somewhere in my chest, tangled up with everything I'd never said out loud. Because telling her wouldn't just mean admitting who Graham was to me. It would mean admitting who I'd been with him. The version of myself that learned to speak more quietly. To want less. To stop talking about food like it mattered, like it could be a future, instead of a hobby that took up too much space. He hadn't told me outright to shrink—but somehow, over time, my ambition dulled, my joy in cooking dimmed, until I almost believed it had been silly to dream in the first place. Saying his name out loud felt like handing over that version of myself too, the one who'd let someone take something she loved and convince her it was indulgent, unnecessary, embarrassing. I closed my mouth instead. Some things still felt too raw to give away. Like if I said it out loud, I'd have to admit how deeply he'd gotten in—and how hard I'd worked to build myself back without anyone watching.

The words didn't come. It felt too pathetic—like admitting I'd let someone take away the part of me that once defined *me*. They knew I'd gone through a breakup, just not with whom.

Memories flashed through my mind. How he used to

call me "kiddo" in public and "unambitious" in private. How he'd sampled every meal I made with a smug smirk and a comment like, *"Not bad. But not ready for prime time."*

He was the reason I stopped cooking. I'd loved it once. I had dreams of opening my own place, or maybe writing a cookbook, or starting a YouTube cooking channel. I wanted to create dishes that made people feel something nostalgic, or homey, or comforting. But after Graham, the kitchen became another place where I got things wrong.

I was the sous chef to his head chef. His employee. His protégé. His hero-worshipping ex-girlfriend. His dirty little secret. No one knew what truly happened between us when I worked for him. That was the way he wanted it. And I had agreed to everything—the secrets, the sneaking around, the lies. He was older—in every way that mattered: age, experience, status. At first, he made me feel seen, but it quickly turned into making me feel small.

I knew he was from Honeybrook Hollow, but I foolishly never put the pieces together and realized he was the same age as Cara and Lucy. God, I was so stupid, of course they knew him.

"He's coming back to town?" I asked, trying to keep my voice steady. "To stay?"

Cara nodded. "Yeah, and apparently the food's going to be amazing. He trained in Paris or something." I knew he did. He talked about it all the time. I couldn't even count on both hands all the times he'd start a sentence with "*When I was in Paris…*" Ugh.

"Yeah, I mean, yeah," I mumbled, for lack of something better to say. "That's great."

"And just saying, Nate won't be the only possibility in town anymore. Like, finding someone to date in a small town can be a real problem sometimes." She gestured to herself with a thumb. "Exhibit A, am I right? I say go for it, keep your options open."

"Absolutely not." The words came out too fast, too sharp.

Cara blinked at me.

I tried to backpedal. "I mean—he's not my type." Which was technically true. I didn't date men who once told me I was *too emotional about crème brûlée* anymore.

"Okay. I'll quit trying to fix you up," she said as she studied my face. "Maybe you're not ready to get back out there. Do you want to talk about your breakup? It's been over a year. It might help to get it out, you know, talk it through. Keeping things bottled up inside is never a good idea—"

"I'm sorry I snapped at you." I swallowed hard. "I'm gonna go feed the espresso machine before it goes on strike."

Cara blinked. "You okay?"

"Fine." I grabbed a bag of beans and got to work. "Totally fine."

Eventually, she left with a hug and a promise to text me later, and I closed up the Coffee Cabin by myself. The last car in the drive-thru had ordered two mochas—

one decaf, one full throttle—and a dozen cake pops—typical Thursday.

By the time I was ready to close up, the sky had turned lavender-gray, and the lights of my grandparents' inn, The Honeybrook—named after the town, of course—twinkled across the parking lot. Every time I visited here as a kid, I cried when it was time to go home. I would have given anything to stay with my grandparents instead of my father, who was more focused on networking events than being a parent, and my mother, who treated my emotions like mildly inconvenient side effects to having a daughter.

After shutting off the espresso machine, I finished cleaning up silently, letting the hum of the refrigerator fill the empty shop. The place always felt different after closing—quieter, lonelier, but it also felt safe in a way that made me linger. I counted the cash drawer twice, just to distract myself, then slipped into my jacket and braved the cold.

My old Volkswagen Beetle wheezed to life like a tired asthmatic bumblebee, but it got me home. My townhouse wasn't much—small, a little drafty, mildly run down—but it was mine, and that was all that mattered to me.

My stomach twisted into knots as I drove.

I hadn't seen Graham since the day I walked out of his downtown Portland condo and left behind the last recipe I ever created.

He used to say I had a "natural touch" in the kitchen, that my food "tasted like memories." But then he'd follow it with a sneer or a backhanded compliment. By the end,

I couldn't tell whether he hated my cooking or just hated that I loved something besides him.

Either way, I stopped cooking. It didn't feel good anymore. I packed up my knives, trashed my journals full of handwritten recipes, and came here. I hadn't cooked a real meal since. Not like I used to

The last straw with him hadn't been big. It hadn't been dramatic. It had been a dinner party, the kind Graham loved—linen napkins, too-expensive wine, people who laughed easily at his stories. I'd cooked, spending the afternoon on a dish that was warm and familiar, that reminded me of my family—chicken pot pie that my grandma had taught me to make. People complimented it. Asked questions. Someone even said, "You should definitely do this for a living." I'd felt something bloom in my chest then—small but hopeful. Pride. Possibility.

Graham had smiled and draped an arm around my shoulders. "She keeps things pretty simple," he'd said easily, like he was translating for the room. "Comfort food. Nothing too ambitious." A few people nodded, laughing awkwardly. I laughed with them, because that's what you do when the person you're with decides the meaning of the moment. Later, when I told him it had hurt, he had sighed and said I was reading too much into it. That he'd only been setting expectations, and that was when I understood it wasn't accidental. He didn't just hurt my pride—he sanded it down. And standing alone in the kitchen afterward, staring at plates scraped clean of the food I'd made, I realized I'd been shrinking for a long time. Ending it wasn't dramatic. It was necessary. It was the only way to stop letting someone else decide how much of me was allowed to matter.

And now he was back. In *my* town. About to open *his* restaurant. Only it was his town too, damn it. I knew that. But he swore he hated small-town life and would never leave Portland.

Was he doing this to spite me? Because I left him? Or was I being conceited even thinking this had anything to do with me at all? I'd lost all perspective when I left him.

I pulled into the cracked parking spot behind my townhouse, headlights briefly illuminating the peeling paint on the back steps. The engine sputtered as I turned it off, leaving a silence that felt too loud. For a moment, I sat there, my hands resting on the wheel, watching my breath fog the inside glass while doubts crowded in. When I finally stepped out, the cold bit through my jacket, and the door creaked shut behind me, echoing my mood. I lingered on the stoop, brooding under the weak porch light, thinking about everything I'd left behind and everything that might happen now that Graham was coming to Honeybrook Hollow.

Waiting for me inside were Remy and Linguine, my two cats who managed to fill the townhouse with more personality than most people I knew. Remy, the older of the pair, was a sleek tortoiseshell with a penchant for curling up in the warmest patch of sunlight he could find. Linguine, on the other hand, was an energetic orange tabby whose mischievous green eyes always seemed to be plotting his next playful ambush. Together, they greeted me with impatient meows and winding tails, their companionship a constant comfort at the end of every long day.

I fed them, changed into sweats, and sank into the couch with a fuzzy blanket and the book Cara had brought me. I didn't open it. I just sat there, trying not to think about anything.

My phone rang on the coffee table.

I expected Cara's name.

I did not expect to see Graham's.

I stared at the screen until it stopped ringing. Then it lit up again.

When my phone lit up with his name, my heart stuttered like it had missed a step. Not longing—never that—but something older, a reflex I hadn't managed to unlearn. My stomach tightened, breath going shallow, as if my body remembered him better than my mind wanted to. I stared at the screen, irritated at myself for the way my pulse jumped, for how a single name could still pull me out of the present. A flicker of unease, the quiet shame of realizing some doors don't close cleanly, no matter how hard you shut them.

It was almost funny how one person could pull me out of my cozy, quiet Coffee Cabin bubble and drag me back into a storm I thought I'd moved on from. I hesitated, thumb wavering, as old arguments and apologies popped up in my head. Part of me wanted to ignore it, let the ring fade into silence, but curiosity—and maybe a stubborn piece of hope—won out. Not hope for getting back with him, because *hell no*. Hope that he would recognize how he treated me and feel sorry for it. Maybe I needed some kind of closure.

This time, I answered, wishing I had blocked his number and wondering for a moment why I hadn't, before realizing it was my stupid sense of optimism hanging on, waiting for the apology that would never come.

"Hello?" I said, already regretting it.

"Eliza," he said, voice smooth and warm. "Hey. I was hoping we could talk."

My stomach tightened. "You're calling me... why?"

"I'm in town. Opening a new place across from the library. I figured you'd hear eventually." His voice softened like he thought I'd be flattered. "I thought we could catch up."

"Graham, we haven't talked in over a year."

"Exactly. That's why we should. I've changed. Things are different now."

I stared at the blank TV screen. "You mean you're charming, ruthless, and ambitious in a new ZIP code?"

He laughed, like I'd just told the best joke. "Still sharp, kiddo. I missed that."

I didn't reply. I never lost my sarcastic edge with him. But even though I was mouthy about it, I had always ended up giving in to whatever he wanted. Honestly, I think he kind of liked it. He must have thought of me as a challenge he could defeat over and over.

"I'll stop by for coffee tomorrow," he said lightly, like it was a casual idea and not a threat to my peace. "It'll be good to see you. You look great, by the way—your picture's up on The Honeybrook Inn's website. You're running the Coffee Cabin? That's so you—cute."

I hung up without saying goodbye. *Cute.* Most people would have taken that like a compliment, but after being with him, I knew he was belittling me. Damn it, I should have known better than to answer.

I turned off my ringer, buried my face in the blanket, and tried not to spiral.

Graham was back in Honeybrook Hollow. He was a big deal in Portland with a string of successful restaurants. But his family still lived here, and his mother was constantly asking him to come back. He had been the quarterback of Honeybrook Hollow High School's football team, student body president, and captain of the debate team. People here loved him. They always had.

His return to town wasn't what I needed; it was just one more reason to feel like an outsider. He'd be the big man in town, and I'd be—whatever the opposite of that was.

I'd never told anyone the full story about why I left Portland. About how I had become an emotional contortionist to stay on his good side. How charming he was in public and how small he made me feel in private. I couldn't tell anyone about him because I was afraid no one would believe me. And who would believe me now if he came back here to play the hometown hero? My family probably would, but then it would be us against the town, and I didn't want to put anyone in an awkward situation.

Who was I, anyway? The grumpy, smartass barista at the Coffee Cabin, that's who.

Before I could fall any deeper into the emotional hole I was digging, my phone buzzed again. I checked it.

> Nate: Hey. Hope you're warm and curled up with a book or something good on TV. Tilly says hi and wants me to tell you that Waffles and Lois miss you.

I stared at the screen, heart squeezing.
Then I typed:

> Me: Tell them I miss them, too. And the Pre-K Princess who brings them everywhere.

Nate replied almost instantly:

> Nate: She's currently asleep under three blankets, holding Waffles like a teddy bear. She wants to bring you a sticker tomorrow after school.

I set my phone down and let Remy crawl onto my lap. Linguine curled up on the arm of the couch like he didn't care, but his purr was louder than the heat rattling from the vents.

For the first time in hours, I felt a little lighter.

Graham might be moving back to Honeybrook Hollow.

But I was here too, and I had just as much right to this town as he did.

I had family here, and friends, and I would absolutely be okay.

Chapter 3
Nate

Errands with Tilly took twice as long as they should have and somehow still felt like the best part of my weekend. The drive into town was slow in the good way, the kind Honeybrook Hollow specialized in. Late-morning clouds hung low but bright, the sun breaking through in patches that warmed the windows just enough to make me crack one open. The air smelled like damp earth and pine, leftover from rain the night before. Tilly sang along with the radio, making up her own lyrics, while I kept one ear on the road and the other on the quiet of the house we'd left behind.

Lois had watched us go from the front window, tail thumping, chocolate-brown eyes full of hope and accusation. She loved the new backyard—had already claimed it as hers—but the fence still needed fixing, one loose panel I hadn't gotten to yet. I told myself she'd behave. I also told myself that about toddlers once, and I knew how that had gone.

"Do you think Lois is okay?" Tilly asked, peering back at the house as we turned the corner.

"She'll be fine," I said. "She's got her toys."

"And the couch," Tilly added helpfully. "And the pillows."

I sighed. "Yes. The pillows." Mental note: add new toss pillows to my ever-growing list of things I need for the house.

Maybe I needed a crate. I didn't love the idea, but I loved the idea of not coming home to chewed furniture more. I added it to the mental list, right under *fix fence* and *buy more peanut butter.*

The hardware store was first. I needed screws and brackets for the fence, but Tilly treated the place like a gallery. She inspected paint swatches with great seriousness—declaring yellow "too shouty" and blue "sad but polite"—and asked the clerk if dogs were allowed inside because Lois liked meeting new people. The clerk laughed and said yes while pointing to a canister of dog treats he kept on the checkout counter.

At the feed store, Tilly waved enthusiastically at the chickens as if they were old friends.

We circled the aisles twice, Tilly leading the way like a seasoned explorer, pausing to deliberate over the merits of each flashlight and garden gnome. I let her pick out a small packet of seeds—sunflowers, her favorite— promising we'd plant them together once the yard dried out. The clerk offered Tilly a cookie for Lois, which she accepted with solemn responsibility, clutching it in both hands all the way to the checkout.

I grabbed dog food and listened to a detailed explanation about why Lois preferred the blue bag over the red one, even though, as Tilly pointed out, "she cannot read, but she *can* feel vibes."

I did not argue with this.

By the time we reached the park, the clouds had thinned, sunlight filtering through the trees and catching on the playground equipment. The grass was still damp, cool, and green, the air alive with the sound of kids laughing and someone strumming a guitar near the gazebo.

Tilly burst toward the slide, then doubled back suddenly to grab my hand. "You're coming too," she said, like it was optional.

I sat on the bench while she climbed, slid, and narrated every move. And then I saw Eliza.

She was cutting across the park with a canvas tote slung over her shoulder, hair loose, sweater sleeves pushed up like she'd been busy and forgot to be anything else. She slowed when she spotted us, lifting a hand in a small wave.

"Hey," she said, stopping near the bench.

"Hey," I replied.

Tilly skidded to a halt in front of her, eyes bright. "We went to *three* stores," she announced. "Daddy is fixing the fence because Lois keeps trying to escape, and also he's thinking about buying her a crate, but he feels bad about it."

I closed my eyes. Briefly.

Eliza's eyebrows shot up. "That's a lot of information."

Tilly nodded. "Lois chewed up a shoe once. But it was an accident."

"It was *not* an accident," I muttered.

Eliza laughed, real and warm, crouching to Tilly's level. "What kind of shoe?"

"One of Daddy's good ones," Tilly said solemnly. "Not the running one."

Eliza winced in sympathy. "That's tragic."

"She also snores," Tilly added. "And Daddy talks to her like she's a person."

I cleared my throat. "Okay."

Eliza looked up at me, smiling. "I talk to my coffee machine. I think you're safe."

Tilly seemed pleased by this common ground and immediately launched into a detailed explanation of our house—how Lois liked the backyard but didn't understand fences, how I cooked but sometimes forgot the importance of ketchup, how we were having grilled cheese for dinner again "because it's a comfort food year."

I let it happen. Mostly because stopping her would've taken effort I didn't have.

Eventually, Tilly darted back toward the slide, satisfied she'd shared everything she knew.

Eliza stayed. "She's amazing," she said quietly.

"She is," I agreed. "Thank you."

Sunlight caught in her hair as she smiled at me, and I stayed on the bench, watching Tilly climb like the world was nothing but possibility. Lois would probably chew something. The fence would get fixed eventually. And for once, the unfinished parts didn't feel like failures.

They felt like proof we were settling in.

Eliza lingered instead of leaving right away, shifting the tote higher on her shoulder. Up close, I noticed the details I always did—the soft sweater in a chocolate brown that brought out her eyes, the way her hair was half-tamed and half-defiant, like she'd run out of time and decided not to apologize for it. She looked tired, but in a way that made me want to offer her a chair and something warm, not in a way that dulled her. If anything, it made her feel more real.

"Heading in?" I asked, nodding toward town.

"Yeah. The Coffee Cabin," she said. "My grandma opened this morning. I woke up with a headache, and she staged a full takeover." Her mouth curved. "She's dramatic, but effective. I'm better now."

"Good," I said, meaning more than just the headache. "I was going to ask if you were okay."

She smiled at that—small, but genuine. "I am. Thanks."

Tilly reappeared long enough to announce, "Grandmas fix everything," before racing off again.

Eliza laughed softly, watching her go. "She's not wrong."

We stood there for a beat, the sounds of the park filling the space between us—laughter, the squeak of swings, leaves stirring overhead.

"I should get going," Eliza said, though she didn't move yet. "But... good luck with the fence."

I huffed. "I'll need it. Most days, Lois goes to my grandpa's when I'm at work or when Tilly's at school. He loves having her. Spoils her rotten." I shook my head. "Today was a test run. For all of us."

Eliza's smile softened. "She's lucky."

"So are we," I said, then caught myself. "I mean—Tilly and me."

"I know what you meant," she said gently.

"Yeah," I said, quietly. And for a second, everything around us felt still, like the morning was holding its breath. She adjusted her tote, the light catching her just right, and I realized these were the things that stayed with you—the unremarkable moments, easy and unguarded. Not because they demanded attention. Because they didn't, the park hummed softly around us—distant laughter, the creak of swings—and she moved through it the same way she always did with Tilly at the Coffee Cabin: patient, warm, never talking down, like kindness was something she carried without thinking about it even though she hid it behind sarcasm and jokes.

"Well," she said finally, stepping back, "tell Lois I'm rooting for the couch."

I smiled. "I won't."

"See you, Nate."

"See you, Eliza."

She headed toward town, and I watched her go longer than necessary, hoping she really did feel better.

It struck me then that she looked different outside the Coffee Cabin—lighter somehow, like the morning hadn't asked anything of her yet, like this version of her belonged to herself. The thought settled quietly in my chest, warm and unexpected all at once.

"Daddy?" Tilly called from the top of the slide.

I looked up.

"She's nice," she added, like this was a conclusion she'd been working toward. "You should make her grilled cheese. Or spaghetti!"

I laughed, pushing to my feet. "Yeah," I said softly. "Maybe I will someday."

Chapter 4
Eliza

A couple of days after running into Nate at the park, I was back in the grocery store parking lot before dawn, the town still dark and quiet in that way that felt like a shared secret. The sky hung low and blue, more night than morning, and the cold bit just enough to make my breath fog as I stepped out of the car and shut the door softly, like Honeybrook Hollow might still be sleeping and I didn't want to be the one to wake it. The town looked different at this hour. No traffic. Nobody milling about. Just streetlights humming and the faint sound of something mechanical in the distance. I wrapped my coat tighter around myself and crossed the lot, my boots echoing more than they should have, each step a reminder that I was up early on purpose. The Coffee Cabin didn't open for another hour, but I liked these mornings—the ones that belonged to me before the world started asking for things.

The automatic doors slid open with a quiet whoosh,

warm air spilling out to meet me. Inside, the grocery store felt suspended in time. Fluorescent lights buzzed gently overhead, casting everything in a pale glow. The floors were freshly mopped, the faint scent of cleaner mixing with produce and bakery bread. A soft, indistinct song played over the speakers, something slow and forgettable, perfect for not thinking too hard.

I grabbed a cart and started down my usual route, hands resting on the handle as the wheels squeaked softly in protest. Milk, eggs, heavy cream, butter—my body moved on autopilot, the rhythm familiar enough that my thoughts wandered despite my best efforts to keep them focused on inventory and prep lists. Mornings like this had a way of sneaking up on me, letting feelings drift in when I wasn't watching closely enough.

I told myself to think about work. About opening the Coffee Cabin. About the day ahead.

I didn't, not really.

I was halfway down the dairy aisle, reaching for my second carton of heavy cream, when I heard my name.

"Eliza?"

It took a second for it to register—low, familiar, threaded with surprise. I turned, carton in hand, and there they were.

Nate stood a few feet away, one hand resting on the handle of a grocery cart, the other tucked into the pocket of a soft gray sweatshirt. A beanie was pulled low over his dark hair, like he'd dressed in the dark and trusted instinct to take care of the rest. He looked tired in the honest, unguarded way—eyes a little shadowed, mouth already curved into a smile anyway. The kind of tired that came from being up because someone else needed you. I wasn't prepared for how good he looked—rumpled and tired, the kind of handsome that sneaks up on you when you're not paying attention. He smiled at Tilly, patient and unhurried, and I had to remind myself not to linger on the way he carried himself, like being kind was something inherent instead of something he pretended to be.

In front of him, tucked into the cart like a prized possession, was Tilly.

She was bundled in a cozy fleece-lined hoodie, a pink beanie slipping slightly to one side, wisps of sleep-tousled hair escaping near her ears. Her stuffed reindeer was clutched under one arm, his antlers peeking out like he'd insisted on coming along. Her free hand held tight to the side of the cart as she peered at me with solemn curiosity.

"Well," Nate said, voice warm despite the hour. "This feels like fate or extremely good timing."

I laughed softly. "You're up early."

"Tilly couldn't sleep," he said, nodding toward her. "So we decided to be productive."

"Good morning, Tilly."

"We ran out of maple syrup." She nodded seriously. "And I said it was too quiet at home. And Daddy makes loud eggs."

Nate winced. "Context matters."

I blinked. "Loud eggs?"

Nate sighed like a man already on trial. "I crack them one-handed. There might be enthusiasm involved."

"They sizzle loud too," Tilly added helpfully. "And he talks to them."

I laughed, unable to help it. "I support encouraging your breakfast."

"Thank you," Nate said. "Finally. Someone who understands."

She glanced into my cart. "Why do you have so much milk?"

"For work," I said. "I'm opening the Coffee Cabin soon."

Her eyes widened. "Where are your whipped cream cans?"

Nate chuckled. "She's very concerned about things like this."

I pointed to the stack of heavy cream nestled in my cart. "I make it myself."

Tilly stared at the cartons like I'd just revealed a magic trick. "You *make* it?"

"From scratch," I confirmed.

Her mouth fell open. She looked up at Nate, awed. "She's fancy."

Nate laughed, the sound low and soft in the quiet aisle. "I was already impressed. We're heading to the diner," he added. "I'm opening in about an hour. My grandma is meeting us later."

"That sounds like a cozy morning," I said, meaning more than the word covered.

"It is." He nodded. And for a second, the grocery store faded into something softer, something warmer.

Tilly shifted her stuffed reindeer higher under her

arm and studied me for a long, serious moment. "I like you," she said decisively. "You smell happy, like flowers and coffee. He thinks so too." She held the reindeer out for me to greet.

Something in my chest tightened in a way I hadn't been expecting. I smiled, steadying my voice as I tried to remember the reindeer's name. *Winston? No. Walter. Definitely not Walter.* "That might be the nicest thing anyone's ever said to me," I said instead, giving it a respectful nod like we were already on good terms.

She nodded, satisfied, and went back to studying the shelves like she was taking mental notes.

We stood there for a moment longer than necessary, carts side by side but facing opposite directions, the early morning wrapping around us like a shared secret. Then Nate cleared his throat lightly.

"Well," he said, smiling. "We should probably let you get back to your very important dairy decisions."

"And you should go make loud eggs," I said.

Tilly grinned. "Extra loud. With grape jelly!"

Nate's eyes softened as Tilly bounced in the cart, hugging her reindeer tight. I glanced at him, catching a flicker of gratitude in his expression—something unspoken passing between us. For a moment, we all stood suspended in the glow of the store's fluorescent lighting, the hum of possibility weaving through the mundane.

"Well," he said quietly, shifting his grip on the cart, "we should probably get going."

"Yeah," I said, smiling. "See you around."

Tilly waved enthusiastically, her reindeer bobbing along with her. "Bye, Eliza!"

"Bye, Tilly," I said. "Stay cute."

Nate held my gaze for a beat longer than necessary. "Have a good day."

"I will," I said. "You too."

We parted with a small wave, heading down separate aisles, but the store didn't feel quite as empty anymore. I pushed my cart forward, warmth settling into my chest, and let myself carry it with me.

The moment loosened its hold. I finished my shopping, checked out while the store still felt half-asleep, and stepped back into the cold morning with my bags cutting into my palms. By the time I pulled up to the Coffee Cabin, the sky was beginning to lighten, the day ready to start whether I was or not. I unlocked the door, flicked on the lights, and let the familiar quiet wrap around me—carrying that small, unexpected warmth with me as I set about opening up.

Chapter 5
Nate

Monday morning came soft and gray, the kind that made everything feel a little slower as I drove Tilly toward Honeybrook Hollow Elementary. I caught myself watching the sidewalks as we passed through town, half-expecting to see Eliza heading toward the Coffee Cabin, even though I knew how unlikely that was. Tilly looked tiny as we climbed the school steps, her backpack tugging at her shoulders, pausing to take it all in. She'd been to Pre-K in Portland, but this felt different—more permanent, more like the life I'd been trying to build for us. Homey and real. Cozy and warm.

Mostly, though, I watched Tilly. I watched her square her shoulders and head inside, and I felt it settle in my chest that this was the point of all of it. A life with roots. A little more time together. And something that finally felt like home.

It was strange how quickly a new chapter could begin

—one minute you were wrapped up in your own worries, the next you were responsible for someone else's entire world. I took a deep breath, letting the morning's uncertainty settle on my shoulders, and reminded myself that this was as much a beginning for me as it was for Tilly. The familiar ache of nerves mingled with hope, a reminder that even on the hardest days, life offered the chance to start over, exactly like we were doing in Honeybrook Hollow.

The parking lot buzzed with morning energy—minivans idling, kids hopping out with backpacks half-zipped, coffee cups balanced on roofs while parents wrangled lunches and coats. I crouched to straighten Tilly's jacket, hyperaware of the way conversations seemed to pause just long enough to register me. It wasn't uncomfortable exactly, just... new. A few moms smiled openly. One gave me a slow, curious once-over like she was cataloging details for later. Someone whispered. I pretended not to notice, because noticing felt like participating.

I caught my reflection in the glass of a car window—rumpled flannel, bed head under a beanie, the same tired-but-put-together look I'd perfected since becoming a single dad. Apparently, it worked. I exchanged polite hellos and accepted a few friendly comments about how cute Tilly was. One mom lingered a second too long and asked if we were new to town. I answered automatically, already thinking about how strange it was to be evaluated like this—as if I were available inventory instead of a man just trying to get his kid to class on time.

The school was one of those red-brick, two-story

buildings that probably looked exactly the same since the sixties, complete with a bell tower that hadn't worked in decades and a row of painted murals along the sidewalk—smiling animals with backpacks, a rainbow, and a slightly terrifying dolphin holding a pencil in its fin. The Pre-K wing had its own small courtyard, fenced with white pickets, scattered with plastic ride-on toys, and one very tired tricycle.

Tilly, for her part, had gone full sparkle for her first day. She wore a purple puffy coat covered in silver stars, a matching knit hat with cat ears, and the sparkly light-up sneakers my mother had "accidentally" bought her when they had gone shopping together. Her backpack was pink with a picture of a cartoon jellyfish named Princess Bubbles, and she clutched Waffles the reindeer in one hand like a fuzzy little security guard.

We'd had the grand tour of the school the week before Christmas break. She had met her teacher and knew where to go, so why was I so reluctant to let her walk through the door?

The air was crisp with the lingering chill of winter, the kind that still clung to your bones. Kids swarmed the steps of Honeybrook Hollow Elementary, their voices buzzing with stories from holiday break and excitement about seeing old friends again. But for Tilly, this wasn't the first day back—it was her first day ever. While everyone else slipped easily into familiar routines, Tilly was stepping into something entirely new, her bright coat and nervous smile setting her apart from the crowd. I watched her, heart twisting, knowing how brave she was to face all of this for the very first time.

One of the moms leaned down with a smile. "Your dad's very handsome," she said to Tilly, like it was a secret meant just for her.

Tilly considered this seriously. Then she nodded. "Yeah. But he's already tired."

I coughed, trying not to laugh.

She tugged on my hand and added, helpfully, "And he's making me grilled cheese for dinner. So he's busy."

The woman blinked. Then laughed. Hard.

Tilly waved once, completely satisfied, and dragged me toward the stairs like the matter was settled.

"Are you sure you don't want me to walk you in?"

"I'm sure." She nodded solemnly. "You can go. I'm brave now. I decided it, and now I am."

I glanced around at the crowd of bustling kids, some clinging to parents and some rushing ahead with untamed excitement. Teachers and staff moved with practiced ease, greeting children and offering reassuring smiles. Watching the orderly chaos, I knew, with so much care and laughter swirling around, that Tilly would be fine here.

I smiled. "I never doubted it. You're the bravest kid I know."

She hesitated, big blue eyes squinting up at me. "But will you come back and pick me up in case it sucks?"

I knelt down so we were eye to eye, feeling the familiar mixture of excitement and anxiety swirling inside me. The moment seemed enormous, more than a school drop-off—this was the beginning of new routines, new friendships, and new places for both of us. I squeezed her tiny mittened hand, hoping she'd feel my reassurance through all the layers, and tried to memorize this image: her determined chin, her wide eyes, the way she stood tall even when she felt small.

"Yes. But I think you're going to have a great day."

"Okay, Daddy. I think so too." She grinned, her cheeks flushed with anticipation and just a hint of nerves. I brushed a stray lock of hair from her face and gave her mittened fingers one last reassuring squeeze. As the school doors loomed closer, she squared her shoulders, holding onto her courage and her reindeer with equal fierceness. I stepped back, letting her take those final steps on her own, feeling both proud and a little wistful as she moved forward, ready to embrace whatever lay ahead.

She walked through the door, her little feet stomping with determination, Waffles, her stuffed reindeer, dangling from one hand like a warrior's flag. I stood there until the teacher waved her inside along with the other kids, then turned to head toward the parking lot with a mix of pride, nerves, and the distinct realization that I now had no excuse to delay the rest of my day.

The Pennywhistle Pantry awaited. I rounded the corner and pulled into my reserved parking spot.

It looked like something straight out of the 1950s—curved chrome edges, red vinyl booths, and neon signs flickering in the windows. The jukebox inside still worked, though it mostly played a mix of Elvis, Patsy Cline, and whatever playlist my grandma had recently learned to stream from her phone via Bluetooth.

Technically, my grandparents had retired, but that didn't stop them from stopping by to help. My grandmother stood outside the side door, smiling at me as I approached. Her knit hat was pulled low over her silver hair, and she was spinning the keys on her finger like a gunslinger. Joyce Winters had always been the type to be up before sunrise, bustling around the diner with a sharp wit and the resourcefulness of someone who's seen—and solved—every possible problem. Even as she cracked jokes while starting the coffee machine, you could tell she was whip-smart, always thinking several steps ahead and ready to tackle whatever the day threw her way.

"Tilly make it through the front doors?" she asked as I caught up.

"Like a pro." I unlocked the second bolt for her and held the door open. "Told me to leave because she was brave, then asked me to come back later in case it sucked."

She laughed. "Smart girl. She's got good instincts."

We stepped inside. The scent of lemon polish, old maple syrup, and cinnamon hit me instantly.

The diner was warm and familiar, like stepping into a happy memory. The black-and-white tile floor gleamed. The curved counter wrapped around the open kitchen, stocked with chrome napkin holders, a glass cake dome, and a vintage milkshake machine that I still hadn't quite figured out how to operate without making a small mess. Red vinyl stools stood like soldiers along the front, and the back booths were tucked under heart-shaped cutouts in the walls that my grandpa had installed during a romantic streak in the 1980s. It was a mashup of eras, and somehow, it worked.

"Thanks again for meeting me," I said, sliding behind the counter. "I figured I could use a refresher before I burn something or get harassed by a customer."

"You'll be fine," she said, starting the coffee machine with the confidence of a woman who'd done it every morning for thirty years. "But I'll hang around anyway, just in case the griddle develops an attitude as it's wont to do sometimes. And I'm not gonna lie. It hasn't been that long, but I miss the old place. Feel free to call me for help anytime."

I pulled the cash drawer and started counting. "It's a lot. The house, the diner, Tilly. All new."

"You're not alone, honey—remember that. Grandpa and I are always a phone call away." She set a mug in front of me, steam curling up in lazy ribbons. "You've taken on a lot lately. But never forget that in this family, we can handle whatever comes." Her words settled over me like a warm quilt, steadying my nerves as I finished counting the bills. For a moment, the bustle of opening up the diner and the weight of new responsibilities seemed a little more manageable, as if the Pennywhistle Pantry itself was quietly rooting for me.

"I know. It feels like everything's been tossed in the air and I'm still waiting to see where it lands."

She looked up from the coffee machine. "You're allowed to feel that way. Don't let it stop you. Never let anything stop you, honey."

I nodded, unsure of what to say, until finally, I muttered, "She lives in Paris now. Opened some kind of clothing shop. I haven't heard from her since Tilly was born."

Grandma stopped fussing with her coffee and focused on me with sharp eyes. "Tilly's mom?"

"Yeah." I didn't say her name. I never really did anymore. In fact, I never really talked about her at all. My parents still didn't know what had gone on between us.

I don't talk much about Tilly's mom. Not because it's a secret, exactly—but because once you know Tilly, really know her, it's impossible to understand how anyone could walk away from her.

At the same time, I respect the choice she made. She knew what she could and couldn't be, and she didn't pretend otherwise. I'm grateful for that honesty, even if I couldn't fully understand it. So, I don't linger there. I try not to pull at that thread too often, because it's complicated, and because wishing her well was easier than wondering why loving Tilly wasn't enough to make her want to be part of her life.

I hesitated, wondering how much to say. The truth was, I'd always been closer to my grandparents than anyone else. This diner has felt like a second home since I was old enough to climb onto one of those shiny red stools; I'd always loved this place. My best memories were baked into the walls, flavored with cinnamon and laughter. It's a comfort to know that no matter what else changed, the Pennywhistle Pantry remained—steady, familiar, and now mine.

Everything—the house, the diner, trying to be both parent and provider—made me feel like I was constantly playing catch-up. Dropping Tilly off at school this morning was the hardest part; her small hand slipping out of mine on the school steps left a hollow ache in my chest that lingered long after I'd waved goodbye. I realized I needed to say it out loud, to admit how overwhelming it all felt, hoping maybe the weight would lift, even just a little.

But underneath all that, I knew there was another reason I needed to say it. I felt like I owed Grandma the truth, especially now that I'd be living so close by. I didn't want to keep anything from her—not when she'd always been my confidant. It felt right to lay it all out, no secrets between us.

"She didn't want to be a mother," I admitted. "That's what she said when it happened. Getting pregnant was an accident, something about antibiotics messing with her birth control. But I wanted the baby. I told her I'd take care of her during the pregnancy and handle everything afterward, so she wouldn't have to do a thing. We broke up after she was born."

"She gave you a gift. How brave of her." Grandma's voice was gentle. "But you knew what you were signing up for when you asked to keep Tilly, didn't you?"

My throat tightened. Saying it all out loud made it

feel more real—something I couldn't brush off with the morning rush or a smile I put on for Tilly. Grandma didn't interrupt; she never did. She gave me the space I needed. I stared down at my hands, tracing lines on the tiled counter, grounding myself in the familiar routines of opening the diner.

"Yeah, I did," I said, voice rougher than I intended. "Not because I thought she owed me, not out of obligation. It was always her choice, and I respected that. I just —I already loved her. I didn't know her yet, but I felt like her dad already—from the second she told me she was pregnant. Is that weird?"

"Not at all." She reached over the counter and patted my hand. "And you're a damn good father, Nate. You knew Tilly was meant to be with you. You fought for her, and you took care of her mama, too. I'm proud of you."

I took a deep breath, feeling like I could finally say something lighter. "Grandma, I, uh, I keep running into someone around town. Eliza, from the Coffee Cabin." She raised an eyebrow, her lips curling into a knowing smile. "She's—great."

Her eyes softened, her approval clear. "She's wonderful. I know her grandma. Mabel is one of my oldest friends."

Before I could question her, the bell above the front door jingled, and we both looked up as the diner's staff started to arrive. Ready or not, the day was beginning, and I needed to step up.

The rest of the morning passed in a blur of coffee

refills, chatting with customers, and a small pancake-related crisis I didn't want to talk about.

As I stood behind the counter, the motions of preparing for the lunch rush brought back vivid memories from years ago. When I was a kid, I spent countless afternoons at Grandma's side in her kitchen, learning to cook. She always let me crack the eggs, stir the simmering soups, and taste the cookie dough straight from the bowl. I enjoyed it—those moments felt special, like a secret language we shared, full of laughter and fun. It was in those lessons that I first felt at home in a kitchen, learning not only recipes but also patience, resilience, and the quiet pride that comes from feeding people you love.

Though I spent most of the morning on my feet, I wasn't actually the diner's cook—we had one, and he was far better at it than I'd ever be. My job was to run the show, keep things moving, and ensure everyone had what they needed. But, like my grandma, I pitched in when it mattered, whether that meant flipping a pancake in a pinch or refilling coffee for the regulars, never above getting my hands dirty when the team needed help. They rarely needed me, though. Probably because most of them had been here for at least a decade. I was lucky they stuck around after my grandparents retired.

The diner slipped into a lull sometime after ten, the breakfast rush thinning to a few lingering mugs and the soft clink of dishes being stacked. I wiped down the counter out of habit more than necessity, watching steam curl from the coffee pot as Grandma refilled a cup for a regular who'd been coming in since before I could walk.

The Pennywhistle settled into its midday rhythm, calm and familiar.

Grandma leaned against the counter beside me, scanning the mostly empty booths. "Slow enough to breathe," she said.

"Feels like it," I replied, wringing out the rag.

She took a sip of her coffee, then glanced at my phone where it sat face down near the register. "You could take a lunch break," she said casually. "I've got things covered."

I hesitated. Not because I didn't want to. Because I did.

"I was thinking about asking Eliza," I said, keeping my voice light. I'd already told Grandma I liked her—there hadn't been anything dramatic about it. Just a fact, stated once, accepted quietly.

Grandma nodded, like I'd told her the weather. "Sounds nice."

That was it. No advice. No nudging.

I picked up my phone, thumb hovering for half a second before I typed. Something simple. Something easy. I hit send before I could talk myself out of it.

Grandma turned back to her coffee like nothing momentous had happened, and the diner hummed on around us. I stood there for a moment longer than necessary, heart steady but expectant, waiting to see if lunch would become a thing.

I pulled my phone from my pocket, staring like it might judge me.

Me: Hey—this is Nate. I know it's short notice, but I'd love to have lunch with you today if you're free. Casual. Thought I'd ask.

The reply came faster than I expected.

Eliza: Hi. I'm… possibly free. But it will have to be later, after the rush. What kind of lunch are we talking about?

I smiled despite myself.

Me: The kind where I promise not to make loud eggs. Burgers. I can meet you at the gazebo in the park.

A pause. Long enough to make me wonder if I'd over-done it.
Then—

Eliza: That does sound tempting. Extra pickles?

My smile turned into a grin.

Me: Always. And I was thinking a cherry pie milkshake, if that's not too much.

Another pause—shorter this time.

Eliza: I could absolutely make room for that. How about two?

I let out a breath and turned away so my grandma couldn't see my face. I'd never hear the end of it.

Me: Perfect. I'll be the guy overthinking condiments.

Eliza: I'll be the one pretending not to judge.

I slipped the phone back into my pocket, the diner suddenly feeling a little brighter, a little warmer. Lunch—at the gazebo, with burgers and extra pickles—was officially a thing.

"I'm glad she said yes," Grandma said mildly from behind the counter.

I looked up. "I haven't told you anything yet."

She lifted her phone, already locking the screen. "Her grandma texted me," she said, like this explained everything. "She's happy too."

I shook my head, smiling despite myself, and went to grab the coffee pot.

Grandma stayed until nearly noon, offering steady backup and casual, yet hilarious chit-chat. The customers loved her, and I hoped she'd keep spending her time here. I glanced around the dining room, watching faces I was beginning to know by heart. There was comfort in the hum of routine, in the familiarity of the regulars who nodded at me over mugs of coffee, in the easy rhythm of people coming and going. It struck me then how much my world had changed, yet how much I depended on these small certainties to keep myself steady.

Now, the lunch rush had wound down, and the diner buzzed with the quieter rhythm of silverware on plates and the occasional burst of laughter from the corner booth. I double-checked the kitchen—prepped, cleaned, stocked—and handed things over to my staff.

I didn't usually duck out mid-day, but this wasn't any lunch.

This was *Eliza*, and I couldn't wait to get to know her better.

I pulled two burgers off the grill myself—one with cheddar and extra pickles for her, one with pepper jack and grilled onions for me. I boxed them carefully with a side of curly fries and grabbed the cherry pie milkshake I'd promised her and a Coke for myself.

Lois was spending the afternoon with my grandpa as she would do whenever I was working, which meant I didn't have to worry about dog hair in the milkshake or a nose smudged against the takeout bag as we ate. Tilly's first day of Pre-K was almost done, and I needed to make sure I wrapped up lunch in time to pick her up. Every other day, my grandparents would take care of pickup and babysitting until I finished up at the diner—but today was mine. I packed everything into the carryout bag and paused, my hand resting on the back counter.

I hadn't spent much time around anyone like Eliza in years--with any woman, actually. I was still a little cautious after Tilly's mom, and how we ended up wanting such vastly different things. But the idea of seeing Eliza again made me smile. Just thinking about her quick wit, the way she rolled her eyes when I teased her, the little laughs we'd share whenever we ran into each other.

It was simple, really. Lunch together, maybe an hour or so of banter, good food, and seeing what happened. I told myself that was more than enough for now.

I grabbed the bag, took a breath, and headed out the back door into the crisp winter air to meet her.

Chapter 6
Eliza

I stared at the to-go cup in my hand like it might give me the answer to life's most pressing question: what the hell was I doing?

"You're going to lunch," my grandmother said, hanging her coat on the hook by the back door and grabbing an apron. "Not walking into battle."

She could pull off a glittery cardigan and a matching knit beret like she was strutting onto a Paris runway instead of just running the Coffee Cabin. She always looked cute and fancy—her outfits were as bold as her personality, and she never missed a chance to add a little sparkle, both to her clothes and her words. Sassy didn't begin to cover it; she could make me laugh even when I was terrified, tossing out jokes and encouragement like confetti at a parade. Maybe that's why I told her all about my date with Nate.

"Says the woman who used to wear combat boots to

disco night," I muttered, tightening the scarf around my neck. "I've seen the pictures."

"That was fashion. This is flirting. Try to have fun."

I tried to steady my nerves, swirling the cup as if the movement could stir up some courage. My reflection in the window looked uncertain, cheeks flushed from both the cold and anticipation. Grandma's words echoed in my ears—reminding me this was supposed to be fun, not a test I could pass or fail. I pressed my lips together, determined not to let anxiety steal the whole afternoon.

She shooed me out the door with a wink and a "Go get him, tiger," before sliding behind the espresso machine like she owned the place. Technically, she didn't anymore; she'd given it to me. But she and the staff at The Honeybrook Inn had run it for years, and in many ways, it would always be hers.

I still couldn't believe I'd told her where I was going— that I was meeting Nate and that it wasn't a big deal, so she'd better not make a thing of it.

The words had practically strangled me on the way out of my mouth. I'd sworn her to secrecy with the kind of dramatic gravitas normally reserved for mafia confessions.

"You breathe a word of this to *anyone*, and I'll start putting decaf in your morning espresso," I'd warned.

Her gasp had been appropriately horrified. "You wouldn't dare."

"Try me."

Now here I was, halfway down the street with my heart threatening to beat straight out of my chest.

The sky was a pearly gray, soft and heavy like it might snow later, and the air had that late winter bite that made you rethink every fashion decision that didn't involve fleece-lined leggings and a heavy winter coat.

I crossed Sycamore Street and slowed down near the library—where a big *Coming Soon* sign hung in the window across the street, advertising *Maison Graham*—then headed toward the park. My jaw tightened as I passed Graham's restaurant, all glass and polish, built to be admired. The reaction was instant and physical—heat in my chest, a hard knot in my stomach. I didn't slow down. Places like that thrived on restraint and performance. I kept walking, choosing warmth over spectacle, substance over shine.

The Honeybrook Hollow town park wasn't huge, but it was one of those small-town treasures that looked like it had been lifted straight from a storybook or an episode of *Gilmore Girls*. A cobbled path looped around the perimeter, winding past clusters of leafless trees and snowy bushes. Fairy lights still wrapped the gazebo in the center, a leftover from Christmas no one had the heart to take down yet. The covered picnic tables near the gazebo offered just enough shelter to eat outside without freezing one's ass off entirely.

In the far corner, the dog park was enclosed with wrought-iron scrolls and had two benches, a decorative fire hydrant, and a well-worn sign that read "*Sit Happens.*"

I spotted Nate before he saw me. He was standing by the gazebo, holding a brown paper bag in one hand and a takeout tray with our drinks in the other, looking like he belonged in one of the Hallmark movies I would never admit to binge-watching.

Tall. Broad shoulders. Dark hair mussed just enough to be interesting. His winter coat was unzipped, and I could see the outline of his thermal Henley underneath—charcoal gray, with jacket sleeves pushed up, even though it was cold, his forearms on full display. He wore jeans that fit far too well and had that relaxed, hometown guy confidence that made me forget my own name for a second.

He caught sight of me and smiled—slow and unguarded, that familiar, crooked grin that felt unfairly personal, like he'd been waiting for me specifically—and something warm and hopeful fluttered in my chest despite my very best efforts not to let it.

Game over. I was toast. He was too hot to be real.

"Hey," I said, stepping under the gazebo while eyeing the huge bag he'd set down. "That's a huge bag. Bring enough food for the entire population of Oregon?"

He held up the milkshake. "We agreed on burgers. I'm just a man following orders."

We sat at the picnic table, and he passed me a takeout box and a carton of fries like it was some kind of peace offering.

I opened the lid. "Extra pickles? You remembered."

"Of course. I stuck to your burger preference text as if it were the letter of the law. I aim to please."

The gazebo blocked the wind, and the wood underneath still held some warmth from the weak midday sun despite the chill in the air.

For a few minutes, we ate in silence—comfortable silence, which surprised me more than anything. It wasn't awkward, it was easy.

"So," Nate said, after a sip of his Coke. "How long have you been in Honeybrook Hollow?"

"A year this spring," I said, dunking a fry into our shared mound of ketchup.

"You like it?"

I shrugged. "I like the Coffee Cabin. I like my grandparents. And I like being close to my sisters—even when they treat me like a wounded baby bird who needs rescuing."

"Why do they treat you like that?" he asked softly.

I smiled, a little crooked, because there wasn't a simple answer. "Because I'm the youngest and I have a history of looking fine while quietly imploding." I shrugged, trying to keep it light. "So now they hover. Snacks appear. Feelings get checked on. I'm a project." I glanced up at him, amused despite myself. "Apparently, I give off strong *needs supervision* vibes."

Nate didn't laugh or ask me to explain further. He just listened. And somehow, that made me feel steadier than all the hovering ever had.

I chewed slowly, suddenly uncomfortable with how warm that made me feel.

"What about you?" I asked, deflecting. "Why leave Portland for a life of diner grease and cherry pie milkshakes?"

He leaned back slightly, elbows on the table. "Because I wanted something simple. Something settled and peaceful. And because the house my grandparents gave me has a built-in pantry that smells like creamed corn and reminds me of my childhood."

I smiled despite myself. "And Tilly?"

"She's everything," he said simply. "She made it easy to walk away from the old life. I want more time with her, not like it was in Portland, when I worked almost nonstop. Eighty hours a week is good money, but it doesn't leave much time for anything else."

My stomach flipped. He didn't say it with bitterness. Just truth.

I took another big bite of my burger, sighing like it was the best thing I'd ever tasted. Honestly, it might've been. Nate's eyebrows lifted in amusement as he sat across from me.

"Was that a food sigh?" he asked.

"Mmhmm," I said around a mouthful. "Better than therapy."

"That's what I was going for. Burgers and break-throughs."

I grinned at him, the sun filtering through the trees overhead, casting shifting shadows across his flannel. "You always this good at emotional manipulation via cheeseburgers?"

"Only with the people I like."

I looked away, smiling at the way my heart stuttered like it hadn't learned how to handle compliments yet.

We chewed in silence for a few moments. The breeze

smelled like pine and grass with exactly the right amount of chill in the air.

"So," I said, nudging his foot with mine. "Brothers? Sisters? Any more Winters kids running around Portland?"

"Nope. Just me. My parents were busy being important, and I was busy turning the Pennywhistle into a second home and begging to visit my grandparents any chance I could."

"You seem like someone who should have a loud sibling or three."

He laughed. "That's what my grandma says. She's always saying I'm too quiet for my own good."

"Yeah, well," I said, picking at my fries. "I have four sisters, and I still feel like I don't belong half the time."

He watched me, his intense brown eyes sweeping over my hair, my cheeks, the curve of my mouth, and then back to my eyes. I felt every point of his gaze, a strange warmth making my chest tighten.

"I don't know," he said softly, almost a murmur. "You look like you belong to me."

I blinked, caught off guard, and my mind stumbled over the words. Did he mean, "You look like you belong, to me"? Or "You look like you belong to me"? My stomach fluttered, and heat crept up my neck. Of course, he didn't mean anything by it.

Instinctively, I shifted back on my seat, brushing a strand of hair behind my ear and trying to look anywhere but him. My fingers fidgeted with the toggle at the end of my coat, my pulse hammering in my ears. I wanted to step away, to make space.

I liked that about him. He didn't perform honesty—he *was* honest. And kind. And funny. And absurdly attractive.

"You're very charming. Has anyone ever accused you of that?" I asked, but I was smiling.

"I have many layers," he answered with mock solemnity.

"Like an onion?"

"Like a really sarcastic parfait."

The wind softly whistled through the evergreens along the back fence.

"You know," I said, "it's kind of weird seeing you without your entourage."

He looked amused. "You mean the four-year-old and the dog?"

"Exactly. You're like a package deal. It's throwing off my whole equilibrium."

"Lois is with my grandpa. Tilly's at school. That means you get my full attention."

My stomach flipped. "Dangerous."

He leaned a little closer, that easy smile tugging at the corners of his mouth. "I think you like danger."

"Mm," I stuck my straw into my mouth, trying to think of something to say. "I like this milkshake. Don't get cocky."

"Oh, I'm already there. You agreed to lunch. I brought you curly fries and a cherry pie milkshake. At this point, I'm just showing off."

I tried not to look directly at his rolled-up sleeves. Or the way the breeze kept ruffling his dark hair. Or the dimples that appeared when he smiled like that—like he knew exactly how good he looked and wasn't above using it for evil.

He sipped his Coke, then gave me a sideways glance. "So, how long did it take you to admit to your grandma you were meeting me?"

I groaned. "Ugh. I told her this morning and swore her to secrecy. She practically squealed." I squinted at him over the rim of my cup. "Wait—how did you even know about my grandma?"

He grinned, feigning innocence. "Small town, remember? Word gets around."

"Busted," I muttered, but I couldn't help smiling.

"I'm honored that you told her. Mine knows too, by the way. She suggested it."

"Well, I'm supposed to be on my best behavior. She made me promise to wear lip gloss and not say anything too sarcastic."

"Failing spectacularly on that second one."

"I know," I said, deadpan. "You bring out the worst in me."

He laughed and leaned back on the bench. "I think you might bring out the best in me."

That shut me up for half a second. He didn't say it in a flirty way. He just said it. Quietly. Sincerely. Like it was a truth he hadn't meant to let slip.

I looked away, unsure how to respond. My mouth went dry.

"Anyway," he said, glancing at his phone, "I should get going. First-day pickup. Marshmallows are required."

I nodded. "Right. Can't compete with Pre-K and marshmallows."

He smirked. "You might surprise me someday."

I rolled my eyes but couldn't hide the grin tugging at my lips. Together, we gathered the empty containers and napkins, stuffing them into the trash bag in companionable silence. It felt surprisingly easy, like we'd done this a hundred times before, even though it was only the first.

"I suspect," he said with a teasing glance, "that underneath all that sass and sarcasm is a very soft core."

I blinked at him, caught off guard, and let a small laugh slip out to cover my awkwardness. "You're ridiculous."

He grinned, stepping a fraction closer. "Maybe. But it's true."

I shook my head, smiling despite myself. "We'll see about that."

He brushed his hands down his jeans. "Well... I really should run. But this was fun."

"Yeah," I said, a little breathless, not wanting to admit how much I'd enjoyed it. "It was."

He gave a small, easy nod. "See you soon?"

I managed a grin. "We'll see."

He didn't leave right away. For a moment, he lingered there, close enough that I could see the way his gaze softened—like he wanted to say something more, or maybe do something more. The look he gave me made my breath catch; it was full of hope and possibility, and I found myself wishing he wouldn't go just yet.

I tried to think of something clever to say. Something cool and breezy. What came out was: "Text me later. I mean, if you feel like it."

He grinned. "Oh, I'll definitely feel like it."

Before he turned to leave, he hesitated again, close enough that I could feel the warmth radiating from him. Then, so gentle it made my heart flutter, he bent and brushed a soft kiss against my forehead. My cheeks burned, my insides went all syrupy, and I couldn't stop the tiny smile that crept onto my face.

I told myself it was the moment. Just the way he was —kind, handsome, and impossibly easy to be around. Nothing more.

Then he winked—an actual wink—and strolled off like he hadn't just rearranged every rational thought in my head.

I watched him go, the path crunching under his boots, the breeze teasing the edge of his jacket. His warmth lingered at the table, a phantom of sun and spice and cherry pie milkshake. My fingers itched to check my phone, like maybe he'd already texted even though I know he didn't. Like maybe this thing—whatever it was— was real and not just something my heart had invented out of loneliness and milkshake-induced euphoria.

I sighed, grabbed the bagged up trash, chucked it in the can, then started walking back toward the Coffee Cabin.

The town square was mostly quiet now, except for

the wind rattling the bare branches and the occasional bark from the dog park. Winter in Honeybrook Hollow was a peaceful kind of beautiful—gray skies, warm lights in shop windows, and the smell of pine and frost lingering in the air. I was beginning to understand why my sisters loved it here so much.

I pushed open the back door of the Coffee Cabin and stepped inside to see my grandma at the counter, carefully rearranging the gift card display like it was a high-stakes game of coffee-themed Tetris.

"Well?" she said without looking up. "Did you kiss him?"

"Grandma!"

She turned around with an entirely unrepentant smile. "What? I have a vested interest in your happiness."

"First of all, you swore secrecy. This was supposed to be a low-key, stealth lunch. No big deal. Not a date. You were sworn to grandma-level secrecy."

"I didn't tell anyone. Okay, yeah, I told Joyce. But she already knew, and she can keep a secret, don't worry."

"Joyce? Is that Nate's grandma?" I trailed off, acutely aware that there were hidden threads connecting everyone in Honeybrook Hollow, like roots beneath the frozen ground. It seemed my grandma's circle of influence stretched farther than I realized, touching corners of my life I thought were private. I glanced at her, searching for any hint of mischief in her eyes, but she just grinned at me as if she'd orchestrated my entire life from the time I got into town.

"Yes."

My mouth dropped open. "Until today, I was unaware you knew his grandma. How well?"

"Of course, I know her; this is a small town." She waved a hand as if I had asked if she knew how to breathe. "Joyce and I grew up together. We were terrible teenagers, but somehow survived and became very good at meddling in other people's lives."

I narrowed my eyes. "Oh my God. Is nothing sacred in this town?"

My accusation hung in the air between us, but Grandma didn't even flinch. If anything, her eyes twinkled brighter. "Let's just say, in Honeybrook Hollow, nothing escapes the grandmas." She winked conspiratorially. "Especially when it comes to ensuring our favorite people find their happiness." Suddenly, I wasn't sure if I should be exasperated or grateful for her persistent involvement. "I mean, someone had to tell Nate that this place had the best coffee and cocoa in town, right?"

"You're a menace. She is, too. Dang."

She smiled sweetly. "A helpful menace. And don't act like you didn't have a good time. You came back all flushed and dreamy."

"Did not."

"Did too."

I groaned and slumped against the counter. "Why did I ever tell you?"

"Because you love me and I love you and I gave you this entire Coffee Cabin to run to make you stay in town with your family where you belong, duh."

She handed me a fresh cup of tea without asking if I

wanted it, steam curling up to warm my cheeks. I accepted it with a sigh and took a sip. She seemed to always know what I needed. Maybe what I really need to do is believe in *this*. This place, this family, this life I was so afraid to let myself sink into.

"Just... don't say anything, okay?" I muttered. "It's not a big deal. It was lunch, that's it. And I don't know what it is yet. He's nice. I like him. I don't need a parade."

"Fine. No parade." She paused. "How about a very small marching band?"

"Grandma!"

She laughed, and I couldn't help it—I laughed too.

Maybe I'd made a mistake telling her. But as I stood there, sipping her delicious tea and letting the warmth chase off the last of the cold, I also couldn't deny this tiny spark in my chest. A flicker of something that felt suspiciously like hope.

Which, honestly, was far more terrifying than any marching band or parade could ever be.

Chapter 7
Nate

The Coffee Cabin looked almost ethereal in the cold morning light—warm glow spilling out of the windows, steam curling from the vents, and the smell of espresso drifting across the parking lot like a promise I actually believed in.

Cars were stacked three deep in the drive-thru lane, engines idling, defrosters humming. Honeybrook Hollow was fully caffeine-dependent before nine a.m. I parked in one of the two short-term spots up front—someone had just vacated the other one, with tires crunching over thin ice as they backed out.

I'd already dropped Tilly at Pre-K, where she'd marched inside wearing glitter socks, her star hoodie, and the confidence of someone who had thoroughly conquered the concept of "show and tell." Lois had been delivered to my grandfather for a long morning walk, tail wagging so hard her entire body moved with it.

For once, I was on time. Early, even.

And for reasons I wasn't prepared to examine too closely, I found myself headed toward the Coffee Cabin window like a man magnetized.

The covered porch heater buzzed warmly, cutting the edge off the cold. I took a seat on one of the stools at the walk-up window and watched Eliza move behind the counter.

She was wearing a fitted long-sleeve shirt under her Coffee Cabin hoodie, sleeves shoved up to her elbows. Her hair was twisted up in that messy, half-fallen way that shouldn't have been attractive but absolutely was. Her leggings bore a light sprinkle of powdered sugar, and her winter boots, worn and well-loved, gave her the look of someone ready for anything.

I should've been exhausted. I was exhausted—my eyes gritty from a late night at the diner finishing payroll, my shoulders aching from leaning over the service counter too long, but sitting there, watching her tuck a loose piece of hair behind her ear and call out an order to the drive-thru? I felt awake for the first time all morning.

She turned, noticed me, and paused long enough to raise one eyebrow.

"You know your diner serves coffee, too?"

"Doesn't taste as good as yours, and I wouldn't have the pleasure of your early morning snark."

"Mm-hmm." She turned to grab a cup. "You look tired."

"I am tired."

"But you're still going to flirt with me, aren't you?"

"Obviously."

That earned me the smallest, fleeting twitch of her lips before she focused on the espresso machine again. I watched her from my stool as she worked—quick, efficient movements, tapping the portafilter, steaming milk, wiping the wand with practiced precision. It was the kind of rhythm someone got from doing something they were good at, even if they pretended they didn't care.

Her grandma, Mabel, stood nearby taking orders from the drive-thru window, and when she spotted me watching her granddaughter, she gave me a knowing little smile.

"You're early today," Mabel said.

"Lucky timing," I replied.

"Eliza doesn't admit it, but she likes it when familiar faces show up in the morning," Mabel said conversationally. "Some people bring good tips. Some bring warmth. Some bring—"

"Grandma," Eliza said sharply without looking up.

Mabel held up her hands. "I was going to say some bring consistent coffee orders. Heavens. Black coffee, right? Dash of sugar?"

"Yeah," I answered with a chuckle. "Please."

Eliza groaned under her breath, but the corner of her mouth softened.

"It's fine," I said. "I'm used to grandmas liking me more than their granddaughters do."

"You're too much," Eliza murmured. "How am I supposed to handle all this charm?"

She handed me my coffee a moment later. Her

fingers brushed mine—barely—but it was enough to send a faint jolt through my tired brain.

"You really do look sleepy today," she said, leaning on the counter. "Everything okay?"

"Yeah," I said. "We're finally settling into a rhythm. Tilly's getting the hang of school. Lois is sleeping through the night more. The diner doesn't feel quite so overwhelming anymore. Small wins, even though payroll was a beast last night."

"You look a bit overwhelmed," she said, softer now.

"Okay, I confess. I am," I conceded. "But also... I'm good. Happy. Mostly."

She nodded slowly, studying me, something shifting in her expression for just a second.

"I was thinking," I said, clearing my throat. "Now that things have calmed down a little... maybe we could try a second date. This weekend? If you're free."

Eliza froze. Not dramatically. Just a small, subtle stillness—like she was surprised I'd asked, or surprised she wanted to say yes.

"Nate," she said quietly, "you're busy. You have so much going on. Are you sure—"

"Yes," I said immediately.

She blinked, surprised. It made me wonder what had happened in her life to make her doubt her appeal.

I tried again, calmer, less eager. "Yeah. I'm sure."

Her mouth curved—not a smile, exactly, but something more careful. Hopeful.

"Okay," she said. "We can make plans."

Which I'd learned was Eliza-speak for *I want to, but I don't know if I should.*

I nodded. "That's all I'm asking."

From inside, Mabel tapped an order slip onto the counter and called, "Honey, if you don't say an immediate yes to that one eventually, I'm putting decaf in your morning latte and telling everyone it's a medical necessity."

"Grandma!"

Mabel hummed innocently.

I laughed, taking a sip of my coffee as warmth spread through my chest—some from the drink, most from her.

"See you tomorrow morning?" I asked.

Eliza hesitated a moment. Then—"Yeah," she said quietly. "See you tomorrow."

And somehow, the day didn't feel quite so overwhelming anymore.

I drove through Honeybrook Hollow with my coffee in the cup holder and Eliza still very much on my mind.

The streets were already lively—dog walkers wrapped in coats, older kids with backpacks heading toward school buses, and the glow of Sycamore Street storefronts casting a golden light on the sidewalk frost. Even in winter, this town moved at the easy rhythm of people who felt they belonged. I'd always appreciated that about it—how it made space for you without expecting anything in return.

But today, something felt different.

Seeing Eliza this morning had knocked something loose. I kept replaying the way her voice softened when she looked at me. The way she noticed that I was tired. How she didn't shut me down when I asked her out again. The flicker of something warm in her eyes—hesitant, sure, but real.

I wanted more of that.

I wanted her.

But wanting her and deserving her felt like two different things.

I turned into the alley behind the Pennywhistle Pantry and parked in my usual spot. The back entrance was already propped open with a bucket of potatoes—my grandma's trick to keep deliveries moving quickly—and the comforting smells of butter, bacon, and coffee met me before I even stepped inside.

"Morning, Nate," my grandmother said from behind the griddle. "You're late."

I checked the clock. "It's 7:48. Nancy was in charge of opening today. So technically, I'm early."

"Ahh, fair enough," she called back.

"Morning, Nancy," I called, giving a wave to one of my grandma's oldest friends as she whisked past the pantry shelves. Nancy had worked at the Pennywhistle for over twenty years, and there wasn't a trick or secret in this kitchen she didn't know. She could flip a pancake with her eyes closed and settle a lunch rush squabble with just a look. Seeing her here always made the place feel more like home.

"I love this place in the morning," Grandma said, voice filled with nostalgia. "So I decided to stop by." I was glad she was here. Her presence brought a steady warmth to the place, anchoring my day before I even tied my apron.

I smiled and shrugged off my coat, slipping into the diner's familiar rhythm. Stainless steel counters gleamed under the overhead lights, biscuit dough was being rolled out at the prep station, and someone had already queued up a playlist of '50s rock and roll. I gave the old jukebox in the corner a pat as I walked by. My grandfather had loved that jukebox. He claimed it made the hash browns crispier.

The place was humming. We had regulars in booths by the windows, a couple of tourists checking out the pie case, and the line cook humming along to "Great Balls of Fire" while flipping pancakes. It was chaotic and warm and comforting in the way only a good kitchen could be.

I grabbed the coffee pot—strong enough to wake the dead—and leaned on the counter to watch for a customer who needed a refill.

The talk around town today was about the Honeybrook Hollow Taste-Off. Apparently, the flyer was now posted in the town square, the date was set, and my grandmother insisted it would be good for me to enter. Said it was tradition, the Pennywhistle entered every year.

The Taste-Off was the kind of event that drew everyone out of their routines and into the park, where booths were set up beneath strings of colorful lights. I remember going to a few of them when I was here visiting as a kid. All the local restaurants entered their best dishes, each hoping to impress the crowd with something special. People wandered from booth to booth, sampling everything from savory casseroles to decadent desserts, and cast their votes for their favorites at the end of the night. It always brought the community together—neighbors chatting over bites of pie, families sharing plates, and old friends reminiscing about past competitions.

My grandparents had won a few times with their classic recipes, and their framed certificates still hung proudly in the diner's hallway, a testament to the Pennywhistle Pantry's place in Honeybrook Hollow's heart.

I wasn't sure how I felt about entering. It was my first year, and I was still learning the lay of the land. But Grandma was already talking smack like we were front-runners.

And now there was this new restaurant opening across from the library. Rumor had it, the owner was a big-deal chef from Portland. Probably wanted to bring "elevated cuisine" to Honeybrook Hollow. I didn't know much about him, but the town seemed excited. Curious.

I should've been worried about competition.

But all I could think about was Eliza.

How she'd looked this morning. The way she'd hesitated—like she was toeing the edge of something new—with me. And how badly I wanted to be the one she trusted enough to step over that edge with.

I poured myself a cup of coffee and looked out at the morning crowd. This place was starting to feel like mine. This town was starting to feel like home. And maybe I was finally ready for more.

Chapter 8
Eliza

The early afternoon lull was settling in at the Coffee Cabin when I saw him--Graham, striding up like he hadn't spent the last year tearing through my heart. My stomach twisted, my hands clenched the counter, and for a moment I couldn't breathe. Same confident posture, same award-winning smile, same smug charm, and yet I wanted nothing more than to turn and run the other way. Or hurl every coffee cup on the shelf at him. He was tall, broad-shouldered, with dark blond hair that never seemed to fall out of place and a jawline so sharp it could slice through ego and expectation alike. He had that polished, confident look that made people trust him without question, and a smile that could sell lies wrapped in velvet.

"Afternoon, Eliza," he said smoothly, like we were old friends instead of awkward exes. "Heard the coffee here is the best in town."

My smile was automatic, professional. "We haven't burned the place down yet, so I guess that's something."

Behind me, Grandma gave a small hum as she wiped down the pastry case. She hadn't looked up, but I could feel her curiosity brewing stronger than the espresso.

"I'll have a tall drip, whatever's fresh, and maybe something sweet," Graham said, leaning slightly on the counter.

"I'm fresh out of *sweet*," I muttered under my breath as I turned to pour his coffee, wishing he would leave.

"What was that?"

I smiled again, wider this time. "Nothing. We've got lemon scones and almond croissants."

"Perfect. I'll take one of each. I love trying new things."

I handed him the bag and cup right as the back door opened and Cara walked in, holding a shopping bag from her bookstore.

"Well, look who's back in town," she said brightly, her gaze landing on Graham as she stepped up behind me at the window.

He turned with his politician-level charm and extended a hand over the counter. "Cara Darlington. You haven't changed a bit."

She laughed. "Liar. But I'll take it. Last I heard, you were some big shot up in Portland. What are you doing back in Honeybrook Hollow? I heard the new restaurant opening up is yours."

"It is. Right across from the library. Hoping to bring a little fine dining flair to town."

Cara's eyes sparkled. "We could use some of that. Everyone's already talking about it."

"Yeah," a customer in line said dryly. "It's the hot topic in town for sure." My eyebrows shot up. Maybe I wasn't the only one not thrilled to have Graham in town.

They ignored me, chatting like old classmates at a reunion. Which, technically, they were. I busied myself straightening napkins and resisting the urge to roll my eyes so hard they got stuck.

Graham thanked me again, nodded politely to Grandma, and left with a wink I pretended not to notice.

"Wow." Cara turned to me, smiling. "He's still as good looking as he was back in school."

"Mmhmm." I mumbled.

"You sure you don't want to date him?"

I nearly choked on air. "Why would you even ask that? Maybe *you* should date him."

"No. He's not my type." She shrugged. "He's yours. Broody. Tall. Slightly arrogant."

"Well, thanks. That's flattering. And that's not my type anymore. Not for a long time."

Grandma chuckled softly, carrying an order to the window.

Cara leaned on the counter, watching me closely. "You know, he was always very charming. Just saying."

I busied myself with wiping down the counter again. "You want a latte or just gossip today?"

"I'll take a latte and a walk with Grandma. We're heading down to the bookstore for book club. You should come after you lock up."

"Maybe." *Nope.*

The book club gathered in the cozy back corner of Cara's bookstore, a mismatched circle of plush chairs and tea-stained mugs. Most members were seniors, including Joyce, who I now knew was Nate's grandma, whose laugh always rose above the rest. The meeting was a mix of gossip and literature—discussions of neighbors and grandkids blended with lively debates about the monthly mystery novel.

Someone always brought a new blend of herbal tea, and the conversation often wandered from plot twists to whose son was dating whose daughter, before looping back to the book—come to think of it, that's where they probably hatched their plan to get Nate to come to the Coffee Cabin and meet me.

Needless to say, Cara's book club was less about the reading and more about the company, stories, and secrets shared over steaming cups and dog-eared pages. I'd attended a few times. But now that I had this whole Graham secret to deal with, I'd be staying far away from their prying eyes.

I made her a latte and watched the two of them leave, chatting and laughing like Graham hadn't just charmed the pants off the place.

By the time I was locking up, the last few cars had gone through the drive-thru with their usual oddball orders—triple-shot soy caramel latte with no caramel, decaf espresso over ice with oat milk foam. The espresso machine hissed out its last bit of steam, echoing the unease quietly brewing in my chest. I wiped my hands on a towel, stalling, letting the silence wrap around me as the distant sound of laughter faded from the street outside. With everyone gone, the place felt too large for my worries and the secret pressing against my ribcage.

Inside, it was quiet again. Peaceful. But not empty.

Because now, Graham was back in my life. And judging by the way he'd looked at me, he was going to make it a thing. But the worst part wasn't that he was here in town. It was that I hadn't told anyone, I'd kept it a secret exactly like he wanted. And it felt like something he would relish in holding over my head with every charming and polite wave he bestowed upon my family.

I shut off the lights and locked the door. Remy and Linguini would be waiting for me at home. I just needed one night of peace before everything got complicated. Or until I spilled my guts about what an idiot I had been over him.

Outside, the sun was setting in honeyed streaks over the rooftops, casting a glow across the parking lot as I stepped out with my keys in hand.

I wasn't even halfway to my car when I noticed him.

Leaning against the hood of a glossy black SUV parked two spaces over from my old Beetle was Graham.

Perfect posture, that expensive coat, and a smile that seemed to suggest he thought he'd get whatever he wanted from me.

"Hey," he said, like this was normal. Like we had ever been normal.

I stopped short. "Why are you standing by my car?"

He raised a hand in a mock-surrender gesture.

"Didn't want to bother you while your family was around, since they obviously don't know about us. Thought I'd catch you after work. I wanted to talk to you."

Of course, he did. And of course, he'd waited. If Cara and my grandma were around, he couldn't reveal his true personality and attempt to bully me into giving in to whatever he wanted.

"About?" I asked, not moving.

He looked around, as if to say, *Right here? In public?* "I need to clear the air. We're going to be neighbors, kind of. I thought it'd be good if we weren't tense around each other. It would also be good if we kept things under wraps. Right?"

I crossed my arms. "We're not neighbors. You're opening a restaurant across from the library. I run a drive-thru coffee shack. This isn't an episode of *Friends*." I rolled my eyes, crossing my arms. "Good God, no, I don't plan on telling *anyone*. I can't imagine anything I'd want less than to broadcast our little arrangement to everyone I know." I grimaced, a full-body shiver working through me, as I let the sarcasm drip from every word, hoping he'd finally catch the message.

For a brief heartbeat, the charm vanished, and its place was a flicker of something cooler, like he wasn't used to anyone denying him in such a way. But just as quickly, he shrugged, masking it with his usual polish, and chuckled. "That sarcasm was always adorable. Good to know some things haven't changed."

I rolled my eyes, smirking, feeling the tiniest surge of

satisfaction. He could pretend all he wanted, but I knew the moment had landed exactly where it should. I was opening my mouth to deliver a line that would absolutely shut him down when a familiar voice called across the lot.

"Eliza!" It was Tilly.

I turned. Nate and Tilly were coming from the sidewalk, cutting across the corner of the lot on their way to the park. Tilly was holding Nate's hand, her bright blue jacket zipped all the way to her chin, strawberry blonde ponytail bouncing with each step. Lois trotted alongside them, leash in Nate's other hand, her tail wagging with what looked like equal enthusiasm and judgment. Dogs definitely could sense evil, or at least jerks.

Of course.

The difference between the two of them couldn't have been more striking. Nate wasn't polished, hiding behind a facade of kindness. He was *actually* kind. Nate was real.

Where Graham's confidence was calculated, Nate's was quiet and unassuming. He didn't charm people—he saw them. Heard them. Remembered their favorite pie flavors and the names of their dogs. And when he looked at me, it wasn't with that practiced gleam that Graham always had in his eyes. Nate looked at me like he was trying to memorize every expression I made—or at least that's how it had always felt.

Nate slowed when he saw us—me and Graham, frozen in the parking lot. His eyes flicked from Graham to me, and something shifted behind them. Polite. Guarded.

Great.

Tilly, on the other hand, had no sense of awkwardness. She tugged on Nate's hand and marched straight toward us like she was on a mission.

"Hi, Eliza!" she said brightly. "Lois wanted to say hi, too!"

Lois barked once in agreement and wagged her entire body.

"Hey, Tilly," I said, crouching to pet the dog because that was less complicated than looking Nate in the eye.

"She's been asking if you'd be at the Coffee Cabin all day," Nate said lightly, voice even. "And I told her you would probably be closed. We were heading to the park."

"Hi, I'm Graham," said Graham, ever the opportunist. He stepped forward and extended a hand. "Friend of Eliza's."

The lie stung like lemon juice on an open cut. He was no friend of mine.

Nate shook his hand. "Nate Winters."

Graham gave a smooth smile. "You new in town? You look kind of familiar."

Nate nodded. "Took over the Pennywhistle Pantry from my grandparents."

Graham's eyebrows lifted like he'd just realized he was slumming it. "Ah, the diner. I remember it well. Hard to believe it's still around."

"Hope to keep it that way," Nate said, his tone pleasant but firm. He turned to me. "Anyway. Didn't mean to interrupt. Just saying hi."

I opened my mouth, ready to explain, to say something that would make it clear Graham was not someone I wanted to be caught standing next to—but nothing came out.

"Nice meeting you," Nate added to Graham, and then turned to Tilly. "Come on, sweetheart. Park's waiting."

"Bye, Eliza!" Tilly called, waving with both hands.

"Bye, sweet girl," I said, my voice a little hoarse.

I watched them walk away, Nate's hand back in Tilly's, Lois trotting happily behind them.

Graham gave a low whistle. "You into him?"

I didn't answer. I turned and unlocked my car door.

"You've got a new type," he added casually.

"No," I said, opening the door and sliding in. "I've got a tolerance level. And you used up all of yours."

He stepped back, hand over his heart, like I'd wounded him. "Fair enough. But you'll see, Eliza. This town loves a success story."

I slammed the door.

And I hated that, even as I drove away, I couldn't stop thinking about the look on Nate's face when he saw me with Graham.

Not angry. Not even jealous.

He was distant and it hurt.

Like maybe I'd closed a door I hadn't even known was open for me.

By the time I pulled into my townhouse complex, my grip on the steering wheel had officially become a stress position.

Remy and Linguini were waiting at the door, their tails flicking with enough attitude to remind me that I was late for dinner—*their* dinner.

"I know," I muttered, kicking off my boots and heading straight for the kitchen. "You've both been tragically neglected. I'll expect a formal complaint filed with HR."

Remy gave a chirp. Linguini tried to leap onto the counter and promptly knocked over a spoon. Chaos. Comforting, familiar chaos.

I fed them and stood in the kitchen, staring at the microwave clock like it owed me an apology. Graham had some kind of nerve. Showing up at my car. Acting like we were friends. Acting like he hadn't taken something I loved and twisted it until it no longer felt like mine.

And Nate...

Ugh.

Why hadn't I said something? Told him Graham was my ex. That he was the reason I'd lost the part of myself that once dreamed in recipes and handwritten menus.

But no—I'd stood there like a statue, letting Nate walk away thinking—who knows what he thought. But I know it wasn't good.

I flopped onto the couch, curling up with my blanket that smelled like cinnamon and espresso. Linguini promptly climbed on top of me like a purring hot water bottle. Remy took his usual spot on the armrest, watching me like a judgmental roommate.

My phone buzzed on the coffee table.

Cara: I just saw Nate walking past the bookstore. He waved. Still handsome, right? Don't you kind of want to fix him up with someone? Yes, that's a hint…

I stared at the message, my fingers hovering over the keyboard. I wanted to tell her. Desperately. But the words wouldn't come.

Instead, I sent:

Me: Yeah, maybe.

She replied with a heart emoji. I threw the phone onto the couch and groaned into my blanket.

I felt like a teenager again—shut out, unsure, and suddenly suffocated by secrets. Only now the stakes were higher, because the person I was shutting out wasn't some guy I had a crush on. It was Nate.

And I *liked* Nate. Liked him in a way that made my heart trip over itself and my brain scramble. Liked him in a way that felt scary and honest and so far out of my comfort zone, I might as well be on the moon.

But now there was Graham. Smiling. Lurking. Charming the town like he'd never been anything but golden.

And me?

Now I was lying to everyone who cared about me and pretending it was fine.

Remy meowed, the sound sharp and scolding.

"You're right," I told him. "I hate it too."

A knock at the door made all three of us jump. I paused, my heart stuttering.

Nobody ever knocked at this time.

I padded to the door and peeked out the side window.

Grandma.

I opened it and stepped aside. "Come in. I was busy wallowing in poor life choices."

"Excellent," she said, breezing in with a bakery box. "I brought emotional support pie."

"Piper's?"

"Of course, straight from her bakery. Chocolate chess pie, my favorite. Now tell me everything."

I blinked. "Everything?"

She arched a brow. "Eliza Mae Darlington, I changed your diapers and taught you how to fake a fever to get out of school. You think you can keep secrets from me?"

I sighed. "Nate and I had lunch."

"I know."

"I told you, but I also told you not to tell *anyone*. I'm not used to anyone knowing about me," I added in a whisper.

"I haven't said a word about it. I know you like him a lot. I can tell," she said, opening the box and handing me a fork. "I would never tell that kind of secret, not even to Joyce. Could you imagine that conversation?" She laughed. "Although she'll figure it out soon enough. That girl has eyes like a hawk and a matchmaking soul."

"I figured. She's exactly like you."

She sat beside me. "So, what's the problem?"

I hesitated. "An ex. From before. He's back. He's opening a restaurant here."

She went very still. "*That* ex? *The* ex is Graham? He's the dick?"

"The one and only. And Grandma, nobody knows about him and me—I mean nobody. It was a secret. Don't say a word. It was bad—"

"I won't. I'll keep your secrets, sweetheart." She reached for her fork. "We'll poison his coffee next time he comes in. A little laxatives never hurt anyone, and diarrhea will keep him busy for a couple of days. Keep him out of your hair while you bring Nate some cookies or something."

I snorted. "We can't poison his coffee. Oh my god."

"Then we'll add extra shots, get him good and wired so he'll have to run the extra energy off."

I let out a laugh that turned into a sigh. "I'm scared, Grandma. Of messing things up. Of not being enough. Of trusting the wrong person again."

She reached over and squeezed my hand. "Eliza, sweetheart. You are *plenty*. And if someone can't see that, it says more about them than it ever could about you."

I didn't answer. I just leaned my head on her shoulder and let her hold me.

For a few minutes, we sat there in silence, the pie growing cold on the table, the cats curled around our feet.

And in that quiet, I realized something. I needed to tell Nate the truth about Graham. Not because I owed him, but because I didn't want to start something real or even something casual on a foundation of secrets. I wasn't ready to get involved, not fully, but if there was ever a chance for this to go anywhere, he deserved to know.

Chapter 9
Nate

Dinner at Grandma and Grandpa's was exactly what I needed after a long day of half-burned bacon, a broken syrup pump, and a delivery mix-up that left us short a dozen burger buns. At the Pennywhistle, I was the boss, the problem-solver, the guy everyone looked to. Here? I got to sit down, breathe, and eat real food that I didn't have to plate myself.

It had been a few days since I'd seen her with Graham. I hadn't brought up the subject of seeing her again, and even though I felt bad about it, the whole thing made me back off. I guess I was feeling insecure—maybe more than I'd like to admit—but seeing them together left me second-guessing everything.

I'd seen them together long enough to know there was history there. Not the obvious kind. No tension you could point at, no raised voices or lingering touches. It was in the way Eliza went still, like she was bracing for something, and the way Graham filled the space as if it already belonged to him. I recognized it because I'd lived it before—the moment you realize someone else still has a claim on the room, even if they don't deserve it anymore.

So, I backed off. Not because I wanted to, but because if she had unfinished business with him, she deserved the time and space to deal with it without pressure from me. Whatever had happened between them wasn't mine to untangle, and until she told me otherwise, the kindest thing I could do was give her room to breathe.

Outside, the air was crisp as I walked up the path to their new place in the senior living condos. The building was a low brick rectangle, neatly landscaped with trimmed evergreen hedges and pots of purple pansies by the front door. I could see warm light spilling from their windows, the blinds half-open, revealing framed family photos clustered on the sill and one of those goofy garden gnomes Grandpa insisted on bringing from the old house. Inside, everything smelled like cinnamon and lemon cleaner, the kind of welcoming scent that made it feel like home even though they'd only recently moved in. There was a small foyer with a coat rack overflowing with scarves and coats. It wasn't the same as their old place, but somehow, it still had the comfort I remembered.

The kitchen smelled like rosemary and butter, a comfort that eased the tension in my shoulders. For the first time all week, I felt myself relax, grateful for the familiar warmth of family around me. Grandma had made roast chicken with mashed potatoes and the kind of green beans that still squeaked when you bit them.

Grandpa was in his usual chair at the head of the table, carving slices of chicken like he was leading a holiday feast instead of a casual weeknight dinner. Tilly sat beside him, swinging her legs under the table, telling him all about a paint catastrophe in art class.

I sat across from her, letting the warmth of the room settle into my shoulders, letting my guard down for the first time all day.

"So," Grandma said, after a few minutes of small talk and second helpings, "I assume it's a yes, and you're entering the Honeybrook Hollow Taste-Off? You haven't brought it up, and I'm pressing the issue."

I nodded. "Yeah. Figured it'd be good for the diner. And for me. A little competition won't kill me."

"Might kill Graham," Grandpa muttered, not looking up from his plate. "This town already has a fancy place; the restaurant inside The Honeybrook Inn has been good enough for this town for decades. That boy was always too big for his britches."

Grandma shot him a look but didn't disagree. I liked that—they disliked Graham too, and I wondered if anyone else in town felt the same. But I didn't ask, I didn't want to gossip in front of Tilly.

"I've got a few ideas," I said. "Trying to find the balance between nostalgia and showing off what the Pennywhistle can do under new management."

Grandma's expression was all approval. "You should ask Eliza Darlington to team up."

I looked up from my plate. "Eliza?"

Tilly's eyes shot to me. "Do it! You'll totally win."

"Maybe, sweetheart," I answered her. "I have to think about it."

"She used to love cooking," Grandma said casually, like she wasn't dropping a conversational bomb. "You wouldn't know it by what she's doing now, but Mabel told me she used to talk about opening her own restaurant someday. I wonder what stopped her. She went to culinary school and everything."

I hadn't realized she used to cook—not like that. I'd only ever seen her behind the espresso machine, rolling her eyes and handing out sass with her fancy coffee drinks. But now that Grandma mentioned it, I could picture her in a kitchen. Focused. Passionate. Maybe a little bossy.

I leaned back in my chair. "You think she'd actually want to help me compete? Why wouldn't she do it for herself, for the Coffee Cabin, or even The Honeybrook Inn's restaurant?"

"The Coffee Cabin doesn't have the menu for it, and the Honeybrook never enters; they're always one of the sponsors. Plus, Mabel emcees almost every year." She smiled like she was two steps ahead, which she usually was. "If someone gave her the chance and the right reason, it might bring Eliza back to cooking. Mabel told me she used to have big dreams..."

"Hmm. It's something to think about." My mind went straight to her hands—how they moved when she handed me coffee, how she brushed her hair back when she was annoyed or flustered or both. I'd been keeping my distance lately, showing up at the Coffee Cabin after drop-off but not pushing for more. She'd seemed unsure after I saw her with Graham. Guarded. And I hadn't wanted to rush her. But the truth was, I liked her. More than I probably should. And now I wanted to know what had made her walk away from something she used to love.

"She's talented," Grandma added gently. "Mabel is always bragging about her. Don't let her pretend otherwise."

I nodded, not trusting myself to say anything right away. Because I was thinking about the way Eliza had smiled at me the last time I'd seen her, like she was thinking about saying something but stopped herself.

Maybe I wasn't the only one holding back.

"I'll think about it," I said. "I promise."

Grandma's smile said she knew I'd already decided.

After dinner, Tilly begged to stay the night with Grandma and Grandpa. She was already in pajamas before I got to the front door to leave.

"She needs a little spoil time," Grandma said, kissing Tilly's head. "And you need a night off."

She wasn't wrong.

I hugged Tilly, promised we'd do pancakes in the morning, and headed back to my place with the strange, unfamiliar freedom of an evening alone stretching ahead of me.

The house felt too quiet. I put away the clean dishes that had been sitting in the rack for two days, started a load of laundry, and made a grocery list that included everything from bananas to light bulbs to whatever healthy cereal Tilly had decided was suddenly "yucky".

After stuffing the laundry into the dryer, I tugged on my running shoes and pulled a hoodie over my head. The sky outside had dipped into that deep blue of evening, and the air held the kind of cold that bit just enough to keep you moving.

Running through Honeybrook Hollow always made me feel like I belonged here. Familiar streets, friendly porch lights, the smell of fireplace fires, and pine. I took the long way through town, cutting past the library and slowing near the corner lot where the renovation was almost complete on Graham's new restaurant.

It made my stomach twist in a way I hated. My mind was loose in that way it only got when my feet hit the pavement. The restaurant was all glass and glow—polished, posed, trying a little too hard to be impressive. I didn't feel jealous. Not even curious. Just... alert.

The kind of alert you get when something looks right on the surface but doesn't sit right in your gut. I'd learned to trust that feeling a long time ago—in courtrooms, in negotiations, in rooms where charm was used like leverage. Graham had that same energy. All sharp edges wrapped in confidence; eyes that measured instead of met. I lengthened my stride and kept going. Whatever Graham was selling, I knew one thing for sure—I didn't like the way it felt to be anywhere near it.

I kept jogging until I reached the park. The gazebo stood quiet and empty, the benches dusted with frost, and the trees still bare except for a few stubborn brown leaves clinging to branches.

I was halfway through my usual loop when I spotted Eliza up ahead and nearly tripped over my own feet.

She stood on the path like this was the most normal thing in the world, bundled in a light jacket, holding two leashes that led to cats. Actual cats. One, a brown tabby, moved with deliberate purpose, surveying the ground like he was mapping it for later reference. The other—an orange tabby with far more enthusiasm than coordination—had already wrapped his leash once around a signpost and was blinking up at it in confusion, clearly surprised by the consequences of his own curiosity.

I slowed to a stop, catching my breath as I tugged one earbud free.

"Are you moonlighting as a professional cat-walker," I asked, nodding at the leashes, "or is this a very niche fitness trend I missed?"

"They're mine," she lifted her chin as if that settled it. "They needed enrichment," she said calmly. "They're not thrilled."

The orange cat chose that moment to flop onto his side, leash tangled around one leg, as if staging a protest.

I laughed, real and unguarded. She tugged gently on the leashes, murmuring to them with quiet patience, like this kind of chaos was just another thing she knew how to handle. It was unfair how cute she looked doing it—hair wind-tousled, cheeks pink from the cold, completely unembarrassed. The kind of person who didn't try to be charming and somehow managed it anyway.

She smiled, but there was a sadness threaded through it, subtle enough that most people would miss it. I didn't. It stirred something protective and reckless in me—the need to ease her burden, even for a moment. I wanted to make her laugh so badly it felt like a promise forming in my chest. Not because I thought I could fix her, but because I found myself wanting to be the one who made her smile for real.

"Of course." I crouched a little, hands on my knees. "I've never seen anyone walk cats like this. Is this a daily act of bravery, or did they unionize and demand fresh air?"

"Not daily, but enough to make people think I'm an oddity," she said. "When they start looking at the windows like inmates planning an escape, then I have to take them out."

The brown tortoiseshell—sleek, alert, all coiled muscle—fixed me with bright, assessing eyes, tail flicking like he might actually launch himself at a squirrel just to prove a point. The orange tabby sat squarely on the path, round and unimpressed, paws tucked under his chest like a grumpy loaf of bread, glaring at me like I'd personally offended him by existing.

"That one hates me," I said.

"He hates everyone," she replied. "It's his brand."

I smiled despite myself. "And the other?"

"He thinks he's in charge."

"Ah," I said solemnly. "Like Lois—and Tilly. Relatable."

She snorted into her coffee cup, then tried—and

failed—to look annoyed. The knit hat pulled low over her hair made her eyes stand out, dark and warm, and the long coat wrapped around her in a way that made my chest do something inconvenient.

I straightened, suddenly aware of my heartbeat for reasons unrelated to jogging. "So," I said lightly, "do they bite, or should I risk a hello?"

"They don't bite," she said. Then, after a beat, "Usually."

The brown one leaned forward, curious. The orange tabby turned his head away in clear disdain.

"Good to know," I murmured. "I'd hate for my legacy in this town to be the guy taken down by a leashed cat in a park."

Her mouth curved, soft and real this time. "You'd recover. People here are very forgiving."

"Depends on who's telling the story," I said, meeting her gaze. "You look... nice."

It came out quieter than I meant. Honest enough that she probably knew I settled for nice to be polite, or proper, or whatever.

She blinked, just once. "You're sweaty," she said, deadpan.

"Wow," I said. "Straight for the throat."

"And yet," she added, eyes flicking over me in a way that absolutely did not feel accidental, "it's working for you."

The orange tabby cat huffed like he disapproved of her flirting. The brown one stepped closer to my shoe, sniffed, and decided I was acceptable.

"See?" I said. "I've been vetted."

She smiled, standing there with her coffee and her cats and that look on her face that made the whole park feel smaller, quieter. Like I'd found something I hadn't known I was looking for.

"Careful," she said softly. "They get attached."

I held her gaze. "So do I."

I meant it as a joke. Mostly. But something in her expression shifted anyway—surprise first, then a softness she didn't rush to hide.

"Well," she said, clearing her throat, "that makes three of you."

The brown tabby chose that moment to rub against my ankle like we were old friends. The orange one flicked an ear and continued pretending I didn't exist.

"Wow," I said. "I've been accepted into the inner circle."

"Don't get cocky," she warned. "That one"—she tipped her chin at the orange-colored loaf—"is still deciding whether you're a threat."

"I respect his process."

She laughed again, quieter this time, and took a sip of her coffee. Steam curled between us, the air sharp with cold and pine and whatever bakery down the street had started warming up. The park was almost empty—except for a couple walking a dog in the distance, and a jogger passing on the path like we weren't standing in the middle of a moment.

"So," I said, because silence with her felt charged

instead of awkward, "is this part of your routine? Coffee. Cats. Mild intimidation of strangers."

"It depends on the day," she said. "Sometimes I just intimidate strangers at the Coffee Cabin."

"Efficient."

Her eyes lifted to mine, and there it was again—that look like she was deciding whether to step closer or take a step back. I stayed where I was. Let her choose.

"You run every day?" she asked.

"Most days," I said. "It helps me think."

"And today?" she prompted. "Did it help?"

I shrugged. "Today it helped me find you."

Her breath caught. "That sounds suspiciously close to flirting," she said.

"Is it working?"

She glanced down at the cats, then back up at me. "Maybe."

The brown cat sat down decisively at my feet like he'd made a ruling. I smiled.

"I feel like I should say thank you," I said to him.

"He prefers tributes," she said. "Treats. Blind devotion."

"I can manage devotion."

Her mouth curved, slow and knowing. "Careful, Nate."

I liked the way she said my name. Liked the way she didn't say anything else after that. How she stood there with the words stretching out between us, warm in a way that had nothing to do with the steam from her coffee.

I watched the way she handled them—gentle, steady,

unembarrassed—and felt the familiar tug of a question I kept not asking. Graham hovered at the edge of my thoughts, something unfinished I didn't know enough about. I could ask. Or I could let it be. And for now, letting it be felt like the kinder choice.

"I should let you finish your walk," I said, even though I didn't want to.

She hesitated. "We're looping back toward town."

"Yeah?"

"Yeah."

I fell into step beside her like it was the most natural thing in the world. The cats tolerated it. She did too. And as we walked, close enough that our arms brushed now and then, I had the strangest, quietest thought: This. Me and her. *This* could be something.

I couldn't help but grin, imagining her leading this little parade through the frosty park, getting side-eyed by boring dogwalkers. "Well, you're definitely making this place more interesting. What are their names?"

"Remy and Linguine."

"*Ratatouille.* Right? Their names." I laughed, and she glanced up at me through her eyelashes. The sharp edges of her expression softened, just for a second. "Tilly loves that movie. I do too, if I'm being honest."

"It's one of my favorites."

I remembered what my grandma had said about her cooking and smiled at her. She stopped and studied my face—not the way customers looked at me, not the way people in town looked at the guy who took over the Pennywhistle—but the way *Eliza* always looked at me.

Like she saw too much and didn't know what to do with it.

"Kid-free night?" she asked.

"Yeah. Tilly's having a sleepover at my grandma's. I was going to do exciting things like fold laundry and buy milk, but decided to go for a jog instead."

"You know how to get wild."

I hesitated, shifting my weight from foot to foot. The night felt unusually quiet, punctuated only by the distant hum of cars passing and the faint jingling of the cats' collars. There was a comfort in the silence between us, a sense that we didn't need to fill every moment with words. Still, I found myself searching her face for answers I wasn't brave enough to ask for yet. I wanted to ask her out again. I wanted more with her, but wasn't sure if asking would put pressure on our—whatever it was we were doing.

"I've been thinking about something," I said carefully.

Her brow lifted. "Oh yeah?"

"I want to ask you something. But not here. Not while your cats are watching me."

Her smile froze—hesitant, like maybe she didn't know what to do with flirting that didn't ask for anything in return. As I looked at her, a flicker of worry crept in. There was a heaviness in her eyes tonight, a sadness she tried to mask with laughter, but I could feel it lingering between us. It made me want to ask if she was really okay, even though I knew she'd brush it off.

"Go home," she said eventually, tucking her chin

down into her scarf. "Buy your milk. Fold your socks. Maybe I'll let you ask me later. And uh—I need to talk about something with you too. Stop by in the morning for coffee?"

I nodded. "Okay." And then, because I couldn't help myself, I added, "You look good tonight, Eliza. More than nice—beautiful."

She didn't say anything. But I saw the smile she tried to hide. Before I could leave, Graham turned the corner, jogging in our direction. She didn't see him; her back was turned, but the cats circled her legs, their leashes tangling as they paced, suspicious of every breeze and twig snap in the dark.

Eliza tugged her coat tighter around herself and nudged Remy back gently with her foot. "You sure you don't want to adopt one? He growled at the vacuum this morning and then tried to fight it."

"I respect a man who knows his enemies," I said, smiling as I kept my eyes on Graham and hoping he'd pass us by.

She laughed under her breath, the kind of laugh you only earned if you'd known her more than five minutes. The quiet, real kind.

"I should let you go," she said. "You have things to do that don't involve cats on leashes."

"Laundry can wait." I paused. "Though if I keep running into you like this, I might pretend I forgot detergent just to get out again."

Her lips quirked. "That's a terrible line."

"Still worked. It got you to smile at me again."

And then the rhythm shifted.

Footsteps. Loud ones. Quick and sure, coming up behind her on the path.

Graham jogged up—his breath steady, like he'd emerged from a lifestyle magazine ad titled *Joggers Who Steal Your Girlfriend.*

Except she wasn't my girlfriend—yet.

His eyes flicked to me for half a second before settling on Eliza. "Evening," he said smoothly.

"Hey," she replied, voice neutral, but the way she shifted her weight toward me said everything.

I didn't move, just watched as he slowed to a stop. He gave me a nod—barely polite—and then turned his whole body toward her like I wasn't even there.

"I saw the lights were on at the Coffee Cabin earlier," he said. "I meant to stop by. Still figuring out the best espresso in town."

"My coffee is obviously the best, but I think you'd feel more comfortable at this cute little upscale place, about 140 miles that way,"

He laughed as if she'd flirted. She hadn't. I couldn't figure out their dynamic.

Eliza rolled her eyes, but her lips quirked at the edges, betraying a hint of anger. The air felt charged—competitive, yes, but also threaded with something unspoken between all three of us. For a moment, the evening seemed to pause, each of us sizing up the scene and where we belonged in it.

Remy and Linguini were fully on alert now—Remy

giving a low growl and Linguini half hiding behind Eliza's legs.

Graham didn't notice. Or didn't care.

He turned his smile on me. "Still getting your footing at the Pennywhistle?"

I raised an eyebrow. "Footing's solid."

"Good," he said, too quickly. "Would hate to see the place fall apart. Especially with the Taste-Off coming up. You're entering, right?"

There it was. He regarded me as competition. He looked at me like we were already standing at opposite ends of a battlefield, aprons on, spatulas drawn. But why would he care about the Pennywhistle and me? We were not the same type of restaurant, and there was plenty of room in Honeybrook Hollow for both of us.

I kept my expression flat. "I'm looking forward to it."

"I'm sure you are."

He turned his attention back to Eliza. "We should catch up soon." He took a step closer to her, that greasy smile still fixed in place—

"Shit!" He yelped, hopping back as Eliza's little brown devil released his ankle from between needle-sharp teeth and sat down again, looking deeply unimpressed.

One glance at Eliza's expression, bright with barely contained delight, had me quickly turning my head, feigning interest in something over my shoulder as I stifled my own answering smirk.

Graham straightened, face tight, forcing a laugh.

"Guess I should keep moving. Gotta keep the heart rate up."

Eliza didn't smile. She simply adjusted her grip on the leash.

"Plenty of town to run in," she said coolly.

And then, with a final nod to me that barely qualified as acknowledgment, he turned and jogged off down the path like some damn swan-necked shadow.

I watched until he disappeared into the trees, tension buzzing behind my ribs.

When I looked back at Eliza, her expression was unreadable.

"Friend of yours?" I asked carefully.

She gave a too-quick shrug. "Not really."

I wanted to ask more. I wanted to know why he looked at her like that, and why she looked like she wished the sidewalk would crack open and swallow him whole. But I didn't push. Not yet.

Remy was still growling.

"Your cat has good instincts," I said. "I don't like that guy. Don't know why—yet."

"I'm sure you'll find out soon." She huffed out a bitter laugh. "Remy's been wrong about people before, but not often."

I took a slow breath. The air had gone colder.

"Well," I said. "I should go pretend to do laundry."

She nodded. "I should go pretend I know how to walk cats."

I hesitated, then gave her a softer look. "You know, if

you ever want to talk about that guy—or anything else—I'm around."

Something flickered in her expression. Gratitude, maybe. Or regret.

"I know," she said quietly. "Thanks, Nate."

As I walked away, I tried not to glance back.

I failed.

She was still standing there, cats wrapped around her like a forcefield, watching me go.

The silence pressed down, thick as fog. I felt the weight of her words settle between us, questions swirling in my mind that I didn't dare voice. For a heartbeat, I considered going back—saying something, doing anything to lighten the moment. But instead, I kept moving, each step feeling heavier than the last.

And all I could think was—what the hell was that?

"He's my ex," she called.

Her voice rang out, slicing through the hush like the clang of a bell. I stopped short, heart stumbling in my chest. The words echoed in the chilly air, raw and unapologetic, settling into the space between us with the finality of a confession neither of us could take back. I waited, uncertain, as the realization sank in and a current of understanding passed between us, heavier than any silence. I froze, then headed back in her direction.

Chapter 10
Eliza

"I dated him," I said, voice sharper than I meant it to be. "Graham. He's my ex."

Nate had already slowed, but that stopped him in his tracks. He turned, brows raised, searching my face like he didn't quite believe it.

I hesitated, bracing myself. It was all out there now—no more half-truths, no more sidestepping the subject. For a second, we stood in the quiet, the moment filling the air between us. With so many things unsaid and the faint hope that maybe someone would understand. That someone could see through the cloak of charm Graham always hid behind.

"I should have figured it out," he said eventually. "The way he looked at you and the way you looked like you wanted to disappear."

I let out a breath. "Sorry. I didn't mean to bark it out like that. I just—since he got to town, he always shows up at the worst possible time. He always manages to make everything complicated, even when he's just passing by. It's like he has a radar for my worst moments, and somehow, he always finds me when I least want to be found. I wish I could say I was over it—that seeing him didn't bother me—but it's never that simple, is it?"

"Things like this rarely are. Believe me, I know." He stood still for a beat, then gently gestured ahead with his chin. "Wanna walk?"

"Where?"

"The Pennywhistle's closed. But I've got my keys with me. If you don't mind a dark diner. We could put the cats in my office."

"Sounds like my kind of night." I shrugged, pressing my hands into my pockets, searching for the right words. "Sure. I could use a change of scenery." Something about the idea of sitting in that familiar diner with Nate made the tightness in my chest loosen, if only a little. At least there, the ghosts of old arguments and unresolved feelings might seem less sharp, softened by the quiet promise that maybe, for a little while, I wouldn't have to pretend everything was fine.

We walked in silence down the sidewalk, the sky turning purple above the streetlights. The early evening air had that wintry, cinnamon-tinged chill Honeybrook Hollow always seemed to deliver this time of year—sharp and nostalgic, like a snow globe memory.

I glanced down at Remy and Linguine, the cats weaving impatient circles around my ankles, their leashes taut in my grip. They seemed to sense the tension in the air, each twitch of their tails mirroring the restlessness I felt inside. They padded quietly beside me as Nate and I made our way down the sidewalk, their presence oddly comforting in the thick silence between us.

When we reached the Pennywhistle, Nate unlocked the side door and flipped on a couple of lights—soft ones, the kind that made the chrome gleam and the red leather booths glow like something out of a retro pop art print.

He didn't say anything, guided me to the back, and gestured to his office door.

I took in the quiet space—the faint hum of the fridge, the scent of lingering maple syrup and bacon grease, the cozy hush that wrapped around me like a blanket. The Pennywhistle felt lived-in, loved. And even empty, it was warmer than most places I'd ever called home.

"Be good," I whispered and unclipped Remy and Linguine's leashes, grimacing as they ignored me and hauled ass into Nate's office. Remy darted behind his desk like he owned the place, while Linguini pounced on a box of tissues before darting off to catch up with Remy.

"So," Nate said as we headed to the front of the diner. "Graham, huh?"

I winced and slid onto a barstool. "Please don't say it like that. I know." The words slipped out with a raw honesty I rarely allowed myself to express. Somehow, I trusted Nate. I decided not to question it.

He nodded, pouring us glasses of water and letting the moment settle between us. He didn't push, and for once, I didn't feel the need to fill the silence with excuses or self-deprecation. Instead, I stared at the swirling patterns in my water glass, tracing the neon reflection on its surface. Nate remained nearby, steady and unhurried, as if the quiet itself was its own kind of conversation. I felt the urge to say more—not about Graham, but about the possibility of finding joy in something simple, even if it was only this simple glass of water in the Pennywhistle with the nicest man I'd ever met.

"I'm sorry. I have no reason for it, but I don't like him." He finally said as he raised a brow. He wasn't smug about it, just curious, like he cared about me and was willing to listen. "You don't owe me an explanation. But if you want to talk about it, I'm here."

I sipped my water, then set it down. "I was barely out of culinary school. He seemed impressive, confident. I thought he believed in me."

Nate's brow furrowed. "Thought?"

"I was his sous chef. I worked for him in Portland. We kept it a secret. He supported me right up until my ideas became inconvenient. I wanted to open something casual and warm, that was my dream. Either that or write a cookbook, start a social media page, I don't know—I had a lot of thoughts, different things I wanted to try. He said I was wasting my talent. Said I wasn't thinking big enough."

"He said that? To you? When you were sharing your dreams with him. Huh." The *huh* came out dripping with hostility.

My eyes shot to his, and I nodded. "Yeah," I whispered, wondering why, of all people, I was confiding in him. "He said that among other things. He never yelled. He wore me down. Compliments with caveats. Support with strings. He was older than me, and everyone loved him. He made me think I was special, and at first, being with him felt like a gift. I didn't get a lot of, um, that feeling as a kid. It wasn't until later that I realized there were way too many strings attached ever to be healthy. He said no one would understand or approve of our relationship, and I believed him, so I kept quiet."

Nate's jaw clenched. "He hurt you," he bit out. "I'm rarely wrong about people, Eliza. I was right about him. He's arrogant, unkind, and careless with people's feelings. I don't like the thought of you with someone like that. Tell me everything."

"He chipped away at me. Questioned everything. My instincts. My cooking. My confidence. Until eventually I stopped trusting myself and let him do the thinking for both of us."

I swallowed. My chest felt tight now, the truth pressing in from all sides.

"When I left, I told myself I'd lost my passion. That I'd just grown out of it." I gestured vaguely toward the Coffee Cabin. "So, I came here. Made my life smaller. Safer. Coffee. Muffins. Cake pops. A menu that never changes. A space where everything is controlled and predictable and no one gets to tell me I'm doing it wrong."

I shook my head, anger creeping in beneath the sadness.

"I never really admitted how much of myself I locked away in that little hut until now. How much I settled. How I let one man convince me that my dreams were impractical, indulgent... replaceable." My voice wavered, then steadied. "And the worst part is realizing I helped him do it." I finally looked at him. "That's what scares me. Not him. But the fact that I let it happen."

He was quiet for a long moment. Then, softly, he whispered, "You are not even on the same planet as mediocre. And you are enough. Never doubt yourself. You are more than enough."

I looked up, startled. I let his words linger, feeling their weight settle somewhere deep in my chest. For the first time in ages, I found myself wanting to reach for something more—not success or validation, a small piece of happiness carved out from this moment. Maybe it was the neon haze of the diner, the quiet between us, or simply the way he looked at me—like I was someone worth rooting for.

"You're sharp," he said. "Smart. Funny. And you've got this whole *I don't care what you think* energy that I know is mostly for show—because you care a hell of a lot more than people realize. I see it."

My heart lurched in my chest as his words settled over me, warm and unexpected, like a sunrise I didn't know I needed. For a moment, the old ache of disappointment loosened its grip, replaced by a cautious hope I barely recognized. Was it possible to believe in myself again—because someone else finally saw me, truly saw me, without agenda or judgment?

"I'm not saying that to flatter you," he added. "I'm saying it because you should hear it from someone who actually sees you, and I've had my eye on you since before Christmas. You're incredible, Eliza. I wish you could see yourself the way everyone else does."

I swallowed. "That's dangerously nice of you."

Something in me shifted, a fragile thread of hope weaving through the sorrow I'd carried too long. The diner's hum faded into the background as I let myself imagine a future that wasn't defined by past disappointments. Maybe I could try again—take a risk, trust my instincts, or even dare to dream without fear. Nate's presence made it feel possible, like the world had opened a small window just for me.

His smile was soft. "Danger's my middle name. Didn't I mention?"

"Pretty sure it's something boring like Andrew." For a second, I let myself believe him. Maybe he was right—maybe there was more to me than bruised pride and mediocre muffins. The weight on my chest eased a little, replaced by a warmth I wasn't sure I deserved. I managed a shaky smile, the kind that felt like a first step outside after a long winter.

He huffed a laugh. "Rude. And it's Joseph. Nathaniel Joseph Winters."

"Eliza Mae Darlington," I replied.

We both smiled, and the silence that followed felt different this time—thick with possibility, like something was pulling us together.

He stepped around the counter, slow, deliberate, and leaned against the stool next to mine.

"Eliza Mae Darlington. Beautiful."

I met his gaze. Big mistake.

Those brown eyes were gorgeous. And the way he smelled—soap, coffee, and a trace of vanilla from the diner was irresistible.

"We don't usually see each other without Tilly," I said quietly. "Like, lunch that one time and a few other times here and there."

"I know, and I want more."

The air between us buzzed. My breath hitched in my throat.

He didn't move closer, not quite. He just stayed there, waiting. Letting me decide.

So, I did.

I stood and kissed him.

Quick. Warm. Just enough pressure to know it was real, but not enough to shatter the fragile thread of whatever was blooming between us.

When I pulled back, he was still there, eyes searching mine, lips curved.

"That was definitely not mediocre," he said.

"Shut up," I muttered, a grin I couldn't fight quirking up the corner of my mouth.

"Okay," he whispered. "But only because I want to kiss you again."

I blinked. "You're very confident."

"Nope," he said, and his smile turned a little crooked. "I'm just really sure about you."

And damn it if my heart didn't flip like a pancake on a hot griddle.

The silence stretched between us, thick and charged. Every heartbeat seemed to echo in it, making the air electric and alive, as if the room itself was holding its breath with us. I could feel the tension humming, begging to be broken and promising something new was waiting on the other side of it. And before I could second-guess myself, I leaned in—and kissed him again.

It wasn't tentative this time.

It was heat and want and breathless need, the kind of kiss that spoke in tongues—of missed chances and long stares, of bad timing and better hopes. My hands landed on his chest, the warmth of him bleeding through to my fingers. He kissed me back like he'd been holding it in. Like I was the only thing on his mind. Like I was already his.

His mouth moved against mine with slow, coaxing insistence. He was pushy, he was confident and I liked it. He tasted like coffee and something sweeter I wanted more of. When he deepened the kiss, his hand came up to my neck, his thumb brushing the edge of my jaw in a way that made my knees go weak.

I tilted my face toward him, wanting more. Needing it.

His other hand slid to my waist and tugged me closer. I let out the quietest sound—half gasp, half groan—and he kissed me harder, like I'd undone some tether in him.

"God, Eliza," he murmured against my mouth. "You're gonna wreck me, aren't you?"

My pulse was a runaway train. "Better than mediocre, huh?" I whispered, breathless.

He pulled back just enough to look at me, eyes dark and stormy. "Not even in the same universe as mediocre."

We stared at each other for a beat, both of us breathing hard. The air was thick with everything unspoken—desire, hesitation, fear.

He stepped back slowly, hands lingering for a moment at my waist before he let go. I missed the weight of them instantly.

"We should go," he said, voice low and rough. "You're tempting me to ask for more than we're both ready for."

"Right," I said. My lips still tingled. "Go. We should."

"I have to get Tilly in the morning. But I—" He scrubbed a hand through his hair. "I don't want to mess this up."

"You haven't," I said before I could stop myself.

He smiled. "Good, this means something to me."

"To me too," I confessed breathlessly.

He stepped back slowly, hands still warm at my waist. "Yeah, we should go," he said, voice lower now, like he didn't really want to leave.

"Yeah." I swallowed, still breathless. "Totally, we should."

We headed to the office side by side, the moment oddly companionable, and he opened the door to reveal exactly the level of cat-related trouble I'd expected.

Remy leapt onto the desk, giving us a long, disapproving blink like a judgmental chaperone. Linguini knocked over a pencil cup and bolted for the doorway, skidding on the tile like a drunk toddler.

"They're not used to being anywhere else," I said. "Just my tiny townhouse. Maybe I should have kept them on their leashes. They probably made a mess of your office."

"It's alright," Nate replied, gaze still fixed on me. "Totally worth it."

I huffed out a laugh and shook my head. "Come on, walk me home before they show you what they're capable of and create true havoc."

Nate clipped the leash back on Linguini and headed for the door. "Right," he said, doubling back to switch off the lights. "Can't have your cats starting a one-night-only pancake riot in my kitchen."

I leashed up Remy with a laugh. "They're more cat biscuit boys, but fair."

He grinned and held the door open. "Lead the way."

The air had that fresh, woodsmoke-sweet crispness Honeybrook Hollow always seemed to wear after dark, like the whole town was perpetually one step away from transforming into Stars Hollow.

Nate walked beside me, hands in his pockets, still looking way too good to be true. We didn't say much, but it wasn't awkward. It was like the silence between us had weight now.

When we reached the bottom of the hill near my front door, he slowed. "This is good," I said.

"Like I'm not going to walk you to your front door," he scoffed.

"Gentleman."

He slipped his hand into mine as we walked the rest of the distance to my door. "Thanks for letting me kiss you," he murmured.

"Thanks for making it wonderful."

He grinned. "You say that like I'm done with you."

Before I could respond, he backed me against the door and dipped in again, stealing one more kiss, this one softer and slower. Like a promise he wasn't ready to say out loud. I squeezed his hand, feeling something spark and settle between us, a warmth that made the cool night seem softer. For a moment, we stood there, holding each other's gaze, letting the quiet say everything words might have tangled. The world felt small and safe, the porch light painting gold halos on Nate's hair, and I realized I didn't want to go inside just yet.

Nate leaned in, hesitating long enough for me to catch the way his eyes softened. The porch was quiet except for the distant rustle of leaves and the cats weaving between us. When his lips met mine again, the kiss was gentle and lingering, a slow exploration that spoke of patience and promise. It felt unhurried—like neither of us wanted the night to end. My breath caught, and for a moment, time slipped away, leaving just the two of us in the golden circle of the porch light.

As we lingered there, the cats twined around our ankles, meowing with approval as if they liked Nate, too. Their little meows punctuated the quiet, and Nate laughed, reaching down to scratch behind Remy's ears.

I wanted to keep leaning into him, memorizing the way his breath mingled with mine in the chilly air. It didn't feel like an ending—more like the kind of beginning that slipped in quietly, surprising you with its simplicity. The moment stretched, sweet and fragile, and

I could almost hear the soft hum of possibility in the quiet night.

He opened the door for me. "Goodnight, Coffee Elf," he said, both teasing and quiet, like a promise.

I couldn't help but laugh at the nickname Tilly had given me, the sound bubbling up warm and easy.

I flashed him a mischievous smile and teased, "Goodnight, Diner Dad."

His laughter was soft and inviting, making me want to lean in closer. When I did, I pressed a gentle kiss to his cheek, feeling his skin beneath my lips and the way my grin widened against him. The moment felt lighter, sweeter—just us, wrapped in a quiet goodnight and possibility.

Chapter 11
Nate

It had been almost a week since I kissed Eliza on her porch, and I still hadn't figured out how to think straight around her. Every time her name popped up on my phone, my stomach did that weird little drop that made me feel like a teenager again. Our texts had turned flirty—soft banter, quiet check-ins, the occasional emoji that said more than either of us wanted to admit out loud.

This morning, I wasn't working a breakfast shift, and Tilly was happily settled at school, after a drop-off drive filled with chattering about construction paper hearts and glitter glue. Grandma and Grandpa were on Lois duty for the day, which meant I had exactly one window to swing by the Coffee Cabin and see Eliza in person—without a four-year-old running interference.

The winter air was crisp, the sun spilling pale light over the town, making the snow piles glitter. There was a nervous energy thrumming in my veins as I parked outside the Coffee Cabin. I caught my reflection in the car window—hair a little messy and in need of a trim, shirt maybe not as crisp as it could be, but my grin was impossible to hide. I took a deep breath, trying to play it cool while my heart beat faster than it had in ages.

The place was already busy, the drive-thru was packed, and the walk-up window was seeing a steady stream. Still, Eliza was all I could focus on.

She was behind the window in a burnt orange sweater under her apron, hair up in one of those messy knots that made me think about how easily it would come undone. She moved fast—efficient, focused—but every so often she paused to laugh with a customer or shoot a sarcastic grin at someone she knew. Her whole face lit up when she smiled, and I wasn't the only one who noticed. The guy in front of the line nearly forgot to grab his latte because he was too busy staring.

I almost told him to keep walking and stop staring.

Bypassing the line, I stepped up to the window. She saw me and gave me a look that made my pulse jump. Not a smile exactly—but something warmer. Quieter. Like maybe she'd been waiting for me. "I'm just saying hi," I assured everyone in line.

"Hey, stranger," she said, wiping her hands on a towel. "Thought you were avoiding me."

I leaned an elbow on the counter. "Nah. Just working. You know, trying to make sure the town has pancakes and pie and all that."

Her mouth curved. "I'd hate to get in the way of your civic duty."

"I missed seeing you." The words came out easier than I expected. "I figured I'd try my luck this morning. Maybe get some coffee, see a pretty girl. Start my day off right."

She rolled her eyes but didn't look away. "Flattery before caffeine? Bold move."

I grinned. "It's part of my charm. Anyway, I'm going to get to the end of the line before I cause a riot."

Before she could answer, a familiar voice cut through the moment.

"Eliza."

Graham.

I hadn't even seen him walk up, but there he was—hands in his pockets, hair perfect, jacket expensive-looking and tailored within an inch of its life.

Eliza stiffened as I stepped into line, not wanting to start anything with him.

"Morning," she said, a little too bright. "Didn't expect you."

He stepped up to the walk-up window without a care, as if there wasn't an entire line of people waiting for coffee. "Thought I'd grab a cappuccino and let you know we're finishing the trim work today. The grand opening is imminent, and you will be invited."

"That's fast," Eliza said, glancing pointedly at the crowd of customers. "Congrats."

"Thanks." He smiled at her, totally ignoring every-one. "You'll come, won't you? I want you to see what I've built. Maybe even give me some notes."

I clenched my jaw.

"Wouldn't miss it," Eliza replied, a little too smoothly. Her voice held enough hesitation that I caught it—and apparently, so did Graham.

"I'm serious, Eliza," he added. "I've got something special planned for opening night. The mayor's coming. The chamber of commerce. It's going to be big."

Someone behind us in line cleared their throat loudly. I turned just enough to see an older woman elbowing her husband.

"I thought she was seeing Hot Diner Dad. Are they fighting over her?" she whispered. Not quietly.

"I saw them together in the park. With her cats," someone added.

"We did too," the husband muttered. "He's Joyce and Winston's grandson. Good folks." He turned to me. "You're a good boy. We love the Pennywhistle. You're doing a great job."

"Thanks," I mumbled, turning red as I contemplated running off into the distance, but Graham's presence kept me where I was.

"Mm-hmm," she said. "Graham came back to town too big for his britches. Like he doesn't have to wait in line like the rest of us. Team Diner Dad."

There was a tense pause, the kind that made the whole crowd lean in a little closer. Even the hiss of the espresso machine seemed to quiet down, as if everyone was caught in the undercurrent of their exchange.

I shifted my weight and ducked my head, pretending I was somewhere else, anywhere else.

Graham flicked his eyes toward them, clearly annoyed, but said nothing.

"Yeah, I know you can hear me," she huffed when she caught Graham looking at her. "I'm friends with your grandma, Graham. Mrs. Woods, remember me? You used to tag along with her when we played cards."

I looked at Eliza again. Her cheeks were pink—not from the cold. She looked pissed.

"If you want coffee, you'll have to get in line like everyone else," Eliza informed him, her tone flat and clipped, eyes already back on the espresso machine.

Graham slid onto a stool at the counter anyway. "I can wait until it clears."

From where I stood in line, I watched Eliza's jaw tighten. She didn't look at him this time. "Suit yourself," she said, already calling out the next order, like he was a problem she'd decided not to engage with.

He sniffed and sat on a stool.

I didn't say anything. Not yet. I stood there, waiting my turn, watching her work, letting Graham sit there and stew in whatever weird little power move he thought he was making.

After another minute, Graham finally turned toward me, flashing that effortless smile that probably made investors hand over blank checks. "Pennywhistle's looking good. Still planning to compete in the Taste-Off?"

"I am." I gave him a steady look. "You?"

"Of course. Got a little surprise planned." He winked at Eliza. "And some high expectations."

"He always did like attention," Mrs. Woods announced behind us, her voice steady.

His smile didn't falter, but something flickered behind his eyes. "Good thing I'm excellent at delivering," he shot back, smiling at her as if he had a chance to charm away her hostility.

"Right."

The whispering behind us hit a fresh high.

"Is she dating them both?"

"God, I hope so. This is better than *Days of Our Lives*."

Eliza didn't even blink. She slammed a to-go lid on a cup and leaned one forearm against the walk-up window.

"No," she said, voice flat as yesterday's drip coffee. "I'm not dating anyone. Not him. Not the other him." She pointed at me. "Not your cousin Steve. Not even myself at this point." She raised an eyebrow, "But if I ever do decide to date someone—let alone two someones— you'll know, because I'll stop looking like I sleep in cat hair and maybe start wearing more makeup. Anything else?"

A few nervous laughs.

One person backed up a step.

"Didn't think so." She nodded once, all business.

From my spot in line, I bit the inside of my cheek to keep from smiling. God, she was incredible. Sharp and funny and done with the nonsense in a way that didn't invite debate. The air shifted around her—laughter dying off, curiosity retreating—and I felt an unexpected swell of pride that had nothing to do with being involved and everything to do with watching her take her space back.

I didn't say anything. Didn't joke. Didn't jump in to defend her, even though part of me wanted to. She didn't need backup right now—she needed the circus to move on. I could tell she hated being a spectacle, hated having her life treated like entertainment. So I stayed where I was, quiet and steady, hoping she could feel the support without it turning into one more thing she had to manage.

Someone inhaled sharply.

Someone else snorted.

She handed over a cappuccino to the next person in line with a polite little nod that completely mismatched her words. "So, unless one of you is here to tip generously, or contribute something useful to society, maybe stop speculating about my love life like it's your morning soap opera. *Days of our Lives*, my ass," she muttered.

She turned, started making the next order, and lobbed a dish towel onto the counter behind her.

Someone let out an actual cackle.

Graham didn't laugh. I did.

Because damn.

His jaw tensed, his arms folding across his chest like he was trying to make himself look broader.

"Sounds like you've got your hands full," he said flatly. "Busy morning."

"Oh, you know me," Eliza said, flashing him a grin so sharp it could slice bread. "Always juggling something. Muffins, espresso, men, apparently..."

A customer in a puffer vest murmured, "She's better

than Netflix," to her friend as she took her drink and backed away, eyes still on the drama like she didn't want to miss the season finale.

I was trying not to laugh—and failing. Eliza's mouth was pure fire, and I wanted to kiss it. Instead, I kept quiet and waited, because I knew her well enough by now to know she wasn't done.

Graham's eyes flicked to me, then back to her. "Anyway," he said, "if you ever want to come by the restaurant before the grand opening, I'd be happy to give you a preview. Walk you through the kitchen, let you see how much has changed since Portland."

Her smile didn't reach her eyes. "Hmm. Tempting. But I'm pretty busy here."

That got a bark of laughter from Mr. Woods, behind me in line.

"Always with the jokes," Graham muttered, trying to play it off. "Cute."

"Bold choice opening across from the library," Eliza added, taking the next customer's order. "You'll have to keep the noise down. All those food critics whispering in hushed tones."

Graham chuckled, but it was stiff. "Eliza, always a pleasure." He stood to go, acknowledging me with a nod that was less polite and more dismissive.

"Graham," I said, nodding back. My voice was calm, yet my jaw was clenched. Watching him walk away stirred something primal, protective.

He paused briefly, perhaps expecting Eliza to say more, but she was already focused on her next task—her energy shifting, but not fading. I watched him go, feeling a flicker of relief and something sharper, protectively stirring in my chest.

"Next!" Eliza called, pivoting with perfect poise and absolutely zero chill beneath the surface. Her cheeks were flushed, and she wouldn't look at me.

I waved Mr. and Mrs. Woods and the rest of the line in front of me and waited until she handed off their drinks before stepping up to the window. "You okay?"

"I'm fine," she said, too fast.

"Eliza."

She sighed, finally meeting my gaze. "No, I'm not okay. That was a nightmare. Thank you for witnessing it in real time." She wiped a spot on the counter with unnecessary force. "I hate how smug he is. Like he thinks he still has some hold on me. Like he knows something no one else does. And the line today? Really? What the hell was that?"

"Forget the line. They're a bunch of gossips. Graham is nothing. Don't worry about him."

Her shoulders dropped an inch. "How can I not?"

"I know what I see. And I see someone strong enough to slice through him with her words alone."

She rolled her eyes. "Don't flatter me, I'm already exhausted."

I grinned. "I wasn't flattering you. I'm just trying not to kiss your smart mouth through this window."

That got her. She bit her lip, the corner of her mouth twitching. "You're impossible."

"And you're irresistible. Kind of a problem."

She shook her head, but there was a hint of relief in her eyes now, as if my words had chipped away at some of the tension. The distant hum of conversation felt softer, almost fading into the background for a moment. I leaned in a little bit, letting the silence hang between us, comfortable for once.

The line was gone now, the last few customers lingering on the sidewalk and picnic tables with their drinks and a thirst for gossip. I didn't care. I just wanted to see her smile again—really smile.

"Want me to come by after the lunch rush?" I asked. "Bring you something to eat? Give your sarcasm a break?"

She looked at me for a long moment, then finally nodded. "Yeah. Okay. But only if there's pie involved."

"Cherry," I said. "Obviously."

She snorted. "Fine. But if you're bringing pie, better bring two slices, I'm not sharing."

"Are we soulmates? I don't believe in sharing dessert," I joked, earning a small smile.

"Maybe we are," she murmured, cheeks pink as she slid my takeout cup of coffee across the counter.

"I'll let you get back to work," I said. "But if you need anything..."

She looked up, eyes meeting mine. "I know where to find you."

I smiled. "Don't forget it."

Then I stepped back.

She didn't say anything. Just watched me go with that little half-smile that made my stomach twist in the best way.

From the tables, someone muttered, "God, kiss her already."

Eliza called back without missing a beat. "Maybe he will. Tune in next week."

As I walked away, the tension in my chest didn't ease. Something about Graham—about the way he looked at her like he still had a say in her life—made me want to head to his restaurant and say screw it to being polite.

I didn't.

Not yet.

But if he kept hovering around her like that, I wasn't sure how long my patience would last.

I didn't go straight back inside the Pennywhistle after leaving the Coffee Cabin. Instead, I stood outside the back door for a moment, hand on the knob, breathing in the sharp, pine-tinged morning air like it might settle something in me. It didn't.

Graham's smug face was still burned into my retinas. The way he'd brushed past me like I didn't exist. Like I was nothing but another background prop in whatever performance he thought he was starring in. And that look Eliza had given me—like she wanted to disappear—was enough to make my jaw clench all over again.

I finally pushed the door open and stepped into the kitchen, where the sounds of breakfast prep were already in full swing—eggs sizzling, a whisk clinking against a metal bowl, someone humming along to the classic rock playlist Grandma insisted on. I found her at the far end of the counter, rolling out pie dough like she was preparing for battle.

"Morning," I said, trying to shake off the last of my irritation.

She glanced up. "You look like someone just told you we're out of bacon."

"Worse," I muttered and headed for the coffee machine.

The kitchen crew greeted me with nods and a few knowing looks—probably because I was radiating whatever blend of "annoyed" and "protective" that I hadn't fully managed to swallow down.

I tossed my takeout cup into the trash, poured myself another cup of coffee, and leaned against the counter, scrolling to Eliza's name in my messages. I had to check on her.

Me: You good?

The three dots blinked for a second, then stopped.

I stared at the screen, as if it might offer some kind of explanation.

When it didn't, I slid the phone back into my pocket and took a long sip of coffee, the burn a welcome distraction. I busied myself checking the day's orders and reviewing the shift schedule, but the moment kept replaying in my head—Graham leaning into the window like he owned it. Like he still had some kind of claim on her.

He didn't.

I knew that.

But watching him act like he did made my blood simmer.

"Eliza's working?" Grandma asked casually as she slid a tray of pie shells into the fridge.

I grunted in the affirmative.

She looked up again, sharper this time. "Did something happen?"

"No," I said too quickly. Then sighed. "Yes. Kind of. Graham was there."

Her eyes narrowed. "That boy again? My good friend Eleanor Woods said he's nothing but trouble. He did a real number on her granddaughter back when they were in school. Hmph."

"Yep. I do not like him."

"Someone needs to remind him he's not as charming as he thinks he is."

I smirked. "You volunteering?"

She wiped her hands on a dish towel and gave me a look that was half pride, half challenge. "I'd pay money to see him try that smug act on me."

That made me laugh—finally, a real one. Grandma always knew how to cut straight through the noise.

But underneath the amusement, the unease still lingered.

Because the truth was, Eliza hadn't told anyone about Graham. And for whatever reason, she'd told me. Trusted me with that truth. And now here I was, standing in my own kitchen, wishing I could do more than glower at a man who hadn't earned a single second of her time.

I texted again.

Me: If you need a break later, I'll bring
you a pie. Or a milkshake. Or both.
Forget waiting until after lunch.

No dots this time.

I shoved my phone into my back pocket and grabbed a clean towel to polish off the counter by the pass window. I could hear the morning rush building out in the dining room—forks clinking, someone laughing, the front bell chiming.

But my focus was shot.

Because the truth was, I didn't just want to bring her pie.

I wanted to be the one who made her feel safe. Wanted. Like she was more than the scars she carried.

And if Graham thought he was going to stroll into town and try to mess with her?

He'd have to go through me first.

Chapter 12
Eliza

By the time the drive-thru line thinned out, I'd reheated my coffee twice and still couldn't swallow it past the knot in my throat.

Graham had barely even looked at Nate. Barely acknowledged him—except to act like he didn't exist. But his voice had dripped with superiority, and I knew that tone. It was the same one he used to use with me in Portland, whenever I got too loud, too independent, too *much.*

I also knew what it meant now.

He saw Nate as a threat.

Which meant he wasn't going to ignore him for long.

My phone buzzed a few minutes after Nate left.

> Nate: If you need a break later, I'll bring
> you a pie. Or a milkshake. Or both.
> Forget waiting until after lunch.

I stared at the screen longer than necessary, the tightness in my chest easing a notch. The noise of the morning felt farther away somehow.

> Me: I'm okay. Just… tired of being a topic. Thanks for asking.

Three dots appeared, disappeared.

> Nate: I get that. For what it's worth, you handled it like a pro.

I smiled despite myself, thumbs moving before I could second-guess it.

> Me: That actually helps. See you around?

> Nate: Anytime.

I fidgeted with the levers on the espresso machine, wiping and re-wiping the already spotless counter. My stomach twisted. If Graham went after Nate or the Pennywhistle Pantry—even in subtle, underhanded ways —he wouldn't just be hurting a man who didn't deserve it. He'd be hurting Tilly, too. He'd be putting Nate's livelihood at risk.

And that made me want to scream.

Graham wasn't just my ex here. In Honeybrook Hollow, he was part of the town's history. The golden boy who'd grown up on these streets, left, made something shiny and successful of himself, and came back with money and confidence and a smile people trusted without question. I'd only lived here a little over a year—

long enough to be known, not long enough to be untouchable. In my head, the math was simple and cruel: people like him got the benefit of the doubt. People like me learned to stay careful.

Nate was everything Graham wasn't. Honest. Kind. Steady. And that made him vulnerable in ways Graham would exploit without a second thought. The idea of Graham's influence and money pressing against a place like the Pennywhistle—a place that actually meant something to this town—made my chest tighten until it hurt. Nate didn't posture. He didn't play games. He just showed up and worked hard, like decency was enough to protect him.

I couldn't even tell my family. Not because they wouldn't believe me—but because they would. They'd go scorched earth without hesitation, and Graham would smile through it, shake hands, tell his version of the story until I was the problem for making things uncomfortable.

I loved my sisters for that fierce loyalty.

But I couldn't risk it.

I couldn't risk letting them provoke someone who knew this town better than I did—who had roots and reach and the kind of quiet power that didn't have to announce itself to do damage. Carrying it alone felt safer than watching everything I cared about get caught in the crossfire.

I closed up the Coffee Cabin in a daze, wiped down the counters for the third time, and locked the door behind me with trembling fingers.

I didn't know what to do.

So I did what I always did when the walls started closing in.

I wandered to Paper & Pine, Cara's shop. Sitting on the corner of Sycamore Street, its tall front windows glowed warm against the gray Oregon sky. Inside, floor-to-ceiling shelves of mismatched wood bowed slightly under the weight of well-loved books, the air carrying the soft scent of paper, pine, and Cara's shortbread cookies baking in the back. I hoped the smell of books and peppermint tea would do something to calm the spin cycle in my brain.

Cara looked up from behind the counter, where she was carefully arranging a stack of journals that said things like *Plot Twist* and *This Is Fine* on the covers.

"Hey," she said, squinting at me. "You look like you've either committed a crime or you're about to cry."

"I haven't decided which way to go yet," I muttered, kicking snow off my boots and unwrapping my scarf. "Do you have anything that fixes life? Or at least makes it quieter in my head?"

"Fantasy, mystery, or self-help?" Her eyes softened, her compassion evident even through her teasing. She reached under the counter and produced a tin of her famous shortbread, sliding it toward me with a gentle smile. "Here. Sugar is medicinal, at least that's my philosophy." The kindness in her gesture made my chest ache in a way I hadn't expected, and for a moment, I let myself breathe in the comfort of her presence and the hum of the shop around us.

"I was hoping for witchy time travel or maybe a cook-book that doubles as an escape plan."

"Ah," she said, nodding gravely. "The existential dread shelf. Back left, next to 'murder but make it cozy.'"

I snorted and headed toward the back corner of the shop. Cara's store was all reclaimed wood, warm lighting, and small signs in her curly handwriting tucked between books: *"You need this."* and *"Romance lives here, you know you want it."* A patchwork armchair sat near the window with a crocheted llama pillow tucked into the side, and there was a rolling cart labeled *"Blind Date with a Book"* decorated with red heart stickers and wrapped in brown paper packages tied with twine. Of course, she was on theme for Valentine's month.

She went into the back room while I browsed, running my fingers along the spines as if they might hold answers. I couldn't even tell her what was bothering me. She liked Graham. She thought he was charming. She didn't realize what he'd done to me, how he'd chipped away at me piece by piece until I no longer recognized myself.

Cara reemerged with a steaming cup and two books.

"One's a romance where the main character gets revenge by becoming wildly successful. The other is about a woman who moves to the woods to scream and make cheese."

"Both sound perfect," I said.

She tilted her head, watching me too closely. "You okay?"

I paused. "I'm fine."

"That's your lying voice."

"I don't have a lying voice."

"You do. It's your serious, I'm fine, definitely not spiraling voice—the one with no hint of sarcasm and bereft of jokes. You want to talk?"

I opened my mouth. Closed it. Then forced a smile. "Maybe later."

She didn't push. Just sat at the little reading nook under the window and kept an eye on me.

By the time I picked out two paperbacks and a mug that said *Book Babe*, Cara had locked the front door and flipped the sign. I raised an eyebrow.

"Lucy texted. She's on her way with pizza," she said. "We're doing a cozy sisters' night right here, and you're staying."

I didn't argue. Honestly, it sounded better than sitting at home spiraling while Remy and Linguini knocked things off counters for sport.

Moments later, the sound of a key turning in the lock and hurried footsteps echoing across the wooden floor was followed by a dramatic entrance as Lucy appeared, juggling a pizza box and a tote bag bursting with drinks and snacks. Her hair was pulled up in a high ponytail, cheeks flushed from the cold. With a triumphant grin, she appeared and announced, "Party's here!" The room instantly felt warmer, her infectious energy filling the cozy space. "What's the emergency?" she asked. "Do we hate someone? Are we hiding a body? Because I have a tarp in my trunk."

Cara and I stared.

"What?" Lucy said. "I'm a children's author. You'd be surprised how often my job inspires very specific fantasies."

I snorted. "No emergency. I just needed books."

"And comforting snacks. And distraction. And possibly a bodyguard." Cara added.

Lucy's eyes narrowed. "Something is different about you. Eliza, are you crushing on someone?"

I froze. "What? No. What?

Cara blinked. "Wait a minute. Is this about Nate?"

Heat rose in my cheeks, but I tried to play it cool, grabbing a slice of pizza as a distraction. The truth was, my thoughts had been a tangled mess ever since that last conversation with him. I could still hear his laugh, see the way his eyes crinkled when he smiled. Not that I was going to admit any of that to my sisters.

She watched me carefully, then declared, "It's Nate. Pieces are clicking into place in my brain. He's at Coffee Cabin a lot, even more than a caffeine addict would be. I see him walking down there all the time. He has the jitters, and it's because of you, not the coffee."

"What? No," I blurted, my voice cracking like a preteen boy.

"Oh my god," Lucy whispered, practically vibrating. "You're crushing on the hot diner dad. I heard some things around town—involving you and him and some not-so-subtle flirting, not to mention something happening during the morning rush today? I think it's amazing. Grandma likes him, you know. She told me she did when we were walking Larry and her pugs the other day." Larry was her llama, the main character in her children's books.

"I'm not crushing on him—or anyone."

"You so are."

Cara leaned back, smug. "And I bet he's into you, too. I mean, who wouldn't be? You're gorgeous and hilarious. And you have a great ass."

"Stop it. I might die if you keep this up. I'm not kidding."

Lucy grinned. "This is the best thing that's happened to me all week. I love, *love*—everything about it, watching it happen, the beginning phases, the blushing, the denial, all the feels. This is the best. But I'll stop. Just promise to tell me all about it when you are in the acceptance phase."

"It's not a thing," I insisted. "We're friends. That's all."

"Uh-huh," Cara said, biting into her slice of pizza. "And I'm Taylor Swift."

Lucy pulled out her phone. "Do we need to do a background check on him? Google him? Deep dive his social media?"

"He doesn't have social media," I muttered with an eye roll.

"So you've checked?" She teased with a smirk. "Anyway, that's even better. I like a mystery."

I groaned and flopped back into the armchair, one hand over my eyes. "Why did I come here?"

"Because we're your sisters," Lucy said. "And because deep down, you know we love you and would do anything for you. And you know we're going to like him, too. I already do, in fact. His daughter is adorable, and she's a *Larry the Llama* fan, as you know, since you sent them my way during the tree lighting ceremony at Christmas, now known as clue number one."

I peeked between my fingers, seeing Cara and Lucy watching me with matching grins, waiting for another reaction. For a second, I almost considered spilling everything—every confusing flutter and all the secrets I'd been keeping. But the words tangled in my throat, too heavy to speak, so I laughed it off, trying to sound normal. "You two are ridiculous, you know that?" I tried to play it off like I was fine. I couldn't tell them about Graham. About what happened with him. I wasn't ready. Not yet.

The conversation faded as we turned our attention to the pizza, sharing quiet bites between us. The easy silence felt warm, and for the first time in days, I found comfort in their company, letting my worries slip away as I laughed and ate dinner with my sisters.

But the guilt didn't go away.

It stayed, coiled in my chest like a warning.

Because the more I started to like Nate, the more I had to lose.

And Graham would try to ruin it all because that's the kind of selfish jerk he was.

Later that night, once I was home, a heaviness settled in my chest. Guilt and fear tangled together until it was hard to tell where one ended and the other began. I stared at my phone for a long time, my thumb hovering over Nate's name, knowing that whatever I said next would change something.

The truth pressed down on me in a way I couldn't ignore—if I let this keep growing, I'd only be pulling Nate into the wreckage Graham had left behind. Into the quiet threats and small-town power plays, I didn't know how to fight yet. And Nate had too much to lose. Tilly had too much to lose. I wasn't worth the kind of trouble Graham could bring to their door. Not worth the risk of sour looks or whispered doubts or anything that made Nate's life harder simply because he cared about me.

That thought hurt more than I wanted to admit, because some part of me believed it. That I was still too tangled up, too unsure, too bruised in places that hadn't finished healing. That wanting Nate didn't magically make me ready for him—or good enough for the steadiness he offered so freely.

My fingers shook as I typed, my heart aching with every word. I told him I couldn't see him anymore, that having Graham in town had cracked something open I thought I'd already sealed shut. I told him I had things to work through and that I didn't want to hurt him or complicate his life. Hitting send felt like letting go of something fragile and rare—something I hadn't realized how badly I wanted until I convinced myself he deserved better than the mess I still was.

The message disappeared, replaced by the quiet certainty that it was done—and regret hit me almost instantly. Like a hollow drop in my chest, as if I'd stepped off something solid without meaning to. I set the phone face down, then flipped it back over a second later, like it might change its mind and come back with a different ending.

It didn't.

I pressed my palm to my sternum, breathing through the ache, already missing him in a way that felt unfair. Missing the steadiness. The friendship. The kindness. The version of myself that felt braver by simply standing near him. I told myself this was what protecting people looked like. That choosing distance was the responsible thing.

Even as every part of me wished I'd waited—just one more minute—before letting go.

Chapter 13
Nate

It had been a little over a week, but Eliza's text still hit me like a punch to the gut.

I can't see you anymore. Seeing Graham again reminded me of that. I'm sorry. I just need a little space. Please don't hate me...

I didn't hate her. Of course I didn't. But I'd be lying if I said the message hadn't been gnawing at me ever since I received it.

I hadn't been back to the Coffee Cabin since I got it. Hadn't brought Tilly for hot cocoa or stopped in for a quick hello. I wasn't sure if I was giving her space or just avoiding her because I didn't know what to say. I'd never kissed someone with as much intensity as Eliza. I'd never felt the way I was feeling right now, except for her. I didn't want it to end.

I reread it three times before shoving my phone in my pocket and walking into my grandparents' house like I wasn't unraveling inside.

I wanted to fix it. Protect her. Do something. But I'd seen the way she looked at Graham—tight-lipped and pale, like she was bracing for a hit she couldn't dodge. Something told me he'd hurt her in ways she hadn't said out loud yet.

And that made me want to deck him.

I knew she wanted space. But every part of me—the overthinking part, the loyal-to-a-fault part, the heart-in-his-throat part—wanted to barge through her walls anyway. Just to remind her, she wasn't alone in this.

"Dinner's almost ready," Grandma said as I walked into the kitchen, her apron on and hair pinned up like she was still running the diner instead of feeding three and a half humans and a dog.

Tilly ran past me in a blur of sparkles and leggings, Lois hot on her heels. Grandpa leaned back in the recliner with the newspaper, half-watching the chaos with a smile that said he wouldn't change a thing.

We sat down around the table fifteen minutes later—Tilly between Grandma and me, Lois parked strategically under the table for the best chances of catching dropped food.

I poked at my meal while everyone else dug in.

"You look like someone told you your birthday was canceled," Grandma said, handing me the garlic bread.

"I'm just tired," I lied.

"Mmm," she replied, not buying it for a second.

"Lois is tired too," Tilly offered, rubbing the dog's floppy ears. "She chased a squirrel, and it yelled at her."

Grandpa snorted. "That squirrel had an attitude."

I smiled, but it didn't stick.

After dinner, Grandma was clearing the plates when she glanced up and asked, too casually, "Have you picked what dish you're entering for the Taste-Off?"

"Not yet."

"Did you ask Eliza to enter with you?"

I nearly dropped the plate I was drying. "Uh, no. I haven't."

"You should," she said, busying herself at the sink. "I think the two of you would work well together."

"What do you know? Do you know something I don't?" I hesitated before asking.

The idea of working with Eliza made a flutter start up in my chest, part excitement, part dread. I pictured us side by side in the kitchen, flour on our hands, tasting sauces and laughing—except I wasn't sure we were at the laughing stage anymore. Still, maybe Grandma had a point. Maybe sharing something familiar could help bridge the quiet distance that had grown between us.

Or not.

"Hmm," she hedged. "Not much. But definitely more than you think I do."

I huffed a laugh. "Well, she told me she's not ready to date." I took a deep breath, weighing the possibility in my mind. It felt risky, like stepping onto a bridge I wasn't sure would hold—but there was something hopeful in the thought, too. Maybe if we worked together, we could find our way back to that easy camaraderie we used to share. I glanced at Grandma, searching her face for any sign that this was more than just matchmaking, but all I saw was quiet encouragement.

"Who said anything about dating?" Grandma asked innocently. "You need help, she knows food. Maybe she needs a little reminder that she's still allowed to enjoy herself. Something is different about her. I noticed it when I was picking up some decaf from your grandpa this morning."

"She's not—she's not just—she's complicated. The situation is complicated, too. I can't talk about it too much; it's her business. Not mine to share."

"Well, maybe working with you on something that matters to both of you could be good for her."

I started to argue, but then closed my mouth as my mind raced through possibilities.

Grandpa pushed his chair back from the table and stretched. "Come on, Tilly," he said. "Let's take Lois for a walk and see if that squirrel has any more attitude to spare."

"Okay!" Tilly hopped down and put on her little puffer coat.

When they were gone, Grandma handed me a towel and leaned back against the counter.

"Mabel told me how you look at her," she said softly. "So I know you're disappointed right now. But this isn't just about dating or not dating. Both of you could use a friend."

She reached for a folded sheet of paper beside the saltshaker and slid it across the table. "Here's the application form for the Honeybrook Hollow Taste-Off."

I narrowed my eyes. "I don't know about this. I'm not sure."

"Tell her I can't do it. Blame my bad knee, or tell her my carpal tunnel is acting up. Doesn't matter. You need a partner. She's it."

"That sounds like tricking her."

"It's not tricking, it's nudging. And you're not asking her on a date—you're inviting her to cook with you. She's not running from cooking. She's running from feelings." Her eyes shifted to the side. "I mean, that's my guess."

"Sure. Uh-huh. Your guess. You must have been spending time with her grandma. Is that it?"

She shrugged in answer.

I stared at the form, then looked back at her. "You think this'll work?"

"Give her space if she needs it. But don't disappear."

"She told me she doesn't want to hurt me."

"She won't," Grandma said. "Not if you show her she doesn't have to be alone. Invite her to cook. Make it her idea, if that helps. But don't give up on her."

I scrubbed a hand through my hair. "You really think this will work? Seriously?"

"I think," Grandma said, "that amazing and beautiful things often start in ordinary places. Like a kitchen counter, elbow-deep in cookie dough and pie crusts. No pressure to decide anything more than what comes next. You need to meet each other where you are and see what happens.

I stared at her, heart thudding.

Yeah. I'd ask her to cook with me.

Not as a date.

Just as... us.

Whatever we were becoming before Graham got into her head.

I sat back in my chair, thoughts spinning. Maybe she was right. Maybe Eliza didn't need flowers or romantic gestures right now. Maybe she needed flour, a prep list, and someone to believe she still had something worth sharing.

And maybe—I was that someone.

When we got home, Tilly crashed hard—pink cheeks and soft snores within minutes of being tucked in. Lois curled up at the foot of her bed like the world's most loyal guard dog. I lingered outside her room for a while, watching the steady rise and fall of her breathing. The quiet moments always got me the most.

I stepped into the hall, feeling a strange mix of hope and nerves tangling in my stomach. I gathered the courage to reach out, and I realized how small gestures could mean everything. Maybe this was the start of something—messy, uncertain, but real.

Back in the living room, I sank onto the couch with a heavy sigh and pulled out my phone.

Still nothing from Eliza. And I wasn't sure if that made me feel better or worse.

I stared at her message: *Please don't hate me.* Even in those few words, I felt her doubt, her worry about being "too much". I couldn't hate her. Not now, not ever. If she needed proof, I'd give it a thousand times over.

Eventually, I put my phone down and sat in the quiet

of the room, letting the weight of the day settle around me. The shadows crept across the walls, stretching longer as time passed. I wondered what tomorrow would bring— if it would be more silence, or if maybe it would be a step closer to understanding each other. For now, all I could do was wait, holding tight to the hope that small acts could slowly rebuild what felt fragile.

I finally typed out a message.

> Me: You're allowed to need space. I just hope you know I'm still here.

I hovered over send, then hit it before I could second-guess myself.

A few minutes later, just as I was getting ready to call it a night, my phone lit up with a call.

My heart thudded. I answered immediately.

"Hey."

There was a pause. "Hey," she said back, voice soft, a little scratchy. She sounded tired. Worn thin.

"I wasn't sure if you'd respond," I admitted.

"Me neither," she said. "But I didn't want to just disappear. That's what I used to do. I'd ghost people and call it self-preservation."

"That's not what this is," I said. "You're still here. Talking to me."

She exhaled, a little laugh buried in it. "Don't give me too much credit. I almost hung up twice."

I smiled. "You doing okay?"

"No," she said, honest as ever. "I'm freaking out a little. I can't sleep. My brain's running in circles. And I didn't want to dump this on anyone, but..." She trailed off.

"But you called me."

"Yeah," she whispered. "Because you're the only one who actually sees him for what he is. I mean, that's mostly my fault for not telling anyone but—"

My grip on the phone tightened. "You don't have to explain. Just talk to me. I'm here."

She did. She didn't tell me everything. But it was enough to crack the surface. She told me about how Graham had always made things feel like her fault. How he could twist a moment until she second-guessed herself. I didn't interrupt. I let her speak until the words ran dry.

"I'm sorry," she said eventually. "I didn't mean to make you my emotional dumping ground."

"You didn't," I said. "But I don't want you carrying this alone. And I don't want you shutting down again."

"Yeah. Me neither, I'm sorry I shut down on you."

"It's okay. I care about you, Eliza. I mean it."

"I... I care about you as well," she murmured. I could almost see her cheeks flushing a soft pink, that inherent shyness peeking out from under her usual sharp wit.

"You doing anything tomorrow?" I asked.

There was a pause, the kind that settled between words and made the silence feel heavy. I could hear her quiet sniffs on the line, how she tried to hide them, and it made my chest tighten. I hated knowing she was upset. I didn't say anything. Didn't push. I just listened, letting the stillness speak for me, letting her know I was there and I wasn't going anywhere.

"Not really." She finally answered. "Just work."

"Come to lunch," I said. "Late, like before. No pressure. Just burgers. And maybe a cherry pie milkshake if you eat all your food," I teased to lighten the mood and show her I was here for her.

She hesitated, her breathing barely audible over the line. "I..."

I wanted to reach out to bridge the distance between us, but all I could offer was patience. "You know, it doesn't have to be a big thing. Something normal, something easy. I also have something I want to run by you." I kept my voice gentle, hoping it would make things simpler for her. The invitation hung in the air, not demanding, just waiting for her to pick it up if she wanted.

"I'll think about it," she said.

"Eliza."

"What?"

"Come to lunch," I repeated, softer now. "As friends. No pressure. I'll even let you choose: fries, tots, or onion rings. It's your call."

"Okay. Lunch."

"See you soon."

She laughed then, a soft sound like relief finally seeping in. "Alright, alright. But you have to promise—no questions about my mood, okay?"

"Deal," I said, feeling something in me ease.

Chapter 14
Eliza

By the time I opened the Coffee Cabin, the world had narrowed to manageable things: heat, coffee, routine. It was the only place my thoughts didn't immediately run ahead of me.

I called my grandma the moment the anxiety started whispering its usual lies. She picked up on the first ring.

"Coffee Cabin's yours for the lunch shift," I said. "I've got plans."

There was a suspicious pause. "Plans, huh?"

"Don't make it a thing, Grandma."

"I'm not," she said, already amused. "Except to say I wore lipstick the last time I had 'plans' in the middle of the day."

I groaned. "I'm hanging up now."

"You'd better. And wear something that says you're not just coffee and sarcasm. Go home and put on something cute. No, you're young, change into something tight."

"Oh my god, you're impossible."

"I'll be there in five minutes."

"Thank you." I ended the call and stood at the counter, questioning my life choices. What the hell was I thinking?

I said goodbye to Grandma at the Coffee Cabin door, her smirk hinting she knew more than she let on. As I slid into my car and pulled onto the road, I could still feel the adrenaline buzzing in my veins. The silence in the car made it easy for my doubts to creep in—had I completely lost my mind? I replayed the morning in my head, the anxious pulse of possibility, wondering if nerves and hope had finally outpaced my common sense. By the time I parked in front of my place, I was half convinced I'd gone temporarily insane—all for a lunch that wasn't supposed to mean anything.

I stared into my closet like it might offer a life raft. My heart ping-ponged between *This is just lunch* and *This is a terrible idea.*

I still wasn't sure why I'd called him. I guess I just needed to hear his voice. Maybe I even missed him. And now here I was—trying to figure out if I could sit across from Nate Winters without falling face-first into my feelings. But most of all, I didn't want to hurt him. Or let Graham hurt him. And then there was sweet, wonderful Tilly to consider, too.

I slipped into jeans, my nicest sweater, and boots that looked like I'd tried without trying too hard. Remy and Linguini sat on the bathroom counter, judging me as I twisted my hair up.

"This isn't a date," I told them. "Just a meeting between two people who kissed like they meant it and then pretended they didn't."

Linguini sneezed. Judgment confirmed.

Nate was already waiting in a booth when I got there —jeans, thermal Henley, faint smell of cinnamon and something warm and woodsy. Like autumn and sin and bad ideas.

"Hey," he said, standing when he saw me.

His smile did things to my insides I wasn't ready for.

"You look nice," I said before my brain could stop me. "You know—for someone not trying to date me."

He chuckled. "You look nice too—for someone pretending she doesn't want to be right here."

Touché.

The table had a view of the dog park, where a golden retriever was gleefully rolling in mud, and a woman in a pink scarf was swearing under her breath. Nate passed me a to-go box from the Pennywhistle. "I got us the special instead of burgers, if that's okay. Pulled pork grilled cheese with apple slaw. And sweet potato fries, just like you wanted. Comfort food. Figured we could both use it."

"You trying to woo me with melty cheese?"

"Is it working?"

I didn't answer. I took a bite and tried not to moan. "This should be illegal," I muttered.

"Wait till you try the sweet potato fries."

"So," I said, unwrapping my sandwich, "how's Tilly today?"

Nate smiled immediately, the kind that showed up fast and stayed. "Good. Very good. She announced this morning that she's officially brave now."

"Based on what criteria?" I asked.

"Snack access and knowing where the bathroom is," he said. "She said those are the cornerstones of confidence."

I laughed. "She's not wrong."

"She also informed her teacher that our dog sleeps in her bed sometimes and that this was apparently relevant to class introductions."

I grinned. "I love her honesty."

"Less so when it's about me," he said, still smiling. "But she waved goodbye like she had a schedule to keep, so I think we're doing okay."

The warmth in his voice settled something in my chest, and for a moment, lunch felt easy again.

I almost let myself relax then—until Nate set down his Coke and looked at me carefully.

"I have an idea," he said. "Something that doesn't involve dating. Just spending time together. Doing something fun."

I narrowed my eyes. "Define fun."

"The Honeybrook Hollow Taste-Off. My grandma is not up to entering this year, and the Pennywhistle has always been at least a finalist. I need a partner. Someone who knows what they're doing."

"And by someone you mean—?"

"You. A little birdy told me you went to culinary school."

I wiped my hands with a napkin. "Yeah, I did. But I haven't cooked seriously in a long time."

"You make muffins every morning."

"Basic muffins."

"You're selling yourself short." He leaned forward. "Help me win. The Pennywhistle is my legacy. I don't want to let my grandparents down. Or the town. I'm feeling some pressure, I admit it."

That got my attention. "Go on," I said slowly.

"I know you're incredible in a kitchen."

My cheeks flushed. "You don't have to butter me up. And how would you know that?"

"Because you're incredible at everything else."

"Stop it—"

"I mean it. Do it for the diner. Or for the excitement of competition. No romance attached. Just you and me. Kicking ass. Casually." He smirked. "Unless you want to get romantic because I'm good with that too."

I shot him a look, but I wasn't entirely unamused. "Fine. Maybe. Let me think about it."

He grinned, triumphant but not smug. "Deal."

He passed me the printed registration form with a grin, as if I'd said yes instead of thinking about it. "We need to decide which dish to enter. Comfort food is obvious, but we could try something fancier if you're feeling bold."

I ran my finger along the categories on the Taste-Off form, trying to distract myself from the way Nate was watching me. "You really think we could win?"

"I think *you* could win. I'm just the guy with the big

kitchen. Though, technically, you could enter the Coffee Cabin and try to beat everyone."

I raised an eyebrow. "You're kind of confident today for a guy who admitted to burning the diner's toast when you first started."

"That was one time. The toaster was lying."

I laughed. "Sure. Blame the appliances." I rolled my eyes, but I couldn't stop smiling. "You're ridiculous."

"And you're stalling," he pointed out, nodding at the form between us. "So, are we doing this or what?"

The warmth in his voice, the ease of him—it made something in my chest unlock. He wasn't pushing—well, not seriously. Just waiting. Hoping, maybe. And somehow, that felt more persuasive than any grand gesture.

I picked up the pen.

Nate leaned back in the booth and gave me that look again—the one that made me feel like I was the most fascinating thing in the room, despite the fry grease smell and the laminated menu stuck under my elbow.

"So," he said, settling back in the booth. "If we're going to cook in front of half the county, we should probably have a plan."

I lifted my brows. "Half the county?"

He shrugged, easy. "Well, it's not just Honeybrook Hollow. A few places from the neighboring towns always enter."

That made my stomach flip—for reasons that had nothing to do with nerves. "Great," I said lightly, circling my mug with one finger. "So now we're impressing people who don't even know our names yet."

Nate's smile tilted. "Even better. No expectations."

"Still," I said, leaning forward despite myself, lowering my voice, "there will be competition. Fancy ingredients. Big personalities. People who think food tastes better if it has a French name."

His gaze dropped to my mouth. It lingered long enough that I forgot what I'd been about to say. "Let them have it," he said. "We'll stick to what we're good at."

"And what's that?" I asked.

His foot brushed mine beneath the table—soft, intentional. My breath caught. "Comfort food. Butter. Garlic. Cooking like we actually want people to enjoy themselves."

Heat curled low in my stomach. "You make a convincing argument."

"And," he added, voice quieter now, "I think we'd be good together in a kitchen."

I laughed softly, more breath than sound. "Careful," I said. "Keep talking like that, and I might start believing you."

"You already do," he said, just as quietly.

He leaned forward then, slow enough that I could have pulled back if I wanted to. I didn't. The table between us felt like nothing at all. His hand slid across the surface, fingers brushing mine as he reached for the pen—and for one suspended, dizzy second, his mouth hovered just shy of mine.

My pulse roared in my ears.

Then someone laughed nearby. A chair scraped. The world rushed back in.

Nate stilled, eyes searching mine, breath shallow. I swallowed, fingers curling around my mug like it could anchor me. When he finally leaned back, the space he left behind felt loud and unfinished.

"Worst case scenario," I said, my voice steadier than I felt, "we eat our mistakes."

His smile was slow, knowing. "Best case?"

I met his gaze, heart pounding. "We give more than just Honeybrook Hollow, something really good to remember."

He looked down at his hands, like he was giving both of us a second to breathe, and I realized mine were still shaking. I pressed my knees together under the table, trying to quiet the storm he'd kicked up inside me. That almost-kiss replayed on a loop—how close he'd been, how easy it would've been to lean that last inch. How much a part of me had wanted to.

Don't, I told myself. *You know better than this.*

But my body hadn't gotten the memo. My lips still tingled like they'd been promised something and left waiting. My chest felt too tight, my thoughts too loud. Because it wasn't just attraction—though there was plenty of that—it was the way he'd looked at me, like I was already something important. Like I mattered to him.

I took a slow sip of tea I didn't taste, and reminded myself why I built walls in the first place. Because moments like that didn't just stir hope. They made you forget how badly hope could hurt.

And still... when I looked back up, Nate was

watching me again, softer now, like he felt it too. And that was the most dangerous part.

"Now *that's* the Eliza I want in my kitchen."

My cheeks flushed. "You already have your grandma."

"She's faking carpal tunnel to play matchmaker, I'm pretty sure," he said with a wink. "But I'm not complaining."

I shook my head and fought a smile. "Okay, so what dish are we entering with?"

Nate leaned in again. "I vote comfort food. You feel like comfort food."

I blinked. "Excuse me?"

"You know what I mean," he said, trying to sound innocent. "You're warm and delicious and leave people wanting more."

I snorted. "That is the worst pickup line I've ever heard."

"It wasn't a pickup line. It was a menu description." He grinned. "And it worked, didn't it?"

It did. Damn him. I rolled my eyes, but my heart thumped a little faster. "I guess it's totally normal for us. Besides, every good team needs both a star and a sidekick."

He bumped my shoulder lightly. "As long as the side-kick gets extra gravy."

I pretended to study the form while my brain scrambled for solid footing. "Fine. Comfort food. But it has to be good. Simple, nostalgic, maybe with a twist."

"What's your go-to comfort meal?" he asked, tracing a finger along the edge of his water glass.

"Chicken pot pie," I said without hesitation. "From scratch. My grandma taught me when I was ten. It's one of the specialties at The Honeybrook Inn's restaurant."

He smiled like I'd revealed a secret. "See, that's what I want. Something real. Homey. With a killer biscuit. Or puff pastry. Or a flaky crust. I'll let you decide."

I raised an eyebrow. "Can you even make pastry?"

"Absolutely not. But I'm very good at grating cheese and staying out of the way."

"You're the dream sous chef," I deadpanned.

"Oh, I'll wear the apron. But only if it says *Kiss the Cook*."

I laughed and tossed a napkin at him. "You are shameless."

"And yet, here you are, planning a co-cooked comfort food throwdown with me like it's totally normal."

That stopped me for a beat.

Because it wasn't normal.

It felt like more.

The way his eyes tracked every expression I made. The way he leaned toward me, like gravity pulled him that way. The way I wanted to reach out and brush the sleeve of his flannel just to see if his body was as warm as his smile.

This wasn't friendship.

This was slow-burn attraction dressed up in biscuits and jokes.

I cleared my throat. "Okay. If I'm cooking with you, I'm in charge of the grocery list."

"Deal."

"And the prep."

"Sure."

"And plating. I don't trust you not to just throw food in a bowl and call it rustic."

He held up his hands. "You wound me. But I accept your terms."

I grinned, then fiddled with the pen again. "We'll have to do a trial run."

His gaze sharpened, but he didn't move. "You mean in the diner?"

"Well, I can't exactly whisk gravy in the Coffee Cabin."

His mouth curved slowly. "You're inviting yourself into my kitchen?"

"I'm inviting myself to beat every restaurant in the county. You're just my very charming assistant."

"Keep talking like that, and I might let you boss me around."

I raised my eyebrows. "*Might?* You *will* let me boss you around."

He tilted his head, studying me. "I probably will."

And that's when it hit me—not just the heat between us, but the strategy. The logic. The sense of control I'd been craving for months.

He leaned in, forearms resting on the table, eyes teasing. "You're a little scary when you talk like that, you know."

"Scary?"

"In a good way. Like, you've got this whole intimidating older-woman energy."

I blinked. "*Older?* Nate, I'm twenty-five."

He grinned, entirely unbothered. "I mean, I figured you were younger than me. I just turned thirty. Which means I'm technically the older one. But if we're going by intimidation factor, you win."

I gave him a look. "You don't seem very intimidated."

"Oh, I am," he said, deadpan. "I'm just hiding it behind extreme charm and the sweet potato fries you selected."

I snorted, but the warmth in his eyes made my chest flutter. "You're impossible."

He shrugged, a crooked smile curving his lips. "You like me that way."

"Maybe I do."

He watched me, that little half-smile daring me to admit how much I wanted this partnership, not just for the win, but for the chance to reclaim a piece of myself.

"This isn't just about cooking," I said, quieter now.

Nate's brow furrowed, like he could tell I'd shifted gears. "I know," he whispered.

"I want to win. I want to prove something."

Nate didn't speak at first, he reached across the table and touched my hand. "Then we'll win."

Simple. Steady. Certain.

God, he made it so easy to believe I could actually do it. And the way he said it made my stomach flip.

I was in trouble.

Because this wasn't just about cooking, it was about proximity. Chemistry. Trust.

And right now, sitting in his booth, planning our team-up for a public competition, I wanted so badly to forget every reason I'd told myself to stay away from him.

Nate must've sensed it too, because his voice dropped a little. "I'm glad you didn't cancel our lunch."

"So am I," I whispered.

He reached across the table and tapped the form. "Let's do this."

And just like that, I was all in.

But as I scribbled my name on the dotted line, a quiet voice in my head reminded me: I couldn't let myself fall for Nate. No matter how easy he made it, or how much I wanted to forget my own rules, I had to keep my guard up. I had to protect him.

Chapter 15
Nate

I unlocked the side door of the Pennywhistle and held it open for her, trying not to look as relieved as I felt. We were going to do a chicken pot pie trial run. It had been a few days since she agreed to enter the Taste-Off with me, and part of me worried she was going to show up and call the whole thing off.

Tilly and Lois were with my grandparents for the evening. A few uninterrupted hours with Eliza sounded like heaven and trouble in equal measure. The diner was dark except for the low glow over the counter, chrome catching the warm light. It felt strangely still—like the Pennywhistle itself was holding its breath.

Then the side door opened, and she stepped inside, a small gust of cold trailing her like a scarf. She closed the door behind her, cheeks pink from the chill, eyes lifting to mine with something soft and searching.

"Hey," she said, letting the warmth sink into her. "How is Tilly?"

I smiled—God, I loved that she asked first thing. "She's perfect," I said. "I just got a text. She already had cookies, started a movie, and convinced my grandma to braid her hair like Anna from *Frozen*."

Eliza laughed, relaxing a degree. "I love that. Cute."

Her gaze flicked up to mine again—warm, thoughtful, something deeper hidden just under the surface. "And you're sure it's okay I dragged you out for this?" she asked quietly. "After... everything?"

"Hey." I shook my head. "You didn't drag me anywhere. I'm exactly where I want to be."

Color bloomed on her cheeks that had nothing to do with the cold.

She glanced around the empty diner—quiet booths, polished counter, the sound of the fridge in back. "It feels different in here after hours," she murmured. "Like the place has secrets."

"It does," I said. "One of them is that it cooks better pot pies when it's just the two of us."

That startled a smile out of her—soft and reluctant, like she was letting herself fall inch by inch.

"Okay," she said, setting her purse on the counter. "Let's do this—mini chicken pot pies. No pressure trial run. No judging."

"Zero judgment," I promised. "Even if we burn something."

She raised a brow. "We?"

"Fine. Even if *I* burn something."

Her smile deepened, and the diner didn't feel so still anymore.

"Okay," she said, rubbing her hands together like she was psyching herself up.

"Zero judgment," I promised. "But also, this is very serious business."

She snorted. "You say that now."

I watched her cross to the prep counter, pulling out ingredients like she already knew where everything lived—like she fit here. That did something to me. Something dangerous. Something I had no business feeling right now. She belonged here; I wanted it to be true.

I cleared my throat. "So, minis instead of full size?"

She nodded, grabbing an apron off a hook. "Mini is cuter. And strategic. People will try more booths if they can taste everything without exploding."

"Spoken like a true professional," I said, tying my own apron. "Plus, tiny food is scientifically proven to make people happy."

"Is that a real study?"

"Yep. Harvard. Probably."

She gave me a smile. A real one—small, soft, and gone too fast.

I kept my voice light. "Just tell me where you want me. I'll be your sous chef. Ingredient runner. Emotional support vegetable chopper, anything you want."

She stared at me for a beat. "You don't have to tiptoe around me, you know."

I swallowed. "I'm not tiptoeing."

She raised an eyebrow.

"Okay, maybe I'm tiptoeing a little. I want to make sure you're comfortable. With all of this." I gestured between us, then grimaced. "The cooking. The contest. Not—I mean—"

"Not how it felt when we kissed?" she finished for me, voice too gentle to be teasing. "The way we started, then stopped, then started again. And now, here we are? With all the feelings we can't deny?"

Heat slid up the back of my neck. "Only if you're not comfortable with that part."

She looked at the dough in her hands, the quiet softening in her shoulders giving her away before her voice did. "I was never uncomfortable with you. The problem has never been you, or how I feel about you."

Something low in my chest loosened.

"Good," I said quietly. "Because I don't ever want you to feel pressured into anything. Not the Taste-Off. Not... us." I inhaled a deep breath to steady myself. "If you need slow, we go slow."

Her breath caught just enough that I noticed. "Nate..."

"Yeah?"

She shook her head like she was clearing fog. "Let's just cook and let whatever happens, happen. Is that okay with you?"

"Cooking I can do," I said, grateful for something to hold. "Cooking is safe. And Eliza?"

"Yeah?" she whispered.

"Anything else that comes up? You're safe with me. I swear."

"I know I am. That's why I'm here." She gave me a small, genuine smile, the kind that reached her eyes and made something inside me settle. We didn't need to fill the silence; the comfort was in the steady togetherness, the wordless promise that we were both willing to try.

The air shifted between us. It felt like it did before she broke things off in that text.

She knew it. I knew it.

Neither of us said a word about it.

"Should we get started?" I asked, and she nodded.

The diner's kitchen smelled faintly of maple syrup, and I think it would forever. I turned on the overhead lights, soft and warm, casting a golden glow over the counters and steel surfaces.

Eliza moved as if she belonged in a kitchen—rolling up her sleeves, pulling her hair back higher, tying on an apron. I watched her come alive again, hands working with practiced ease, shoulders relaxed.

I washed my hands at the deep metal sink, stealing a glance at her as she organized the bowls and measuring cups. There was a comfortable rhythm to the kitchen, punctuated by the scrape of the cutting boards being slid onto the counter, the clink of a spoon against ceramic, and our quiet laughter echoing softly between the tiled walls. The air was filled with anticipation, the kind that turns ordinary routines into something memorable.

It felt different with her here—brighter, like we'd conjured a little sanctuary from the world outside. She set out the ingredients with a practiced ease, narrating each step as if teaching a secret ritual, and I found myself hanging on every word, eager to learn, eager to share in the quiet magic of this moment together.

I took a deep breath, trying to memorize the shape of her in this light, apron strings dangling, the soft hum of the fridge filling the silence. For a second, the world outside faded away—the clatter of our preparation, the tension with Graham, even the storm brewing in my own head. It was just us, the promise of something delicious, and the possibility of a new beginning.

I helped where I could—chopping herbs, slicing vegetables, trying not to stare too long.

We worked quietly for a bit. Our hands brushed once while we reached for the same mixing bowl. She didn't pull away. Neither did I.

I caught her glancing up at me now and then, a smile tugging at her lips, as flour dusted her forearms and the scent of thyme rose in the air. There was a wordless harmony in our movements—passing bowls, sharing the sink, laughing when the dough stuck to her fingers. It was strangely intimate, all these small, ordinary acts stitched together, and I realized how much I wanted this moment to last.

"So," I said, after a beat. "What made you agree to this? Not that I'm complaining."

Her smile was quiet, but full of something stronger than words. "You did."

I looked up.

"I just—" She shook her head. "Being around you is easy. And harder too."

That made my heart trip. "Same."

We finished up the mini pot pies—two of them—then slid them into the oven. She sat at the counter while they baked, sipping hot cocoa and waiting. She curled one leg up into the seat, her eyes flicking toward mine, then away.

"Nate?"

"Yeah?"

"I don't know what I'm doing with you."

I swallowed. "You don't have to know. You don't owe me anything."

"I know," she said, then smiled softly. "But I think I want to." She watched me for a moment, then glanced around the kitchen like she was orienting herself again—the counters, the cooling ovens, the place that had become his. "Can I ask you something?" she said, lighter this time. "About you. Before here."

"Yeah," I said. "Ask."

"You were an attorney, right?" Her tone was curious, not prying. "That feels very... not this."

I smiled a little at that, leaning back against the counter. "It was fast. Constant. Long hours, high stakes. I liked it at first—felt good to be good at something that moved that quickly." I paused, choosing my words. "It was also what my parents expected. Success, momentum, the next rung before you'd even settled on the one you were standing on."

She nodded, absorbing that.

"But once Tilly came along," I continued, quieter now, "everything sped up and slowed down at the same time. I didn't want to miss things. I didn't want her growing up with a dad who was always on the phone, always somewhere else." I glanced around the kitchen again, the Pennywhistle humming softly around us.

"This felt like a way to choose her. To choose a life that actually left room."

Her expression softened, something thoughtful settling in. She took a breath, like she was about to step into deeper water.

She was quiet for a moment, then looked up at me again. "Can I ask you something else?" Her eyes flicked to mine. "You can tell me it's none of my business."

"Ask," I said. Whatever it was, I wanted to meet her there and tell her everything.

She hesitated, fingers worrying the edge of her cocoa mug. "Tilly's mom," she said softly. "Is she... around? Does she ever spend time with her? Only if you want to talk about it."

I glanced past her for a second—to the stainless counters, the prep sink full of warm water, the oven ticking softly. The Pennywhistle kitchen was closed and quiet, the kind of quiet that settled into your bones once the rush was gone. I turned back to her.

"Her name is Juliette," I said. "We dated in Portland. It was easy in a way you tell yourself won't matter later— too easy, too shallow. I didn't understand at the time how wrong that could be." I reached for a towel, drying my hands slowly. "When she got pregnant, she was honest with me. Motherhood wasn't something she wanted. Not now. Not ever."

Eliza stayed where she was, leaning lightly against the counter, listening without filling the space.

"But I knew what I wanted," I went on. "I wanted

Tilly. I asked for custody, and Juliette agreed." My throat tightened, familiar and steady all at once.

Her shoulders eased, like something inside her had unclenched. "You chose Tilly," she said quietly. "All in."

"All in," I echoed.

She stood, stepping closer without seeming to realize she was doing it, close enough that I could smell her perfume, sweet and floral. "She's lucky," she said.

"Sometimes," I admitted, rubbing the back of my neck, "I still worry I'm not enough. That one day she'll wonder why she wasn't enough to make her mom stay."

Eliza reached for me then, her fingers wrapping around my forearm, grounding and sure. "You are," she said immediately. "I've seen you with her. I know what a good father looks like." Her thumb brushed once, deliberate. "And you're it, Nate."

The words settled between us. The kitchen seemed to hold its breath—the hum of the fridge, the faint click of cooling metal, the smell of baked pastry lingering in the air. Neither of us moved.

"Thank you for trusting me with that," she added softly.

I swallowed. "Thank you for asking."

Another pause. Longer this time. Charged.

She glanced at my mouth, then back to my eyes, like she was deciding something she already knew the answer to. "I don't know what I'm doing," she said quietly.

"You don't have to," I said, just as quietly.

Her hand tightened on my arm. "Okay..."

That was it. The last thread holding us still.

She stepped into me, and then she kissed me—slow and sure, like she'd finally stopped arguing with herself.

We didn't speak after that. Not until the timer dinged and the kitchen filled with the smell of golden, buttery crust, herbs, and something that felt like hope.

We pulled apart, breath mingling in the hush that followed, and I turned away right as the oven timer chimed again. With a shaky laugh, I reached for the mitts and opened the oven, the rush of heat brushing my face as I pulled out the pot pies, their golden tops bubbling with promise.

She cut into the pie, and we shared a fork, laughing over who got more of the filling.

When we stood to clean up, she turned. I turned, too.

And then she kissed me again.

It was soft at first. Gentle. Her lips brushed mine like a question, one I answered with a careful hand at her waist. For a moment, all I could feel was the soft press of her lips, the way her hand found mine and held on just long enough to steady us both. The world outside faded, the only sound was our breathing as we lingered there, suspended between this moment and what we might become.

The world narrowed to the gentle pressure of her mouth and the faint taste of sage and thyme lingering between us. My breath caught as her hand settled on my jaw, her thumb tracing a slow, trembling line along my cheekbone. Time stretched, the oven's warmth cocooning us as the quiet of the kitchen wrapped around the delicate spark blooming in my chest.

I let myself hope—just a little as her breath mingled with mine, slow and uncertain, as we drew closer still, letting the moment unfurl between us. I felt her pulse flutter under my fingertips, a steady reassurance that echoed the quiet hope settling in my chest. For the first time in a long while, it was enough just to be here—just to feel her, to share the lingering flavors we'd created together and promises neither of us dared to speak aloud.

I didn't know what to do. The kiss lingered—gentle, electric—hanging in the air between us. I could still feel the warmth of her hand pressed against my cheek, both of us caught between surprise and something like relief.

But I didn't want to push. Didn't want to be one more person who took something from her. So I eased back, heart racing.

"Eliza..."

She touched my chest. "I kissed you. I started it. Don't you dare apologize to me."

"But we said—"

"I know." She sighed. "Let's go slow. Can we?"

I nodded, brushing her cheek with the back of my hand. "Whatever pace you need, I'm here."

The air between us was charged, sweet with possibility, and the last notes of laughter lingering in the kitchen. For a second, neither of us moved, both quietly measuring what this night had given us, and what it might mean tomorrow.

We cleaned in silence after that, moving around each other easily. She laughed once when I dropped a spoon, and I caught her watching me like she didn't want the night to end.

As we stepped outside, the glow from Graham's restaurant down the street caught my attention. Lights on. Movement in the window.

Eliza stiffened.

"Don't," I said gently. "Don't give him your peace."

She glanced up at me, lips parting. "I think he sees us."

"It doesn't matter."

I walked her to her car, opened the door, and waited.

She paused. "Thanks for tonight."

"Anytime."

She got in, rolled down the window. "Nate?"

"Yeah?"

"I feel like I'm starting to remember who I was before him."

I swallowed hard. "Good. Because that woman?" I nodded. "I know she's incredible. Because you're amazing, just as you are, right now."

She drove off. I stood there until her taillights disappeared.

Then I turned. Graham stood in his restaurant window, arms folded, gaze fixed on me.

I didn't give him the satisfaction of a reaction.

I got into my car and smiled. For a moment, the night felt impossibly quiet, the air thick with unsaid words. The distant hum of traffic was miles away, and all I could hear was the echo of her words lingering between us. I took a moment to breathe in the silence, calming the storm inside.

Chapter 16
Eliza

I woke up with the remembered taste of Nate's lips on my tongue.

For a few seconds, I lay still, watching the shadow of the ceiling fan move across the wall while Remy snored like a tiny chainsaw at my feet and Linguini purred on my hip. Last night replayed in flashes—heat from the oven, Nate's quiet laugh, the way his hand had trembled just the tiniest bit when he brushed flour from my cheek. My face went hot.

I'd kissed him.

And then I'd told him we should slow down.

Which, if there were awards for mixed signals, would get me a glittering trophy and a stern talking-to from the committee.

Still, I couldn't stop replaying the way the night had ended: his smile, my hesitation, the charged silence between us. Every detail felt amplified by morning light, making it harder to sort out what I actually wanted. I wished I could bottle that feeling—with all its mess and sweetness—and keep it close for the moments when I doubted myself.

My heart flipped between regret and hope. Had I ruined something perfect or just pressed pause on a story neither of us was ready to tell? The memory of our laughter in the kitchen lingered, grounding me as I tried to find my courage for whatever would come next.

I rolled out of bed, fed the boys, and pulled on jeans, a black long-sleeve T-shirt, and my Coffee Cabin hoodie. I twisted my hair into a knot and leaned my elbows on the kitchen counter, phone in hand, composing and deleting a bunch of different texts:

Sorry about last night?

Not sorry at all, actually.

I'm a chaos gremlin. Please advise.

My phone buzzed before I could humiliate myself.

> Nate: Morning, beautiful. No overthinking allowed today. Last night was good. You're good. We will be good.

I exhaled, a little shaky, a little lighter.

> Me: Is this your way of making me feel better? Because yes, please.

> Nate: Pretty much. And I'm proud of us. Whatever pace feels right to you—I'm with you. I'll swing by the window before work.

I set the phone down and let the relief sit quietly in my chest, warm as a fresh cup of coffee. Then I grabbed my keys, kissed both cats between the ears, and headed out.

The Coffee Cabin wore morning like a crown—strings of lights still twinkling under the roofline, the first smear of sunlight shining up from behind the Inn across the lot. Frost sugared the porch rails. Somewhere, someone's radio was playing an old carol out of season. Honeybrook Hollow didn't really care about calendars when it came to coziness.

I flipped on the brewers, checked the pastry case, and ran a quick test pull of espresso. The early rush arrived in a clatter of snow-dusted boots and wake-me-up energy.

The drive-thru stacked up—contractor truck, yoga leggings SUV lady, the newspaper guy who tipped in quarters and gossip. I moved without thinking: steam, tamp, pour, smile, mild judgment. A rhythm I knew by heart.

The bell above the walk-up window jingled once—low, familiar because I felt his presence before I saw him.

Nate.

He wore a gray hoodie and a lined denim jacket, hair damp from a shower, eyes bright like he'd invented mornings and wanted to share them with the class. My pulse did an unhelpful little hop. His smile was easy, like he belonged here amid the warmth and bustle, and for a moment, I felt the quiet thrill of routine—the simple magic of knowing just who would show up and when.

"Good morning," he said, voice soft enough that it

somehow cut through the noise to become all I could hear.

"Inspection time," I said, lifting a sample spoon toward him. "Today's special: maple cinnamon whip. Not too sweet."

He leaned in to taste it—close enough for the scent of his soap to find me—and gave me a look that landed somewhere between impressed and *you're trouble*. "I'd like that on everything I own." He grinned. "One black coffee. One cocoa with a cloud of that, to go."

"For Tilly?"

"My grandparents are stopping by the diner with Tilly; they're having breakfast together."

He passed over cash, our fingers brushing. Just a graze, but it was enough to make me want to lock up and follow him wherever he went.

"You okay?" he asked quietly while I capped the cups.

"Yeah," I said, meaning it. I hesitated, fingers tightening around the lids, unsure whether he meant the day or something deeper. "I'm okay," I said, keeping my voice light. It was easier than letting anything complicated spill out, especially with the line crawling toward the register. For a second, his eyes searched mine, almost like he wanted to ask more, but he just smiled and stepped aside.

He nodded once, like he'd been waiting for that answer, then stepped back to let the next customer through. "See you later, Eliza."

"See you," I said, and it echoed a little in my chest after he walked away.

He left, and the usual bustle resumed—a steady rhythm of orders, laughter, and the hiss of steam. I straightened up the counter between customers and tried not to linger in that moment, replaying his question and the softness behind it. The walk-up bell chimed twice, each time bringing in another piece of the morning, and I let myself believe for a minute that things could actually be this simple.

The morning thinned to a manageable hum. My grandma popped by with a thermos for me to fill and a kiss to my temple before heading to the Inn to "terrorize the linen closet." The morning rush faded, and I relaxed into the silence as I cleaned up.

That was when the shadow fell across the window.

"Busy morning?" Graham asked, as if he hadn't practiced that effortless, boy-next-door tone in the mirror a thousand times.

I didn't flinch. I wanted to. "Always."

He looked maddeningly perfect—tall, tailored coat, casual scarf, smile set to *pleasant public figure*. The kind of man people assumed could do no wrong because his hair always cooperated and he'd perfected the art of a benign smile.

"I heard you've found a new way to keep busy," he said lightly. "The Honeybrook Hollow Taste-Off. With the Pennywhistle Pantry."

"That's right," I said, keeping my voice even. "We're entering a dish."

"We," he repeated, chuckling as if it were a joke only he got. His gaze slid past my shoulder, taking in the cabin like it was a quaint exhibit. "I would have thought you'd want to keep your name off something like that. You had real potential to make something of yourself, Eliza. At least enter *this* place, or The Honeybrook Inn's restaurant. Come on."

My fingers curled into my palms, nails digging in, hurting just enough to ground me. "The entry is under the Pennywhistle," I said, clipped and final. "I'm helping as a friend."

He leaned an elbow on the sill, too casual, too familiar. "If you want people to forget you left fine dining for a coffee hut, hitching your wagon to a nostalgia diner seems like a strange choice."

There it was—the sugar-laced bite.

My jaw tightened. I forced it to loosen before my teeth could grind loud enough for him to hear. "You're opening across from the library in a small tourist town," I said mildly, though heat flashed behind my eyes. "Bold of you to disparage nostalgia."

A car rolled up in the drive-thru, saving me from saying more. I took the order, rang it through, kept my movements smooth, and my face carefully neutral. Behind my calm, something feral paced.

Graham waited, smile fixed, voice pitched low enough for only me to hear. "You were promising, Eliza. People here might not know that. I do."

I looked at him then—really looked—and let him see the edge I no longer hid behind politeness. "I remember," I said quietly. "I remember everything. That's why I'm not with you anymore."

The smile didn't crack, but his eyes cooled, the warmth draining out of them. "Careful," he said. "Aligning yourself with a competitor is one thing. Trying to beat me in a public vote? That's... unwise."

I leaned closer to the window, just enough for him to understand I wasn't shrinking. "Public votes have a funny way of reflecting what the public actually likes," I said evenly. "And around here? They like the Pennywhistle."

"And you?" he asked softly. "Do you like it? Playing sous chef to a former attorney with a new hobby?"

"What's your problem? I know you're not jealous." I met his gaze, refusing to flinch.

"Of course I'm not jealous. I'm curious. That's all. After all the time we spent together, why are you here? Doing something beneath your talents. At the very least, people know you worked for me. Look at you now."

"Maybe I'm tired of pretending to want things I don't." The words felt heavier in the air than I expected, but I didn't pull them back. "Besides, talents are wasted if you only use them for yourself. Nate is a great guy, and the Pennywhistle is amazing. His grandma can't cook this year, so I stepped in. Not that it's any of your business."

Something behind me, near the back door, rustled; I didn't look. A walk-up customer had drifted near the porch bench off to the side. Another pair of footsteps rounded the corner on the gravel, slowly—maybe people were listening, but I was too angry to care.

I handed a latte to the drive-thru customer and turned back to Graham, my pulse steady now, my grip firm on the counter.

"And furthermore," I said, my voice calm in a way that surprised even me, "I like doing work I'm proud of. With people who don't make pride feel like a mistake—and who don't criticize everything I do."

He leaned in fractionally, voice sweetening, the way it always did right before the knife. "You always were dramatic when you were hurt."

Something clicked.

Not a spark. A *pattern*.

He wasn't here because he missed me. He wasn't here because he cared. He was here because he was threatened. Because for the first time, he could see it—really see it—that I might beat him. That I was good. That the thing he'd spent years minimizing was now standing in his way, tied to a diner this town loved and a competition he fully expected to win.

The realization settled into my chest, warm and steady. Almost... satisfying.

Oh, I thought. *That's why you're here.*

I almost smiled. Almost let myself enjoy the fact that this—*me*—was enough to rattle him.

"Good news," came a voice from the side, cool as shade. "She's not going to be hurt by you ever again."

Cara stepped into view like she'd been summoned, expression pleasant and lethal all at once.

"But," she continued, "she might get very dramatic anyway. And so will we."

Relief washed through me, sharp and sudden. Not because I needed saving—but because I wasn't standing alone. I hadn't been for a while now. I just hadn't fully trusted it yet.

Graham's smile faltered.

And for the first time, I didn't feel small across from him.

"You know who really gets dramatic when they're hurt?" Cara continued. "Men. So dramatic the lot of you," She shot Graham a sharp look, then let her gaze flick down just enough. "Funny how those big egos usually cover... other deficiencies."

She stood just to the side of the porch, arms crossed over a navy peacoat, expression politely lethal. Beside her, Lucy's cheeks were pink, and her eyes were bright and furious in a way that would terrify any sensible person.

"We were dropping off books," Lucy said, too pleasantly, "but I guess we can stay and find out exactly what the hell is going on here."

Graham straightened. "Ladies. Good to see you both. You look well. Nothing is going on, right, Eliza?"

"Everything is fine," I confirmed.

"Mm," Cara muttered, clearly trying not to say anything else.

A man entered the walk-up line—Mr. Hawkins, who taught woodshop at the high school, cleared his throat. "Is this line for coffee or a show? I'll take either."

"Coffee," I said, moving to make his usual order. "A show will cost you extra."

I made his usual and slid it across the sill, heart thudding a steady, furious beat I kept under my ribs. Graham watched me like he was judging the air I breathed.

"You don't have to explain anything, Eliza," he murmured. "Least of all to them. Remember our agreement?"

"I don't have to explain myself? To my sisters? Funny," I said. "That's what I was thinking about you. I don't owe you anything, least of all an explanation for what I choose to do with my life."

His smile thinned. "I guess we'll see what the town thinks at the Taste-Off."

"I look forward to it," I said brightly, which was Eliza for *bring it, you condescending dillweed.*

He tipped two fingers off his brow in a mock salute and turned away, footsteps crisp. The porch felt larger when he left, like someone had cracked a window.

I let out a breath.

"I'm just glad Piper and Paige didn't hear that," I said, forcing a laugh. "They'd be—"

"Enraged?" Piper's high-pitched, pissed off voice floated up from the far end of the cabin, and my stomach did a flip. She and Paige rounded the corner together. "We needed coffee, instead we walk in on some kind of intimidation scene?"

Paige planted her hands on her hips. "He was out of line. Beyond. No one gets to talk to you like that. Like, what the hell? Who does he think he is? I have half a mind to follow him to his dumbass, fancy pants restaurant and kick his stupid ass." She stepped off the porch muttering, "Maybe I will—"

Piper grabbed her arm. "No." Paige shot her a look. "Okay, fine. Maybe later. After we find out what's happening here." They stepped back up and joined Cara and Lucy at the window.

Cara's mouth curved into a snarl. "I believe the legal term for men like him is *gaslighting garbage person*. Is he mad about you entering the Taste-Off? That makes no sense."

"Were you with him?" Paige asked knowingly. "Personally? Professionally? Both?"

"He's just—um..."

What was I supposed to say now?

Lying by omission was one thing. Answering a direct question with a lie—to my sisters—was not something I was willing to do.

"Both." I covered my face for two seconds, then dragged my hands down and smiled helplessly at all of them. "Okay. I love you. Please don't form a vengeance club on my porch."

"Too late," Piper bit out. "We meet on Tuesdays."

I laughed, which was maybe the first time I'd truly felt relaxed all morning. The knot in my chest loosened another notch. I prepared four mochas without asking and passed them out like party favors.

"Let's get into it later," Cara murmured. "This is not the time or the place. She's working."

"Thank you for the backup," I said quietly to her as she stepped closer to the counter.

"Anytime," she said. "Also, as your official bookish sister, I'm obligated to tell you: you don't have to be small to be safe. I'll bring some good self-help books down tomorrow, and we'll get to the bottom of all of this. Together. When you tell me *everything*."

I swallowed. "Noted."

I looked up and caught Paige watching me with that soft, knowing look she only wore for people she'd decided were hers.

The familiar comfort of my sisters' presence enveloped me, making the Coffee Cabin's usual noise seem to fade into the background. Their support was loud in the quietest of ways—a look, a gentle squeeze, a teasing word—and I realized how lucky I was to have them in my corner.

"Will you be okay?" Piper asked. "We can talk later, but I won't leave you upset."

"Getting there," I said. "Full disclosure. I'm entering the Taste-Off with the Pennywhistle. Also, Graham is my ex, and he's a huge dick. And yeah, it was a secret for a lot of reasons..." Tears filled my eyes as I grew overwhelmed, not knowing where to start.

"It's okay," Paige whispered and reached for my hand, squeezing it just once, a silent promise that she was there if I needed her. "We can talk when you're ready. No pressure, okay? We're here."

Cara leaned against the counter, her presence steady and grounding, while Piper watched me with a fierce protectiveness that made my chest ache in the best way. For the first time in ages, I let myself breathe and trust that they'd be here for me.

"We're here. No matter what." Piper's smile turned

sharp and delighted. "Listen, you're going to win the Taste-Off. And somehow, I have the feeling it will wreck him if you do. Just stay out of the dessert category, we all know who's winning that." She gestured to herself, lightening the mood.

"Don't worry, we'll think of at least a dozen ways to wreck him," Paige said. "Nobody messes with family."

Cara laughed and sipped her mocha. "We got you, no worries."

Lucy slid onto a stool at the counter and smiled encouragingly. "We're here for the duration. Go to work. We'll just sit here, drink our mochas, and make sure you're okay while we make our nefarious plans."

Customers kept coming. I kept pouring coffee. The day moved on.

And under the fear and the anger and the stubborn, stupid hope, something steadied inside me.

The line finally thinned, the last latte handed off, and the espresso machine let out a sigh like it was relieved to stop witnessing my personal melodrama. My sisters lingered at the counter, sipping the drinks I'd "accidentally" rung up with the sibling discount of zero dollars.

"You doing okay?" Lucy asked.

"I'm fine," I said, which was mostly a lie but also partly true. "Just tired. And over men who think they're the main character in my life."

Piper slid a fingertip across my knuckles. "We're not going to let Graham mess with you."

"I know," I said. "But I don't want anyone fighting my battles for me."

Paige smiled, fierce and proud. "Too late. We already submitted the paperwork. One battle, coming right up."

I laughed—really laughed—and it loosened something tight in me. Talking to them helped. It didn't fix everything, but it made me feel like maybe I wasn't bracing for an earthquake every time someone said Graham's name.

They gathered their things and got ready to go.

"Text us when you get home," Cara said.

"And if Graham shows up in the morning," Lucy added, "hit him with a milk frother."

"I love you guys," I said, waving as they left.

They left, and the Coffee Cabin settled into that cozy, warm vibe it only had at the end of the day. I wiped the counters, swept the floor, counted the drawer—tiny rituals that quieted the parts of me still worrying.

Outside, my Beetle was dusted with frost.

I drove home, fed the cats, made tea I barely tasted, and sat on the arm of the couch with the lamp casting soft gold over the room.

Then I reached for my phone.

Me: Made it home. Cats say hi. You free?

The typing bubbles appeared instantly.

Nate: Always. You okay?

I let my head fall back against the wall, closing my eyes.

> Me: I'm okay. Sisters in full guard-dog
> mode. Thank you for everything.

A pause. Then—

> Nate: I'm here if you need me. No
> pressure. I'm here for you. I want you to
> know that.

Something eased in my chest—small, warm, steady.

> Me: I know. And I appreciate it. So
> much.

I set the phone down next to me. The tea cooled. The
cats piled onto my lap like furry little weighted blankets. I
let myself breathe.

Mean for You

I'm okay. Sisters in full guard-dog mode. Thank you for everything.

A pause. Then:

Nate? I appreciate the ride home — you know I want to go with you.

Something spilled in my chest—small, warm water already.

Mark it now. And I appreciate... S—
you

Chapter 17
Nate

Morning came quietly and cold, the kind that fogged the front windows of the Pennywhistle in slow breaths. I stood behind the counter with the lights still low, listening to the coffee drip and the heaters tick. My phone lay face up by the register, Eliza's text from last night still on the screen.

I'm okay. Sisters in full guard-dog mode. Thank you for everything.

I read it once more, then slid the phone into my pocket. Okay was good. Guard-dog sisters were even better. I didn't need to rush in and try to fix anything. I just needed to be there if she needed me.

I decided not to waste any more time second-guessing if it was right to want her—I simply knew I did. The certainty settled quietly inside me, warm and uncomplicated, like a favorite song played low in the background. I liked her so much it sometimes made my heart stumble, but there was no rush, no pressure; I was content to wait for her, hopeful and patient, knowing she'd come to me when she was ready. It was enough just to care, enough to want, and to hold that longing gently until the moment was ours.

I turned the lights up, rolled out the pastry case, checked produce, and made a mental list for the lunch special. The place now looked like a second home—chrome gleaming, red booths, napkin holders shining from last night's wipe-down. Outside, a few early birds shuffled past in puffs of steam and small-town gossip.

By the time I opened up, the first wave had already formed a loose line. Mr. Hawkins ordered the lumberjack breakfast and said he'd heard there'd been "a bit of theater" at the Coffee Cabin. I told him the pancakes were extra fluffy today and left it there. Two guys from the fire department came in next, trading rumors about a new restaurant's "grand" this and "soft opening" that. I slid plates across the pass and kept the tone light.

Grandma arrived midmorning, and I swore the bell rang with a brighter jingle for her than for anyone else. She wore a lavender cardigan and a grin that could have powered Sycamore Street.

"Your coffee is weak," she sniffed, already pouring herself a cup. "Which means your nerves are strong. Tell me."

"My coffee is perfect," I said, passing her the cream. "You're just dramatic."

"Yeah, always. Your grandpa's bringing Tilly to the playground later today once they wrap up their project for her class."

She gave me a sideways look, the kind that saw right through the veneer. "You're humming thunder today, sugar. Is it that Graham?"

That Graham. She knew something. "I'm fine," I lied, then told a nearby table to holler if they needed more syrup.

"Okay, fine. You're *fine.* I know, honey." She patted my hand. "Anyhoo, fine and steady are good. She needs someone steady, and it's going to be you."

"I know, I'm patient. I'm waiting. I'm sticking around just like you said." I eyed her suspiciously. "You know something, don't you?"

"I probably know more than you do," she answered with a smirk. "But I'm not telling tales out of school. You'll find out everything when *she* tells you. Not when *I* do. One thing Mabel and I have learned over the years is to be discreet. Or at least mostly discreet."

She left with a wink and an extra biscuit wrapped in a napkin. The lunch rush hit a minute later, the kitchen finding its rhythm the way it always did when the bell started dinging, and the noise turned into a song. It grounded me. This would always ground me. The more time I spent here, the more I loved it.

That Graham came in at one o'clock sharp.

He chose the middle booth—the one that couldn't help but resemble a stage under the pendant light—and removed his scarf with a flourish like everyone was expecting him. Tall. Tailored. Waiting for a reaction. A couple of heads turned. It was obvious he wanted them to. I kept working.

"Welcome in," I called over, using as neutral a tone as I could manage. "We'll be right with you."

He gave me a two-finger salute and slid into the booth, back straight, arm draped along the top like it was a photo shoot.

When I stepped over with a menu, he waved it away. "Surprise me with your signature," he said, like a dare. "If you have one."

"The brisket melt," I said, writing it down. "Onion jam, house aioli. Fries okay?"

"That depends." He tilted his head. "How crisp is your idea of *crisp?*"

I smiled benignly. "The kind that doesn't ask for notes."

His mouth tightened in a way only people who knew what kind of man he was would see. "Then yes. And a club soda with lime. I have a meeting soon. I'm kind of in a rush."

"Coming up."

I didn't hurry. I also didn't dawdle. When the sandwich landed, it was a showstopper, like usual—melted cheese, steam curling up, the crust just shy of dark, a pile of fries like golden confetti. I set it down. He didn't thank me. He stared at the sandwich like it should be nervous.

He ate half the melt and a few fries, then set the sandwich down very precisely. I was refilling the sweet tea urn when his voice floated over, pleasant as static.

"It's still a lovely little place."

"Appreciate it," I said, still working.

"Charming. Nostalgic. A time capsule." He dabbed

the corner of his mouth with a napkin. "If I were you, I'd protect that carefully."

I wiped my hands and walked over. "We intend to."

He leaned back. "May I offer some friendly advice?"

"No," I said, and smiled so he'd think I was joking.

He smiled back with a chuckle, like we'd agreed on something. "Eliza looks well."

There it was—the point of his visit.

"Yeah. She always does."

"Mm." He tapped his glass. "She's a bit sensitive about her past, about how things ended for her in Portland. I'd hate to see her dragged into performative rivalries. Or put on display."

"Then stop showing up to her place and talking at her."

He blinked once, slowly, as if recalibrating. "You don't quite understand how this works here, Nate. Honeybrook Hollow loves a hometown success story. They've been waiting for me to come back and give them a restaurant."

"They've had a hometown favorite for going on forty years," I said, nodding at the room. "They didn't have to wait."

A smile, thinner now. "You're busy. Running a small business is—"

"—*my* business," I finished. "Which is why I'm going to keep mine running and let you discover that we can coexist without all this bullshit."

He laughed softly, like we'd reached the witty banter portion of the afternoon. Then he leaned forward, elbows on the table, and let the nice peel back just enough to show the blade under it.

"Don't get tangled up with her," he said. "You'll end up regretting it."

I met his gaze and let the smile ease right off my face. "She's an adult. You don't have a say in her life. And you sure as hell don't get to tell me what to do with mine."

He held my stare for three beats. Four.

"Just some friendly advice," he said again, lighter. "Like I said."

"Here's mine." I kept my voice level, conversational, hiding the threat that simmered beneath. Low enough that he could hear me clearly, and the three closest tables could pretend they didn't. "*You* stay away from her. She's already starting to forget you exist."

The fork on the next table clinked. Someone's chair scraped. The room didn't go silent, exactly—it went intentional. They were listening.

Graham, to his credit, didn't flinch. He took another sip of his water, set it down, and smiled like a man collecting data. "Confident," he murmured. "That'll be useful—for a while."

"It'll be useful *forever*," I scoffed. "Dessert?"

He considered declining. Then pride told him not to be the one who walked away. "What do you recommend?"

"Cherry pie," I said. "Classic."

I comped it because I set the tone in this place, not him. He ate half, paid without comment, and slid out of the booth with that exact same stage posture. On his way to the door, he paused at the counter and set down a heavy, cream card embossed in gold.

"By the way," he said, voice smooth. "Grand opening, day after tomorrow. Industry friends, a few local leaders. You should come by, get a taste of what a *modern* kitchen feels like."

I glanced at the invitation, didn't touch it. "I'll try to stop by. But I might be too busy feeding the locals right here."

His smile thinned. "Suit yourself."

"Break a leg," I said.

He paused, hand on the door. "The sandwich was better than expected," he said. "The fries were... ambitious."

"Glad you enjoyed your lunch," I said, light back on. "We'll keep a booth ready for you."

He left without further word.

"Y'all good?" I asked the staff.

The restaurant settled back into its usual rhythm— booths wiped down, the steady hum of conversation replaced by the familiar clatter of dishes and laughter from the kitchen. I took a breath, feeling the weight lift off my shoulders as the place quieted. I slipped into the storage room to text Eliza. I needed to see her. I couldn't wait.

I pulled out my phone and typed a quick message to Eliza:

> Me: Hey, any chance you're free
> tomorrow? Want to come over for
> dinner? Or come over and cook with
> me? For fun.

I hesitated for a second, then hit send, hoping she'd say yes.

A few seconds later, Eliza texted back:

> Eliza: What time?

The knot in my chest loosened—her answer was exactly what I'd hoped for. I grinned at my phone, thrilled, and already started gathering my stuff to head home and get ready.

Outside, the street had that early-evening glaze Honeybrook wears in winter—gold on glass, breath hanging, the kind of cold that made you walk faster to get out of it. Across the way, Graham's place glowed behind its papered windows. A shadow moved, or maybe I imagined it. It didn't matter. *He* did not matter.

I locked the door and didn't look again. I turned toward Sycamore. Toward the Inn's porch lights. Toward the outline of the Coffee Cabin tucked under strings of bulbs that were always a little crooked, and then I went home.

Chapter 18

Eliza

For once, the morning was mine.

I woke up without an alarm, the gray winter light easing through the curtains instead of demanding my attention. My grandma had volunteered to cover the Coffee Cabin—insisted, actually—waving me off with a smile that said she knew more than she was letting on and reminding me, twice, not to rush through my day.

So, I didn't.

I lingered over coffee at my kitchen counter, watched steam curl into the air, and listened to Remy and Linguini thump around the apartment like they were late for something important. The quiet felt strange, indulgent. Usually, my mornings were measured in minutes and muscle memory. Today, time stretched.

I cleaned without needing to, folded laundry, and reorganized a drawer just to keep my hands busy. Every so often, my thoughts drifted back to Nate's easy smile, the warmth of his kitchen, the way he looked at me like I was something that could last instead of something temporary. It felt good—dangerously good—to be seen that way, to be held in that kind of steady regard.

And yet, underneath it all, a familiar worry lingered. Wanting to be worthy of that kind of care wasn't the same as believing I was. Part of me kept waiting for the moment he'd see what Graham always had—that I was complicated, difficult, not quite enough. I pressed my hands flat against the counter, breathing through the feeling, telling myself that being nervous didn't mean being wrong.

By late morning, I showered and changed, choosing clothes with more thought than I wanted to admit. Comfortable, but intentional. Familiar, but soft. The kind of outfit you wear when you're trying to convince yourself you're not nervous.

I checked my phone—no new messages—but I didn't need one. The plan was set. Spaghetti. Cooking together. Nothing complicated.

And yet...

As I pulled my coat on and grabbed my keys, my heart kicked up a notch, like it recognized the moment before I did. This wasn't just a way to pass the day. It felt like stepping into a room where something important was waiting.

I locked the door behind me and headed for the car, the cold air sharpening my breath.

It's just dinner, I told myself.

But my pulse didn't believe me.

I stopped at the mailbox on the way to my car. It coughed up a coupon flyer, a library slip, and—of course —a heavy cream envelope with my name printed in calligraphy on the front.

I didn't open it until I reached my car.

Graham Barton requests the honor... Gold embossing. Cocktail attire. Grand opening tomorrow night. Local leaders. Industry friends. Please come worship at the altar of Me.

"Eat a baguette," I muttered, which sounded tougher in my head.

Nate's place sat a few blocks off Sycamore Street: dignified blue paint, old maple, front steps with the right kind of creak—a pair of tiny rainbow boots waited by the door beside a wicker basket stuffed with dog toys. A crayon drawing had been taped at kid-height: two stick figures, one chocolate-brown blob labeled Lois, a house with too many windows, and a sun in sunglasses. Caption: Our Home.

The door swung open on soap-and-coffee warm air.

"Hey," he said, soft like we were sharing a secret. Gray tee. Faded jeans. Simple white apron. Hair pushed back with his palm. The look on his face did dangerous things to my heart, along with other places.

As I hesitated, the scent of coffee from the kitchen wafted through the air, and Lois ambled over to greet me with a soft thump of her tail. I knelt to scratch behind her ears, feeling my nerves settle a little. There was warmth here that felt effortless, woven into the creaks of the floorboards.

"Hey," I said, stepping further in, the envelope burning a hole in my bag.

His kitchen was every kind of cozy: butcher-block counters, a chalkboard wall of grocery lists and Tilly art, a ceramic canister labeled *Cookie Emergency*. On the island, ingredients stood like a perfectionist had lined them up. Cans of tomatoes, dried basil in a mason jar, a block of parmesan, a loaf of bread wrapped in paper, and the good olive oil. A big pot was already placed on the back burner; a pan was waiting on the front.

He handed me a mug—glitter paint proclaiming Miss Coffee Elf—and pretended not to watch me smile at it. "House rules," he said. "We taste as we go and lie about nothing."

"So, no gaslighting the marinara," I said.

"Exactly." His mouth tipped. "And if you grade my garlic bread, please do it on a generous curve."

We found an easy rhythm—me at the board, him at the stove. I minced garlic while he coaxed the onions glossy and sweet; he tipped the pan like he was asking permission, and I slid the garlic in to bloom. The whole place shifted at once—into comfort, into memory, into the kind of warmth that makes you linger.

"You're humming," he said, like he'd stumbled onto something fragile.

"I am not."

"You are," he said gently.

I froze for half a second, then kept working. "Don't make it a thing."

"I'm not trying to," he said. "I um, I guess I like it when you sound happy."

My chest did that stupid, aching thing. He crushed the tomatoes with his hands, calm and sure, while I rolled meatballs—small and careful, the way I always was, like precision might keep everything from falling apart. He tore basil and told me about Tilly's dance class, about how his grandpa clapped off-beat and earned a deeply offended look from a four-year-old in a pink tutu.

I laughed, then caught myself, surprised by how easily it came.

We bumped hips at the sink. I should've moved. I didn't. Our fingers brushed, and this time the contact lingered—warm and sweet. The kitchen filled with the smell of garlic and herbs, and something softer underneath, I felt like I belonged here with him.

For a moment, I let myself pretend this was normal. That cooking with him didn't feel like stepping into a life I wasn't sure I was allowed to want. That I wasn't already bracing for the moment it might disappear.

He glanced at me then—not rushed, not distracted— and the care in his eyes made my throat tighten.

I kept my focus on the counter, breathing through it, because feeling this felt risky. And because part of me already knew this wasn't just dinner. It was hope, sneaking in when I wasn't looking.

We moved around each other without thinking about it—him reaching past me for the salt, me sliding the cutting board out of the way. He whipped up a vinaigrette, frowned thoughtfully, then held the spoon out to me for a taste.

"Well?" he asked.

I leaned in, tasted, and nodded. "It's good."

"Just good? That's all I get?" His mouth curved, hopeful.

"It's very good," I said. "But I bet you're still going to adjust it," I added.

He nodded once. "Yeah."

"Why?"

He hesitated, just long enough to tell the truth without meaning to. "Because I like knowing I tried my best to make it perfect."

The words settled between us, gentle and heavy all at once.

I swallowed. "You don't have to be so careful with everything."

His eyes met mine, steady and warm. "I know," he said softly. "Just the things I don't want to mess up."

The oven hummed, the kitchen warm and golden, the kind of cozy that sneaks up on you. He brushed a piece of parsley from my sleeve with an absentminded tenderness that made my pulse stutter. Not a big gesture. Just care, offered without asking anything in return.

"You okay?" he asked quietly, noticing my hesitation even when I hadn't said a word.

I nodded too fast, then slowed myself. "Yeah. I am. I just—" I shrugged, searching for the right shape of the truth. "I forget sometimes that things can feel easy."

His eyes softened, like he understood exactly what

that cost me to admit. "Easy doesn't mean careless," he said. "It means you're safe enough to let go."

That almost undid me.

I turned back to the counter, busying myself with the salad, when my gaze snagged on my bag slung over the chair. The stiff edge of the envelope peeked out, all sharp corners and bad timing. I'd been pretending it wasn't there. Pretending it wasn't heavy.

He followed my line of sight.

He glanced toward my bag on the chair. Obviously, he'd caught me eyeballing it like it held a nuclear weapon instead of an invitation to an evening of dread. "Everything okay?"

I wiped my hands, pulled the envelope free, and set it on the counter like evidence. "Graham's grand opening," I said. "He invited me with a pretentious invitation."

"He gave me one too," I said. "At the diner." His jaw tightened for a second. "Do you want to go?"

"Want to?" I snorted. "No. But I'm also kind of curious."

"Curious," he echoed.

"I mean... if he's really as pompous as advertised, there's probably gold-plated toilet seats, and a menu that says, 'Trust the chef.' I feel like I deserve to see that."

His mouth twitched. "You just want to be nosy."

"Absolutely. And maybe prove I'm not hiding."

He shook his head, amused, his eyes soft with understanding. "Okay. But if we're going to snoop, you're not doing it alone."

I met his eyes. "Are you suggesting we go together?"

"Yes," he said, voice low. "Go with me."

The yes came quicker than my caution could protest. "Okay," I said, then added, because honesty had apparently become a house rule too, "If it gets weird, we bail and go to my place for grilled cheese."

"Deal." The tension in his shoulders eased. "We'll be extremely polite for thirty minutes and then commit carb crimes."

"Excellent plan." I swallowed, heat rising to my cheeks for no good reason. "Thank you."

"For what?"

"For making it feel safe. Like I'll be okay if I go."

"You'll be okay," he said in a low growl. "I'll make sure of it."

He checked the pasta, stirred the sauce, ladled a little into a shallow dish, and slid it toward me with the kind of focus that makes people confess things. I tore off a piece of bread and tasted. He watched my face like he was waiting for a series of medical reports or something. I smiled as I chewed.

I put the bread down carefully. "That," I said, "tastes delicious. Perfection."

He didn't move for a breath. Then he reached across the island and brushed his thumb over the corner of my mouth.

"You're wearing it," he murmured.

"Kind of you to point that out," I whispered, but I didn't step back.

The kitchen hummed with the tension between us. The pot bubbled. I felt the yes building in my chest and didn't try to smother it. If we wanted to kiss me, I was going to let him. Heck, I might just make the first move; that's how right this felt.

"I'm trying to be careful," he whispered. "With you."

"Me too," I said. "With you. I don't want to be misleading. This is new between us, and I know I've been—"

"New doesn't have to mean scary," he said, eyes steady. "It can mean good."

I didn't plan it. I leaned in. He met me halfway.

The kiss was soft for a heartbeat—tentative and sweet, careful the way you hold something delicate in your palm. Then his hand slid to the hinge of my jaw, and I forgot how to keep things soft. I rose onto my toes; he stepped closer, crowding me gently against the edge of the island. He tasted like tomato and basil, and the stubborn possibility that maybe I could trust this. When I opened to him, he answered—slow, sure, not pushy—just enough to make my pulse go off the rails, and my fingers curl in his shirt.

A quiet sound slipped out of me. He swallowed it like a promise and deepened the kiss, coaxing rather than taking, one careful degree at a time. Heat curled through me, hungry and terrifying and so, so *right*.

He was the one who eased back, foreheads touching, breaths tangling. "I'm trying to be good," he said, a little wrecked, a little amused with himself.

"You are," I said, equally wrecked. "And I wanted that. So no apologizing."

His mouth curved, thumb stroking once along my

cheekbone like he was memorizing the map. "Duly noted."

"Also," I added, because self-preservation occasionally visits me, "we should probably not make out while the sauce is unsupervised."

He huffed a laugh and stepped back an inch, hands warm at my waist for one last second before he let go. "Saving our dinner," he said as he stirred the sauce. "One respectable simmer at a time."

"Exactly," I whispered.

"I like you here," he said, as if he'd sensed my thoughts. "In my house. In my kitchen. It feels like you're meant to be here."

"Thank you," I said, and felt the truth of it click into place.

Nate wiped his hands on a towel; I smoothed my sweater and tried not to look like my mouth still tingled from his kiss.

"You ready?" he asked, softer than before.

"For spaghetti?" I asked. "Absolutely."

"For..." He gestured between us, helpless and hopeful.

"I'm ready for slow," I said. "And for small. And for this."

Something in him eased—some tightness I hadn't realized he held. He nodded, eyes bright. "This," he echoed, and the word felt like a promise we were allowed to keep.

Chapter 19
Nate

The garlic bread had just hit that perfect, precarious point beneath the broiler between golden and reckless when Lois lifted her head and gave a single, dignified woof. Truck in the driveway. Right on time.

Eliza stood at the stove, cardigan sleeves pushed to her elbows, stirring the sauce with an easy, careful hand like she'd been born knowing how to coax it to perfection. We'd finished the salad together, set the table, and pretended not to notice how often our shoulders found each other in the small kitchen. At the sound of tires on gravel, she glanced at me, then stepped back from the doorway.

"I'll stay out of the way," she said softly, that small, careful smile in place. "Go get your girl."

"Don't leave," I said, barely above a breath. I felt silly, but I couldn't stop the words from coming out.

Her eyes flicked to mine. "I'm right here, Nate. I'm

not going anywhere—promise."

"Okay." I felt stupid, but I couldn't help myself.

I slid the bread out of the oven, cracked the window over the sink, and wiped my hands exactly as my grandfather's pickup rumbled to a stop. The screen door squeaked; I met them in the entryway.

Tilly barreled in first—pink tights, sparkle skirt, dance bag bumping her knee. "Daddy! I got all the steps right today!"

"Because you're amazing and you practice hard," I said, lifting her for a squeeze. Over her shoulder, I caught Grandpa's look, warm, knowing, taking in the house that smelled like an Italian restaurant and a night trying to become something.

He sniffed appreciatively. "That bread smells like perfection. Just like your grandma's."

"Spaghetti night," I said, setting Tilly down. She immediately took off her shoes with the urgency of a tiny diplomat late to a summit.

Grandpa leaned an elbow on the door frame and gave me one of those looks that saw past the paint. "How's that heart of yours?"

"Fine, I hope," I said.

He tipped his chin toward the kitchen—toward the quiet presence he hadn't seen but probably sensed. "You always did give your best things time."

"I'm moving slow," I said, low. "She's worth being patient for. Worth not pushing."

"Good." Two fingers tapped my shoulder, familiar as breathing. "You don't have to convince the right person to stay, son. Just give them somewhere worth coming back to."

"Grandpa!" Tilly stage-whispered, bouncing on her toes. "Can I show Daddy my star hands and tell him about how I didn't mess up even once?"

"Absolutely. I witnessed perfection today," he said solemnly, utterly sincere. "Zero mistakes." He checked his watch. "We're due at cards. I'll clear out."

"You sure you don't want to stay?" I asked automatically.

He winked. "I know when a home-cooked meal is also a moment. Mind your manners, sweetheart," he reminded Tilly, "best behavior."

"I will," Tilly promised, already peeking past me toward the kitchen like a magnet was tugging her.

Grandpa gave Lois a dignified ear scratch and let himself out. The door thunked softly. The house settled.

Tilly pivoted back to me, eyes huge. "Is someone here?"

I nodded. "In the kitchen."

She squealed and sprinted, skidding to a stop on the threshold like she'd hit an invisible line and remembered to be polite. "Hi!" she burst, then tried again, more formal. "Hello. I did star hands at dance class."

Eliza turned from the stove, lifted the spoon in salute, and smiled like she'd been waiting for this all day. "I have heard excellent things about your star hands."

Tilly beamed, instantly trying to make Eliza feel at home. "Do you want to see my room? It has a llama nightlight and a star projector and a secret treasure box, except

I can't tell you what's in it because it's secret, but I *can* tell you it's sparkly."

"Dinner first," I said, laughing.

"Then treasure time," Eliza added, straight-faced, and Tilly nodded, satisfied.

We squeezed around the table. I ladled sauce and meatballs, slid the bread basket within reach, and watched Eliza observe the small ordinariness of it all like it was surprising and a little holy.

"Tell me about dance," she said, as if she'd been asking it for years.

"I jumped over three stickers and only stepped on one," Tilly reported, demonstrating star hands at perilous proximity to the salad.

"Three out of four is very advanced," Eliza said. "I'm sure I would have stepped on five."

Tilly giggled so hard she almost inhaled a noodle. "Don't," she warned herself, then twirled a perfect forkful and grinned. "I have good manners," she announced through a mouthful of spaghetti.

We ate. We passed bread. Tilly created a Parmesan snowstorm on her plate; I didn't stop her. Lois patrolled under the table like a canine shark waiting for scraps. Eliza asked about the sauce recipe, and I told her it was my grandma's. I asked about the Coffee Cabin and watched her hands animate, her shoulders unwind. The room did some of the talking—about easy, about familiar, about *this is what it can feel like.*

Once, she caught me looking. She held the look for a beat. Between us, something settled—recognition, gratitude, a quiet awe—and we set it gently on the table like a fragile thing worth protecting.

"Is this what it's like?" Tilly asked suddenly. Her voice was small, earnest. A noodle dangled from her fork, forgotten. "Like... having a mom?"

The room went still.

My chest tightened so fast it almost hurt. I felt the question land before I could think, felt the weight of it press into all of us at once.

Eliza froze, too. Just for a heartbeat. Then her eyes went bright, glassy in a way that made my throat burn. She blinked once—steadying herself, the way people do when they're holding something precious and breakable —and when she spoke, her voice was soft but sure.

"I think it's like having people who see you," she said. "And want you. And keep showing up." She smiled at Tilly, warm and soft. "You don't have to be a mom to do that for someone. You only have to care. And I care about you, Tilly. I'm really happy to be having dinner with you tonight. Thank you for letting me."

Tilly considered that with the seriousness only kids manage, then nodded, decisive. "Okay," she said. "Like Daddy cares." Another nod. "And Grandma and Grandpa."

"Exactly like that," Eliza said. Her voice didn't crack —but her eyes did, shining with tears she refused to let fall. I saw her swallow, saw the effort it took, and something in me shifted, permanent and fierce.

I leaned over and kissed the top of Tilly's head, breathing her in for a second like I needed the reminder.

"You matter more than anything," I said quietly, and felt it settle in my chest as truth instead of reassurance. She smiled, small and satisfied, and went back to her noodles like she hadn't just cracked something wide open in the room. Eliza sat very still beside me, her hand curled tight around her fork, eyes shining in that brave way that meant she was holding herself together by choice, not habit.

The air felt different after that—warmer, heavier, like something sacred had slipped into the space between us. We didn't make promises or label it. It was just the unmistakable feeling that whatever this was, it was unfolding faster than we ever could have imagined.

"Also, spaghetti," Tilly added wisely. "Spaghetti matters too. It makes people happy. I'm always happy on spaghetti night—especially this one."

Eliza let out a soft, surprised laugh, the kind that sounded like relief. "That's a very important data point," she said seriously.

Tilly nodded, pleased. "It's science. That's what Grandma says about everything."

I shook my head, smiling despite the tightness in my chest. "Hard to argue with that."

Tilly twirled another noodle and grinned at us both. "We should have spaghetti night together all the time. It's better when there are more people."

For a while, we just sat in the glow of the kitchen, the kind of quiet that feels full. There was no rush to clear plates or hurry bedtime, just the slow settling of comfort around the table. I noticed Eliza tracing the edge of her napkin, Tilly humming softly as she stacked her fork on her plate. Lois let out a sigh, her tail thumping once in contentment beneath the table.

We cleared the table, and I loaded the dishwasher while Eliza put the leftovers in storage containers. Tilly drew on the chalkboard and narrated a story about a llama learning ballet from a fairy mechanic. Lois sprawled in the doorway, eyes half-lidded, waiting for gravity to deliver meatballs. No dessert tonight—just shared orange slices and three small squares of dark chocolate, Tilly declared were "almost as good as real sweets."

After our treat, Tilly dragged her favorite board game out from the hall closet like it was a ceremonial event. The box was battered, corners soft from love, the lid taped in two places. This wasn't a game you bought in a store. This was a game Tilly had made.

She plopped it onto the coffee table with authority and climbed onto the rug, already sorting the mismatched pieces. The board itself was a piece of poster board covered in crayon roads, glitter stickers, and what looked like several abandoned rules crossed out and rewritten in marker.

"Okay," she said seriously, pushing her bangs out of her eyes. "This is *Princesses, Puppies, and Lava.*"

Eliza crouched down, studying the board like she was reviewing blueprints. "That sounds dangerous."

"It is," Tilly said solemnly. "And also, fun."

She held up a crooked little token — a bottle cap with a star sticker peeling off one side. "This one is you."

Eliza accepted it with ceremony. "Excellent choice. I look extremely powerful."

Tilly grinned. "You *are* powerful."

Something in my chest did that quiet ache again.

We played, sprawled on the floor, legs crossed and overlapping, Lois snoring softly from her bed in the corner. Tilly explained the rules with creative liberties, changing them whenever the outcome didn't suit her. Eliza followed along like it was the most important instruction manual in the world, gasping at setbacks, celebrating tiny victories, letting Tilly "help" her even when it wasn't necessary.

At one point, Eliza caught my eye over the glitter-smeared board and smiled — small, private, like we were sharing a secret. *This could be something.*

Halfway through the game, when Eliza's bottle-cap token landed squarely on a glittery lava square that absolutely should've sent her back to the beginning, Tilly paused.

She stared at the board. Then at Eliza. Then back at the board again.

"Hm," she said, dragging the sound out thoughtfully.

I waited for the inevitable rule rewrite that would somehow benefit her.

Instead, she nodded once, decisive. "Okay. You can win this one. That lava pit is a power source this time."

Eliza blinked. "I can?"

"Yeah," Tilly said, like it was obvious. "Because you're new. And because you're nice. And because sometimes people should get to win. Also, it's my game, so I'm kind of the boss of it."

I choked on a laugh. "You *never* let anyone win."

Tilly shrugged, already moving Eliza's piece forward. "I do today."

Eliza's eyes went shiny—fast, like she hadn't expected that kindness to hit her right in the chest. She pressed a hand to her heart dramatically. "I will treasure this victory forever."

"You should," Tilly informed her, while quirking an eyebrow. "It's very rare."

When Eliza "won" the game a few turns later. She celebrated quietly, like she knew it wasn't really about the game. She reached out and squeezed Tilly's hand, gratitude soft and filled with silent humor.

Something in the room shifted then—just a small, solid click into place. And I thought, yeah. They see each other, they like each other, and that mattered more than who actually won.

A gentle sleepiness settled over us like a favorite blanket. The kind that comes not from a busy day, but from feeling safe and comfortable.

I caught Eliza's glance, warm and wondering, as if she was memorizing the feeling too.

Tilly yawned big, sleepy and content, and Lois took her post as bedtime escort, ready to go upstairs, tail wagging softly. The house felt like it was holding its breath, waiting for the next good thing to happen.

Chapter 20
Eliza

Tilly didn't wait for permission.

She grabbed my hand and tugged me toward the stairs with the urgency of someone who had Very Important Things to show me. "Come see my room," she said, already halfway up. "Daddy, let me put the stickers on myself."

Nate caught my eye over her head, a silent *good luck*, and I let Tilly tow me upward.

Her room was at the end of the hall, door thrown wide like it had no secrets. The first thing I noticed was the color—soft blues and warm yellows, nothing too precious, nothing too careful. The second thing was the height of everything. Stickers were scattered along the closet door at exactly Tilly-eye level, crooked and overlapping, some peeling at the corners. Stars. Dinosaurs. One lonely unicorn that had clearly lost a fight with gravity.

"I did those," she announced proudly, pointing. "Daddy said straight ones are boring."

"They're perfect," I said, and I meant it.

Her bed was low and piled high with stuffed animals —bears and bunnies and one very loved octopus with a missing eye. Books were stacked in messy towers beside it, pages dog-eared, bookmarks improvised from ribbons and old receipts. A nightlight shaped like a llama glowed softly on the dresser, casting a gentle wash of light across the room.

It felt lived in. Joyful. Like a place made for a child instead of a photograph.

I thought, unbidden, of my own childhood bedroom —everything matching, everything untouched. The kind of room you weren't supposed to *exist* in too loudly. No stickers. No mess. No evidence I'd ever been a kid at all. Just a space meant to look pretty for my mother's friends to admire when they brought their daughters over for a playdate.

This room looked like love.

"There's my dancing shelf," Tilly said, hopping onto the bed and pointing out her little trophies and ribbons with wild enthusiasm. "And that's where Daddy sits when he reads. He does the voices." She gestured to a rocking chair in the corner, then plopped onto the edge of the bed.

"I do not do the voices," Nate called from downstairs.

"Yes, you do," Tilly yelled back. "You do the dragon ones the best."

I laughed, feeling things I never thought were meant for me. The room felt full of possibility—of scraped knees and bedtime stories, and stickers added whenever someone felt like it. Of a little girl who was allowed to take up space and feel all of her feelings with glorious abandon.

Tilly dove beneath the covers and resurfaced, clutching a very well-loved reindeer with one floppy antler and a sweater that had seen better days.

"And this is Waffles," she said reverently. "Remember him?"

My heart actually skipped. "Waffles the Reindeer?"

She nodded hard. "You know him!"

"I do," I said, crouching so I was eye level with both of them. "I met him first. At the Coffee Cabin."

Her face lit up. "Daddy said you'd remember!" She pressed Waffles into my hands like a ceremonial offering. "He came home with me from the grocery store by our old house. Daddy said he needed a real family."

I swallowed. "That sounds like something your dad would say."

Waffles was softer than I expected, the kind of softness that only comes from being hugged a lot. One button eye was slightly loose, and the stitching on his nose had been repaired—carefully, lovingly.

"He sleeps here," Tilly announced, hopping off the bed and bounding over to the corner of the room. She showed me a little wooden cradle, hand-painted and clearly homemade, tucked beside the bookshelf. Inside it were two other stuffed animals, arranged with the kind of care usually reserved for sleeping babies.

"Oh," I breathed. "He has a cradle."

Tilly nodded as she tucked him in with the other stuffed animals. "Daddy made it. Because Waffles was lonely at night. I can't sleep with him, I throw everything on the floor when I'm dreaming, even my blankets. I'm very kicky."

From the doorway, Nate cleared his throat. "He was having a hard time adjusting," he said lightly, but his eyes were soft. "Big move. New town."

Tilly climbed onto the bed again and patted the blanket beside her. "You can help tuck him in next time," she told me. "He likes it when people tell him he's cute."

Something warm and fragile settled in my chest.

"I'd like that," I said. "Very much."

She grinned, satisfied, then yawned so big it nearly tipped her over.

Nate stepped fully into the room then, resting his hand on the doorframe. "Okay, sweetheart," he said gently. "Time for bed."

Tilly nodded, suddenly all seriousness again. She pointed at Waffles. "He needs a kiss."

I leaned in and pressed a soft kiss to the top of the reindeer's head. "Goodnight, Waffles."

"He wants you to have a good night, too," Tilly told me.

I stood there for a moment longer, taking in the stickers, the cradle, the mess, and the magic of it all.

This room wasn't perfect.

It was loved.

And that realization stayed with me all the way back downstairs, long after Nate's voice faded and Tilly's voice softened into sleep.

Chapter 21
Nate

Eliza's footsteps faded down the stairs, the sound gentle, unhurried. I stood in the doorway of Tilly's room for a second longer than necessary, watching her take in the space.

I hadn't planned for this—this feeling, this hope that edged in where I'd kept things carefully practical for years. I'd built my life around what I could manage, what I could protect. A job with less pressure. A schedule that bent around school drop-offs and dance class. A house that felt solid, predictable. Safe. Eliza slipped into that structure without trying to rearrange it, and somehow made it feel bigger instead. Like there was room for more than survival now. Like maybe wanting something didn't automatically mean risking everything.

I waited in the rocking chair as Tilly darted into the bathroom to brush her teeth and change into her pajamas, smiling as she climbed into bed and scooted her pillows just right, Waffles tucked carefully into his cradle.

She watched me with those too-observant eyes, the ones that missed very little.

"You like Eliza," she said, not accusing. Just stating a fact, the way kids do when they've already solved the puzzle. "Like boyfriends like girlfriends. Like Grandma and Grandpa like each other."

I smiled and crossed the room to pull the blanket up to her chin. "I do."

"I like her too." She nodded, satisfied. "She makes the house feel happy."

That landed somewhere deep. I brushed her hair back, my throat tight. "You make the house happy," I told her. "Every day."

She yawned, eyelids drooping. "She can help too. Like when I'm cranky or something."

"I think she already is," I said quietly.

I clicked off the lamp, leaving the glow of the night-light casting stars across her ceiling. As I leaned down to kiss her forehead, I felt it clearly—this fragile, beautiful possibility. Not a fantasy. Not a plan. Just a feeling that maybe, if I was careful and brave in equal measure, I could build something that didn't just work... but *lasted*.

"Tonight felt like the sparkliest," Tilly whispered.

"I think you're right," I said, kissing her hair. "Goodnight, sweetheart."

"Goodnight, Daddy. Can Eliza have dinner with us again?"

"Absolutely."

"Maybe homemade pizza night will make her happy."

"I think it just might. Love you, Tilly."

"Love you, too, Daddy."

I waited until her breathing softened, then gently clicked the star projector off, the room slipping into a gentle hush. I paused at the door, glancing back once to make sure she was comfortable. The hallway felt quiet as I made my way downstairs.

In the living room, Eliza stood by the bookshelf, fingers tucked into her sleeves, looking at the framed photo of Tilly and me sitting on the front porch while Lois photobombed with her head hanging over Tilly's shoulder.

We ended up on the couch without meaning to, a polite space between us that wasn't as wide as it should be.

Lois had followed me downstairs and settled on her dog bed by the fireplace with her back to us like a very professional chaperone.

"Thank you for tonight," Eliza said after a minute, fingertip worrying a loose thread on the pillow. "That was... I don't have the right word. I keep underestimating my feelings. And you."

"You can keep underestimating me," I said lightly. "It's good for my ego when I do something normal like boil pasta correctly."

She smiled, then let something true out. "I'm not close with my parents," she said. "It's complicated and boring, and it doesn't matter as much as I used to think. But tonight felt like finding a door I didn't know I could walk through." Her eyes lifted to mine, careful. "I needed that."

"I'm glad you're here," I said, because anything else felt like it would tip us too far in one direction or the other. "I want this to feel like a place you can belong. Without effort."

She swallowed. "It does. That's what scares me." Her voice was barely there. "Being with you feels simple. Safe. Like I could let myself want this—and you wouldn't disappear or turn it into something that hurts."

We let that sit. The heater clicked. A car drifted by, leaving headlight stripes across the ceiling, then moved on.

"I'm having feelings about you," she said finally, like confessing to tax fraud. "Just throwing it out there in case I didn't make it obvious before."

I huffed a laugh. "I'm having feelings about you, too."

"They feel—" she searched for it—"real. They feel big and overwhelming. But I don't want them to stop."

"Mine are too," I took her hand and held it. I needed the contact because no matter how much she said it felt real, I was afraid she'd somehow slip away. "I don't want to push you."

"You're not," she said, quick and sure. Then quieter, "I'm pushing myself."

She shifted closer. Not much. Enough that I could see the gold flecks in her blue eyes and the way the tendon in her throat moved when she swallowed.

"I want to kiss you," she whispered, resting her hand

on my chest. "And I want to keep being careful. I don't know how to do both."

"We can start and stop," I said. "We can do small. We can go slow. Whatever pace keeps you okay. You can trust me, Eliza. I promise you."

Something in her loosened. "Small," she echoed. "For now. And I do trust you. I wouldn't be here if I didn't."

I touched her cheek with the back of my fingers, gave her a second to change her mind, and when she didn't, I kissed her—soft and slow, the kind that says *I'm here* instead of *I want.*

She made a small sound and leaned in, and god help me, I wanted more, but I kept it where I'd promised to keep it. When I eased back, she chased me half a breath, then smiled, her lips warm against my mouth.

"This is real," she said again, testing the word for fit.

"Yeah. It's absolutely real, and there's no rush. We have all the time in the world."

We sat with our shoulders touching and our hands not, listening to Lois dream-chuff and the house creak its old, kind bones. After a while, I walked her to her car. The air was cold; our breath hung between us like a cloud.

"I'll see you tomorrow," I said. "We'll survive tiny canapés and whatever fancy crap he decides to show off with, then come back here for leftover spaghetti instead of grilled cheese. Is that okay?"

"It sounds perfect," she said, eyes bright. She rose on her toes, pressed a quick kiss to the corner of my mouth like a secret, and stepped back.

"Goodnight, Nate."

"Goodnight, Eliza. Text me when you get home, okay?"

"I will."

I watched her taillights to the end of the block, checked on Tilly, set the kettle for morning coffee, and stood a minute in a kitchen that smelled like garlic and something I still don't have a better word for than *home*.

I barely slept. I replayed her goodnight over and over, the heat of her kiss lingering like a fingerprint. Everything in the house felt a little lighter, as if her laughter still hovered in the corners, settling into the walls. When I finally drifted off, it was with a kind of hope I hadn't let myself feel in years.

Chapter 22
Eliza

I'd been awake for a while before I realized it was my day off and I could have slept in.

Nate lingered under my skin anyway—not in the obvious ways, though those were there too—but in the quieter ones. The way my chest felt lighter than it had in years. The memory of laughter and careful hands brushing mine, asking for nothing in return. The way being with him hadn't required armor.

That was the dangerous part. It felt so right to be with him, and yet so hard to trust it completely once I wasn't with him.

I padded through the house, letting the morning find me instead of the other way around, coffee untouched on the counter while my thoughts ran ahead. Last night had been warm and safe, so easy it made my heart ache. Nate hadn't rushed me. He hadn't demanded clarity, promises, or explanations. He'd just made it okay to tell him how I felt. Nothing forced.

Nothing owed. Present in a way that made me want to stay.

Which meant, of course, that today was going to be difficult.

Graham's grand opening hovered at the edges of my thoughts like a low cloud, impossible to ignore. I squared my shoulders, determined to get through it steady and intact. I wasn't going to give him more space than he deserved—not in my day, not in my head.

Still, nerves don't listen to reason. They wound tight anyway, whispering worst-case scenarios I'd sworn I'd never believe again.

Nate had made me feel brave last night, and that was the problem. When something started to feel real—safe, even—I couldn't pretend it was temporary anymore.

I finally forced myself into motion because standing still felt like an invitation to spiral. The day unfolded the way days always did—feeding the cats, stepping over Linguini's dramatic sprawl in the doorway, refilling Remy's water bowl before he could glare me into compliance.

Life, stubborn and ordinary, insisted on continuing.

And for once, I let it.

I made toast I forgot to eat and coffee I reheated twice, drifting through my house like I was both present and somewhere else entirely. Every familiar thing felt slightly tilted, as if last night had nudged my life half an inch off its axis.

By midafternoon, I'd cleaned surfaces that didn't need cleaning and checked my phone too often for no reason at all. Nate would pick me up later. That was the plan. Simple. Normal. Except nothing about how my heart raced when I thought about him felt normal anymore. I wanted tonight to be effortless. I wanted to be brave. I wanted not to care what Graham thought—all reasonable goals. None of them were guaranteed to go the way I wanted.

So, when it was finally time to get ready, I treated it like I was donning armor for battle. I showered, dried my hair, chose the dress with care—not too much, not too little. Something that said I knew who I was, even if I was still figuring it out. I caught my reflection once, hands braced on the sink, and took a breath.

Tonight, I told myself, was just a night out, even if it felt like so much more.

I slid into my shoes with a grimace. I hadn't worn heels this high since I left Portland and decided blistered toes weren't a thing I wanted to keep in my life. Tonight, apparently, they were a necessity.

Black dress—simple, fitted, the exact shade of confidence I didn't quite feel. Hair lifted softly at the crown; loose waves pinned to behave. Liner sharp enough to cut glass, lipstick the deep scarlet color of a quiet threat. I spritzed perfume and tried not to think about the dozen different ways this could go sideways.

Remy perched on the vanity like a judgmental stylist. Linguini sprawled on the bathmat, feigning fainting spells. "No notes," I told them, even though they had many.

My phone buzzed.

Nate: I'm outside whenever you're ready. No rush.

Me: Coming. And if I trip in these heels, you never saw it.

Nate: I'll catch you. Then deny everything.

I clicked down the stairs and opened the door to find him in a navy blue dress jacket that did excellent things to his shoulders. Clean shave, hair pushed back, eyes bright. He went still with quiet awe, not performance.

"Wow," he said, voice a little wrecked. "You look stunning."

"You clean up okay, too," I managed, steadier than my ankles in these heels. He offered me his arm like an old movie taught him how—or more likely, his grandfather's example.

Across from the library, Graham's new place glowed like it had hired a cinematographer to light it. Hand-gilded sign. Warm light trapped behind glass. Honeybrook Hollow was already impressed.

Inside, the air smelled like rosemary and butter and ambition. The host knew Nate—of course she did, Graham had personally invited him earlier in the week— and clocked me in the next breath. "Welcome," she said. "Table for two?"

"Two," Nate confirmed.

We landed at a small table with a commanding view: the bar, the open kitchen, the door. Nate's fingers found mine under the table, a single quiet press. "Thirty minutes of politeness," he murmured, "then leftover spaghetti."

"Yes, with extra parm," I said. "Non-negotiable."

The server performed a sonnet about oysters and heritage carrots while the dining room hummed around us. Every table was full—pressed linen, flickering votives, wine glasses catching the light. Laughter rose and fell in practiced waves, the low roar of a place desperate to be *seen* as much as tasted. People leaned close, phones discreetly angled, eyes darting as if this were part dinner, part performance.

Nate ordered sparkling water; I asked for a white wine spritzer because if you're being tortured like this, you should do it with carbonation and alcohol—and bonus, Graham thought wine spritzers had no class.

He arrived as if on cue, cut to fit, smile calibrated to competitive arrogance. "Nate," he said, warmth turned to high. "Glad you made it. Appreciate you accepting my invitation." His gaze slid to me. "Eliza. You look wonderful as always."

"Thank you," I murmured and watched him carefully to see which way he wanted this conversation to go.

He smiled at Nate, mild curiosity in his tone: "Finding your footing yet?"

"Feels solid," Nate replied. "Congratulations on the opening."

"Thank you," Graham said. "It's been a lot to orchestrate. But totally worth it, as you can see."

His gaze slid to me, voice lowering just enough to feel

private. "I'm glad you came. I wasn't sure you would." A pause. "You've been keeping a lower profile lately."

That familiar pressure tightened under my ribs—the old instinct to shrink, to justify myself to him. I kept my smile pleasant and sharp. "Busy enjoying my life," I said. "You should try it sometime."

Nate's thumb brushed my wrist once, calm and soft, a quiet reassurance.

Graham's smile flickered—so fast someone not looking for it would've missed it. "Of course," he said lightly. "Enjoy the restaurant." The words landed with a faint emphasis, like a reminder that we were in his territory. He was already moving again, greeting staff, clapping a cook on the shoulder as if nothing had happened.

I exhaled. "That was restrained. For him."

Nate leaned closer, voice dry. "If that was restraint, I'd hate to see the director's cut. The man is an ass."

I grabbed my drink and sipped it to calm my nerves.

I looked up as the door chimed.

A Darlington sister parade walked in like the place had been waiting for them. They spotted us instantly. Then, like swallows changing direction mid-sky, they headed my way.

Piper reached us first, because of course she did. "You look devastating," she said, kissing my cheek. "We were definitely coming tonight, but with the things we've heard around town, we decided to capital-letter SHOW UP."

Graham, noticing my sisters' arrival, turned around and headed our way.

Great.

"Hi," Lucy chirped, hugging me first, then flashing Nate a smile that was all sincerity. "We're usually very chill," she told him. "Tonight is a dressed-up deviation that could end up decidedly *un*-chill depending on whether the oldest two Darlingtons decide to play nice or not."

"Extremely chill," Cara agreed, calm and observant, her gaze taking in the room like she was cataloging a library. She angled closer to me. "But tonight is for Eliza, and we're ready for—whatever comes up, or whoever decides to start something."

Graham returned for a second lap, confidence still polished but worn thinner now, like he'd already used it too much tonight. "Ladies," he said warmly. "Glad you made it."

Paige took an appetizer from a passing server's tray and popped it into her mouth. "Congrats on the lighting," she said to him, deadpan. "Ambience is ninety percent of a restaurant when the food is tiny and weird."

Lucy smiled, bright and polite. Cara nodded, measured. They had both clocked the tension and didn't comment on it.

"Congrats on the opening," Piper said easily, stepping in just enough to close the circle. "It looks beautiful."

Graham's charm flexed. "I'm thrilled you're here to support our culinary scene."

"We're here to support *Eliza*," Piper said, still smiling.

"And the culinary scene," Lucy added cheerfully. "But mostly Eliza. You'll find out."

His jaw ticked. He turned to me, voice pitched low. "Eliza's always had talent. Shame it didn't translate into something big."

Heat flared sharp and immediate, a spark of anger that wanted teeth. My fingers curled around the stem of my glass, knuckles whitening for half a second before I forced them to relax. I kept my face smooth, my posture loose, like the comment had slid right past me instead of landing exactly where he'd aimed it.

I'd learned that lesson the hard way—he only struck when he thought he could still hurt me. I wouldn't give him that now. Not here. Not in front of Nate. Not in a room full of people waiting to see me react.

So I smiled, slow and deliberate, and took a sip of my spritzer like I had nothing to prove at all.

Paige's eyes went flat—the look that cleared a bar at closing. She moved half a step closer, voice cold enough to chill champagne. "I love this part. Where men think they can say things that sound polite but are really just mean, and we pretend we didn't get it." She tilted her head. "We got it, Graham."

Beside me, Nate shifted. I felt it before I saw it—the tension in his body, the instinct to stand, to put himself between me, my sisters, and Graham. His chair scraped just enough to register, and for a split second, I knew he was about to say something.

Then Piper's hand landed lightly on his forearm. *We've got this.*

Nate stilled, jaw tight, eyes never leaving Graham. A beat later, his hand found mine beneath the table, fingers threading with quiet certainty. He squeezed once, and I held on.

It settled me in a way I hadn't expected. The knowledge that he would step in if he needed to—but trusted me, trusted my sisters, trusted *us*—felt like its own kind of shield.

I lifted my chin a fraction higher.

For the first time, I wasn't standing alone across from Graham.

And he could feel it.

Piper set her clutch on our table and smiled so gently I almost felt bad for him. "Graham, sweetie," she said. "You're not as clever as you think you are. Behave yourself."

A low, delighted chuckle rumbled from Nate.

Graham's smile calcified. "This is a grand opening—"

"Then open grandly," Paige said softly. "Start with an apology."

To his credit—or lack of imagination—he went with placation. "If anything I said was taken the wrong way—"

Piper sighed, as if she were sad for him. "That's not an apology."

"Try again," Cara suggested, serenity edged with steel. "Here's a tip—don't start with the word *if*."

Graham recalibrated, turned to me. "Eliza," he said carefully, "I'm sorry if—" His eyes shot to Cara after she cleared her throat. "*that* my comments came across as unkind. You were poised for greatness and—I'm sorry. It wasn't my intention to hurt your feelings."

I held his gaze. "But it was your habit, wasn't it?"

"I just want to be friends. I'm opening a restaurant here. I don't want any bad blood between us to affect that. Please accept my apology."

I considered his words, searching his face for sincerity. The tension at the table lingered, fragile but shifting, as if everyone was waiting to see if I would extend the olive branch, then decide where to go from there. Piper's gaze was steady, and Cara's subtle nod reminded me that grace could be a choice, not a concession.

"Okay. I accept. Thank you." I knew he didn't mean it, but I didn't care. I just wanted him out of my life.

Nate didn't speak. He didn't have to. His thumb traced that same quiet line along my pulse—*I'm here.*

Graham inclined his head. "Enjoy your evening," he said, and retreated, smile fixed, distance measured.

My sisters didn't gloat. Didn't make a spectacle. They simply joined us at the table. Paige caught the server's eye and ordered a round of champagne for our table and the nearest two. "On me," she said, pleasantly.

Lucy leaned in, voice low. "We can be obnoxious and cause a scene. Or we can sit here and look stunning until it's annoying."

"Let's do both," Piper grinned. "Two birds..."

Paige clinked her glass against mine, her eyes twinkling with mischief. "To fresh starts and fearless women," she toasted softly, the words wrapping around us like a shield. For a moment, the table hummed with a quiet energy, the kind that only family could conjure—calm and sure, a promise that whatever shadows lingered, we would face them together.

"We're actually not staying much longer," Nate answered.

"Good, I'll tell you right now," Piper grumbled. "This place is overpriced and overrated. I bet it won't last a year."

I found my breath. "Fifteen more minutes," I whispered to Nate. "Then leftover spaghetti."

"Extra parm," Nate murmured, like a vow.

We sipped our drinks and let the room fade into the background as we chatted with my sisters.

When we stood to leave, Graham kept his distance—which might've been the first decent thing he'd done since he got into town.

Outside, the air was cold and cleansing. I exhaled and watched a small piece of the past frost float away along with my breath.

"You okay?" Nate asked, opening the car door.

I thought of my sisters, the quiet strength of Nate's thumb against my pulse.

I thought of the girl I'd been in a kitchen where compliments had barbs.

"I think," I said, surprised by the truth of it, "I am."

"Spaghetti?" he prompted.

"Yes." I slid my hand into his, our fingers fitting together like we were made for each other. "And a side of being exactly where I want to be—with you."

He stopped walking.

Not abruptly—just enough that the night seemed to pause with us. He turned, his free hand coming up to my waist, comforting and warm. His thumb brushed the small of my back, slowly, gently, as he always was with me.

"Come here," he said softly.

It wasn't a command. It was an invitation.

I stepped into him, my hands flattening against his broad chest, feeling the quiet strength there, the familiar beat of his heart. He dipped his forehead to mine, breathing me in like this was important to him. Like *I* was important.

"I'm really glad you came tonight," he murmured. "And I'm really glad it was with me."

My throat tightened. "Me too."

He kissed me then—slow and unhurried, the kind of kiss that asks instead of takes. His mouth was warm, sure, lingering just long enough to make my knees weak. When he pulled back, his thumb traced my jaw, like he was committing my face to memory.

"Perfect," he said, voice low. "I've got plenty of the good parm."

I smiled, breathless. "Of course, you do. I'm starting to get the feeling that you'll always have everything I need."

We walked the rest of the way to his truck like that— hands linked, shoulders brushing. He opened the door for me, one hand braced on the roof, the other steady at my elbow, watching until I was settled, like I was something breakable and treasured all at once.

Before he closed the door, he leaned in again, stealing one more kiss—softer this time, a promise instead of a question.

"I'll be right there," he said.

"I know," I whispered.

When he slid in beside me, the space between us felt charged—his hand found my thigh for just a second, like reassurance. Like I was his and he was mine, and he intended to always take care of me.

Behind us, the restaurant still glittered—glass and gold and ambition, all sharp edges and show. Ahead, Honeybrook Hollow curved into itself, porch lights glowing, chimneys breathing smoke, streets leading toward something warm and real.

Toward a house that felt like a home. With a man who made it feel like choosing him was the easiest, bravest thing I'd ever done.

Chapter 23
Nate

The house felt like it had taken a deep breath and held it for me.

One lamp on in the living room. The soft tick of the hallway clock. The smell of coffee clung to the air from this morning, like the walls were reluctant to let it go.

Lois lifted her head from her round knit bed by the bookcase, blinked once, and thumped her tail in dignified greeting.

"Evening, ma'am," I told her, giving the velvet spot between her ears a rub. She stood, pressed her head into my palm, and then shuffled over to greet Eliza. When she stepped in out of the cold, the whole room shifted, like it had been waiting for her. The black dress skimmed her curves in a way that made my pulse stumble, and that quiet, wary smile—soft mouth, knowing eyes—hit me low and slow, doing reckless things to my focus and reminding me exactly how much I wanted her. "Tilly is with my mom tonight," I said, taking her coat. "Sleepover. Cookie baking. Sticker collection shopping. A bedtime that will be ceremonially ignored."

"Here's hoping the sticker gods are on her side," she said, and something in me relaxed.

"Leftover spaghetti still okay?"

"Perfect," she said, like the word had a little relief in it. She hung her purse on the peg by the door and glanced around as if to reacquaint herself with the familiar shadows. I watched her shoulders settle, the day's weight easing off as she stepped further inside. It was the sort of evening where silence felt gentle, not empty, and the comfort of routine made space for something quietly hopeful between us.

Eliza bent down, her hand gentle as she stroked Lois's ears, letting her lean into her touch. Lois's tail thumped again, satisfied, before padding back to her bed. I watched her slip off her heels as she took in the familiar comfort of the room. She glanced toward the kitchen, her smile softening. "Can I help with anything?" she asked.

"I got it. Come with me, and I'll get you a drink."

She followed me into the kitchen, her footsteps quiet on the worn tile. I poured her a glass of red wine—the good kind I'd been saving—and handed it over, my fingers brushing hers just long enough to make my pulse kick.

"To sticker luck," I said, lifting my glass, "ignoring bedtime rituals, and to you being here with me—exactly where I want you."

Her laugh was soft, a little breathless, and when she

looked up at me, she didn't look away. Neither did I. The space between us felt charged.

I took a step closer—slow, giving her time to pull back if she wanted to. She didn't. Her knee brushed mine, her warmth unmistakable, and for a second, all I could think about was how easy it would be to close the distance. Her gaze flicked to my mouth, then back to my eyes, and the look there made my grip tighten on my glass.

She took a sip, still watching me, and I knew—absolutely knew—that the night had shifted into something else entirely. I set my glass down before I did something reckless, turned toward the stove, and pulled the container of spaghetti sauce from the fridge, grateful for the excuse to give my hands something to do besides reach for her.

I reheated the sauce, boiled enough pasta for the two of us, and dished it up with ridiculous drifts of parmesan in the blue ramekins Tilly insisted were "fancy." We curled on the couch with the knit throw over our knees, hip to hip.

We ate in companionable quiet, the kind that felt less like silence and more like understanding. Outside, the wind rattled the window a little, but inside everything was soft—lamplight spilling across the couch, the subtle aroma of garlic lingering in the air, and the easy way our knees brushed beneath the blanket. It was the sort of night that asked nothing extravagant, just the comfort of shared space and the certainty of being wanted.

Finished, she set her bowl on the coffee table and traced the rim of her wine glass with a finger.

I watched her for a moment—the way she tucked one leg under herself, the way her eyes moved around the room like she was taking it in, not judging it. I realized how much of herself she'd already let me see. The messy parts. The guarded parts. The parts she was still figuring out.

It felt right to let her see me, too.

"Can I ask you something?" she said.

"Anything," I said.

"What was it like?" she asked. "Raising a little girl on your own. When she was really little."

I smiled before I could stop myself. "Chaotic," I said. "Exhausting. Terrifying." I shook my head. "I was constantly afraid I was doing it wrong. That I was missing something important." I paused, then added, "I spent a lot of nights googling things at two in the morning. Normal things. Things I felt like I should've already known."

Her mouth softened at that.

"I was still working a lot back then," I went on. "Trying to keep everything moving—job, daycare pickups, doctor appointments, meals. I'd answer emails with one hand while bouncing her with the other. There were days it felt like I was failing at everything simultaneously."

"And you kept going," she said quietly.

"I did," I said. "Because every time I thought I couldn't manage one more thing, she'd do something small—laugh at nothing, fall asleep on my chest—and it reset me." I swallowed. "It forced me to get honest about what mattered. About what I could actually sustain."

She nodded, like that made sense on a deeper level.

"Was that when you started thinking about leaving?" she asked.

"Yeah," I admitted. "Not all at once. I realized that the pace I was keeping didn't leave room for her. Or me." I glanced down the hallway again. "I didn't want her growing up remembering me as someone who was always rushing out the door."

"And coming back here?" she asked. "Was that hard?"

"It was scary," I said. "Walking away from a version of life I'd worked toward for a long time. But it also felt like relief." I smiled faintly. "Like I'd been holding my breath without realizing it. Plus, my grandparents are amazing, and I've always loved the Pennywhistle."

She shifted closer then, just enough that our knees brushed. "I'm glad you're here," she said. The words landed softly, but they held weight anyway.

"Me too," I said.

The room went quiet after that. It was full of shared understanding, of the kind of knowing that didn't need to be rushed or labeled. Sitting there with her, the house breathing around us, I felt something settle into place.

Not sparks. Not fireworks.

Something steadier. Something that felt like being seen.

She was quiet for a moment, then she set her glass

down carefully, like she didn't want the sound to interrupt whatever she was deciding.

"I hope you know," she said, meeting my eyes, "that Tilly is... incredible."

I smiled, but she didn't let me deflect.

"I mean it," she continued. "She's kind. She's curious. She feels safe enough to be herself." Her voice softened. "Kids don't get that way by accident."

Something in my chest tightened.

"You did that," she said simply. "You built that world for her."

I shook my head a little. "I just show up."

She smiled then—small, knowing. "That's not *just* anything."

She shifted closer, her knee brushing mine, and I caught the look in her eyes—respect first, admiration second. Like she was seeing me not as potential or promise, but as proof.

"I don't say this lightly," she added. "I've seen what happens when someone doesn't choose their child. And I've seen what it costs." She inhaled, steadying herself. "Watching you with Tilly... it makes me trust you. Not just because you're a good dad. But a good person. A good man."

The words landed deeper than any compliment I'd gotten in years.

I swallowed. "That means more than you know."

"Good," she said softly. "I want you to know how amazing you are."

And in that moment, sitting in the quiet living room

with the house breathing around us, I felt it clearly—her respect wasn't something I had to earn by being impressive.

She reached out then, hesitating a fraction before her fingers rested against my forearm—warm and steady, like she wanted me to feel that she meant every word. Her thumb brushed once, absentmindedly, and I felt it all the way through me.

I covered her hand without thinking, my palm settling over hers like it belonged there. We stayed like that for a quiet second, neither of us moving, the contact small but loaded with everything we weren't quite ready to say out loud.

It wasn't a promise.

But it felt like one might grow there if we let it.

Lois huffed out a sigh, repositioned. I set my glass on the coffee table.

I brushed my fingers along Eliza's wrist, a question written without pressure. She turned her hand and threaded our fingers together, answering.

"I like you," she said, breath catching. "More than I thought would be possible."

"Same," I admitted, helplessly honest. "And I want to be careful with you."

"I want to be careful, too." She swallowed, then: "But I also want to kiss you until I forget every bad thing anyone ever taught me about myself."

I didn't make a sound, but something shifted inside of me. "I can help with that."

I leaned in slowly, giving her a dozen chances to change her mind.

"Kiss me. Please, Nate."

The first kiss rewrote the tension between us. Now it was soft and sure, instead of hesitant and shy. The second closed the polite gap we'd been pretending was necessary. When my hand slid to the back of her neck, her breath caught, and I stilled.

"Okay?" I asked against her mouth.

"Yes," she said, meaning it, and I felt that yes everywhere.

Her fingers curled against my shoulder, gentle but unmistakably sure. The nearness of her—her warmth, the way she fit into the space that used to be between us—made everything else seem distant and unimportant. I brushed my thumb along her cheek, slow, like I needed to memorize the way she breathed before I earned anything more.

"We don't have to rush," I told her quietly, meaning every word. "Tell me what you need, and I'll match you."

Eliza's eyes softened in a way that hit me somewhere deep and unguarded. "I don't want to rush," she said. "But I don't want to stop, either."

That was all it took.

I kissed her—careful at first, like a promise, then deeper as she leaned into me, fingers sliding into my hair. She let out a soft sigh, which made my pulse trip. Every slow brush of her mouth told me she wanted this, wanted me, and damn, I'd been holding myself back for so long.

Our breathing synchronized, every exhale mingling

in the hush between words. The world outside faded, leaving only the quiet certainty of her presence. I pressed my forehead to hers, letting myself linger in the moment, memorizing the way her eyelashes brushed her cheeks and the flush beneath her skin. Each heartbeat drew me deeper, making it impossible to imagine a reality where we hadn't found this quiet peace together.

Her hands traced my jaw, my shoulders, my chest—tentative, then bolder, like she was remembering what it felt like to want someone without fear. Each touch undid me a little more.

"Eliza..." My voice broke in the middle of her name.

"Don't stop," she whispered. "Please. I don't want to stop..."

I nodded and kissed her again, this time slower, allowing the moment to linger warm and full between us. I eased her back against the pillows, giving her every chance to pull away as I pressed my body to hers. She didn't. She lifted her hips toward mine in a silent response that settled any doubt I had.

We stayed like that—pressed tight, hands everywhere, kissing as though we'd never stop. She pushed lightly at my shoulders. "Sit up," she murmured.

"Tell me what you need. Slow? Or...?"

"Not slow. Not now." She laughed as she trailed her hands down my chest to tug at the hem of my shirt until it was over my head and on the floor. "I want to touch you, too. Can I?"

"Yes. God yes. Touch me. Do anything you want."

I slid my hands over the warm skin of her thighs and

up, raising her dress over her head. She tugged it off and tossed it to the floor.

Her breasts were gorgeous, full, and lush, with rosy little nipples peeking through the cream lace of her bra. I darted my tongue out for a taste. Immediately, she arched into my touch with a sexy little moan.

"More," she moaned as she shoved the cup of the bra down for me.

"Like this?" I sucked hard at her bared nipple, smiling as she ran her hands into my hair and yanked me closer.

"Take me to bed." She pulled out of my arms. "I don't want Lois to watch us."

I stood, sweeping her into my arms to carry her through the house to my bedroom. "I've been thinking about this," I whispered against her lips.

"I have too. I want you, Nate."

Her arms wrapped around me as we crossed the threshold, the soft quiet of the room settling around us like a secret. I paused for a heartbeat, drinking in the sight of her—hair tousled, cheeks flushed, eyes bright with anticipation. The air felt charged, every movement deliberate, and every glance loaded with meaning neither of us had dared to voice until now. I set her gently down on the bed, the mattress dipping beneath our combined weight as she reached for me again, pulling me close and erasing the last bit of distance between us.

I reached for the nightstand without breaking the kiss and pulled a condom from the drawer. She exhaled—a soft, relieved breath that felt like trust.

"Good," she murmured, thumb brushing my lower lip. "Thank you."

"I'll always take care of you. Always, Eliza," I said, because there was no universe where I wasn't careful with her.

The rest of our clothes fell away in a quiet blur of warm skin and whispered yeses. There was nothing rushed about any of it. Just the kind of closeness that felt inevitable. Her fingers trailed over my shoulders. My mouth traced the line of her throat, the curve of her collarbone, each touch asking and waiting.

I slipped a hand between her legs, cupping her in my palm, middle finger tracing her slick opening, then up to find her clit.

"Nate." Her voice was nothing but soft breath in my ear.

"I want to make you feel good. Can I?"

She looked up at me, her eyes bright and unguarded, and for a heartbeat, neither of us spoke. Everything else— the uncertainty, the walls we'd built—had fallen away. I traced my thumb along her cheek and saw the way she smiled, so sweet and so beautiful, the kind you save for moments that feel like beginnings. I felt her heartbeat thrumming beneath my hand, steady and real, and knew this was something we could choose, again and again, no matter what came next.

She nodded, eyes wide, mouth open as she panted softly.

Touching her like this was something I'd never let my imagination get far enough to follow through with. I felt like I was living inside a fantasy. It didn't feel real. The scent of her blended with her perfume, and it was all I could do not to fall apart.

I kissed her, hard, deep, loving how her lips reddened, and her cheeks flushed when I pulled away. She arched into my touch, her breath catching as I moved with a tenderness that made my own heart ache. Every response from her felt like an answer to a question I hadn't known I was asking. I watched her lashes flutter, her lips parting with a shuddering sigh, and I pressed a lingering kiss to her temple—wanting her to feel cherished, wanted, seen.

I slid down, kissing a trail between her breasts, over the soft curve of her stomach, and lower.

"Open for me," I said, smiling against her skin as she threw her legs over my shoulders. "Yeah, just like this." I licked straight up her center, groaning at the taste. She was hot, wet, perfection, and I knew I would never get enough of her.

She clutched my hair and let out a moan as she rocked her hips closer to my mouth. "You're so beautiful," I groaned against the heat of her.

"Please. Get inside me, Nate. I need you."

"You're sure?" I whispered.

Her answer wasn't a word—it was the way she dropped her legs to the sides and tugged at my hair.

She nodded, her eyes searching mine for a final moment of reassurance. "I'm sure," she said, voice low but certain, and any last thread of hesitation unwound between us. We moved together, slowly, letting the trust grow in each gentle touch, every whispered word, as if building something sacred in the quiet dark.

I rose to my knees and slid the condom on. Watching as her lips parted, breath hitching.

I traced a slow line up the center of her body as I leaned over her, my weight on one arm, savoring the way her skin responded to each gentle touch as I settled myself between her legs, rolling my hips to rest between her spread thighs.

"Say the word, Eliza," I murmured, tucking my face into the side of her neck. "I need to hear it again."

"Yes," she whispered, wrapping her arms and legs around me. "Now. Please."

The space between us felt sacred, charged with anticipation and the quiet certainty that we were exactly where we needed to be. In that small space, every heartbeat seemed to echo with the promise of all the things we hadn't said but deeply felt.

I sank inside her body, hardly believing I was lucky enough to be right here, sliding inside the most beautiful woman I'd ever met in my life.

She writhed beneath me, hitching her legs tighter around my waist, begging me without words to get deeper. So, I did, my pulse racing out of control as I slammed my hips into hers.

"God, you feel so good, Eliza."

"More," she moaned, biting my shoulder and digging her nails into my sides.

I propped myself up onto one elbow so I could watch her as I pulled back, then pushed back inside. Again and again, as her mouth fell open and she threw her head back. I ground against her when our hips met, grunting as I held myself back. I'd never felt anything like this before, never been with anyone as amazing as Eliza.

I slid my hand between her legs, pressing with my thumb. Her back arched, and she let out a muffled scream as she slammed a hand over her mouth. It was my name on her lips. Mine. It pushed me over the edge. I took her hand from her mouth and kissed her through it.

The rest unfolded slowly and deeply, like something we'd both been waiting for. Every shift, every touch, every pressed-together moment felt like a promise neither of us said out loud. She held my gaze when I kissed her again, and it wrecked me in the best possible way.

And when the world finally settled around us again, I pulled her into my chest, breathing her in—her hair, her warmth, the soft sound she made when she curled closer.

No rush. No fear. Just us.

She was quiet for a long moment, curled into me like it was the most natural thing in the world. My arm was around her bare shoulders, my hand resting over her spine, feeling the rise and fall of each breath.

I stared at the ceiling in the dark, trying to catch my breath—not from what we'd done, but from what it meant.

Because I was falling for her. Not a crush. Not a phase. Not whatever people called it when they wanted something easy.

She shifted slightly, her nose brushing my collarbone, and I kissed the top of her head without thinking.

"You okay?" I asked quietly, brushing my fingers through her hair.

She nodded, then hesitated. "Yeah. That was more than okay. Just like everything else—you are good at what you do."

I smiled into her hair. "Stay," I said finally. My voice was soft but sure. "You don't have to leave tonight."

She went still in my arms.

"I mean it," I added. "I'll make cocoa or tea or pancakes or anything you like in the morning. Lois will let you pick the playlist for breakfast prep. I'll even give you the good side of the bed."

Eliza's soft laugh warmed the quiet between us. "There's a *good* side of the bed?"

"There is now."

She looked up at me, her eyes unreadable in the dim light, but her voice was soft.

"Okay."

That one word settled something in me I didn't know had been wound tight. I pulled the covers up over her, made sure she was warm, and reached for her hand under the quilt. She laced her fingers through mine without hesitation. We got up, taking turns in the bathroom to get ready for bed.

I'd never wanted to move this slow and stay this close all at once.

We settled back in bed, side by side, the quiet of the house wrapping around us like another blanket. For a while, there was only the sound of soft breathing, the gentle creak of the mattress each time one of us shifted. I could feel the weight of the day melting away, replaced by a certainty that neither of us was in a hurry to break the spell. It was easy, natural—like we'd done this a hundred times before.

She was already half-asleep by the time I whispered, "Goodnight, Eliza."

She didn't answer—but she didn't let go of my hand either.

And I didn't sleep for a long time. Because all I could think about was how good it

felt to have her in my arms, in my house, *in my life.* And how I'd do just about anything to keep her here.

Chapter 24
Eliza

I woke up wrapped in warmth. A solid arm was tucked around my waist, a slow, steady breath tickled the back of my neck, and the quilt was tangled halfway down my legs. For one disorienting second, I didn't remember where I was.

Then I did.

Nate's bed. Nate's room.

Nate.

I blinked in the soft early light coming through the blinds, the scent of cedar and cinnamon still lingering in the air. Lois was snoring faintly from the living room—content and unaware that the entire axis of my world had quietly shifted overnight. For a moment, I just lay there, letting myself soak in the quiet comfort of his presence. Everything felt impossibly still—like the world outside had faded away.

I eased back against Nate's chest, reluctant to move. Last night had been everything. Gentle and sweet.

Heated and sexy. He'd made me feel like more than I ever let myself believe I could be.

I rolled over slowly to face him. His lashes were dark against his cheek, his jaw slack with sleep. One of his hands was resting on my hip. I could've stayed like that for hours.

But reality ticked at the edges of my peace.

Because as much as I wanted to linger in this perfect cocoon, I couldn't pretend that the rest of my life wouldn't come knocking soon enough. Hidden fears and doubts pressed quietly at the edges of my happiness, reminding me that nothing this good ever came without complications. I let out a slow breath, torn between clinging to the moment and bracing myself for what came next.

"I need to go home," I whispered.

He cracked one eye open and smiled. "I was dreaming that we stayed in my bed all day. Unrealistic, I know."

"I have to feed the cats," I said, trying not to melt as he shifted closer, his voice still rough with sleep. "And open the Coffee Cabin."

"Bring them here," he murmured, kissing my temple. "I'll make everyone breakfast."

"I think Linguini would try to steal Lois's bed," I said dryly. "And Remy would try to move into your house permanently."

"Sounds like we'd be a full family by next week."

I smiled, but there was a flicker in my chest I didn't want to examine too closely.

Nate stretched and sighed. "I'll drive you home."

He pulled on a T-shirt and joggers and padded bare-foot through the house while I got dressed, gathered my things, and gave Lois one last pat on the head. Outside, the early morning air was cool and hushed, the world still half-asleep. He held my hand as we walked to the truck, his thumb brushing over my knuckles like he wasn't quite ready to let go yet.

Before he opened my door, he paused. "So," he said, a hint of a smile tugging at his mouth, "just to be clear—this wasn't me accidentally kidnapping you for an extended dinner, right?"

I laughed softly, my heart still doing that unsteady thing. "No," I said. "Though I did enjoy the part where I was fed and emotionally compromised."

He huffed a quiet laugh, then sobered, his gaze lifting to mine. "Last night wasn't just..." He trailed off, shaking his head once. Then he met my eyes, steady and earnest. "It meant something to me."

My throat tightened. "Me too."

"Well," he said lightly, like he was trying to keep things from tipping over the edge, "that's a relief. I was worried I'd imagined the whole thing."

"Don't get cocky," I said. "I'm still processing."

"That's fair," he said, smiling. "Take your time. I'll be over here pretending I'm very cool about it."

He leaned in then and kissed me—soft and slow, unhurried—like he was memorizing the moment. When he finally pulled back, his forehead rested briefly against mine.

"For the record," he murmured, "I'd do that again."

I smiled. "Noted."

The drive was quiet after that, comfortable in the best way—the kind of silence that didn't need filling. When he pulled up in front of my place, neither of us moved right away.

He squeezed my hand gently. "Text me when you're inside," he said. "So I know you didn't vanish into the night."

"I live here," I teased. "I promise I'll still exist."

"Humor me," he said, gaze warm and unguarded. "I like knowing things."

I leaned over and pressed a quick kiss to his cheek. "Have a good day, Nate."

"You too."

The morning light brushed my skin as I stepped out of the truck, heart full, possibilities unfolding behind me—and for once, I didn't feel the need to run from them.

The rest of the morning passed in a quiet haze of routine. Feed the cats. Shower. Try on four different sweaters before giving up and choosing the one Nate once said made me look like a cup of cocoa.

I opened the Coffee Cabin a few minutes late, hair still damp and heart still full.

But by mid-morning, the warm haze of last night had burned off like steam on the espresso machine.

"Hey," a voice said behind me, sharp and smooth all at once.

I turned. Graham.

He stood too close to the walk-up window, hands in the pockets of his sleek coat, expression carefully neutral.

His sudden presence at the window made my stomach twist. I wiped my hands on a dish towel, steadying myself. "Did you need something, Graham?" I asked, careful to keep my tone even.

"Eliza," he said with a smile that didn't touch his eyes. "Your sisters are something else."

I blinked. "They tend to be."

He chuckled, like we were old friends sharing a private joke. "I didn't mean to offend them. I guess I underestimated how protective they are."

I kept my face pleasant. Neutral. "They're my family."

"Well," he said, leaning in slightly. "I just wanted to apologize again for my behavior. Wouldn't want town gossip to make things awkward for you. Or Nate." A subtle jab tucked inside velvet words.

"Thanks," I said, voice light. "I think the town's memory will focus on who really made a spectacle of themselves."

He smiled again. "I'd hate to see you caught in the middle of something messy."

"I'm good at cleaning up messes. Comes with prac-tice, sadly."

His jaw ticked. Then he stepped back and tipped an imaginary hat. "Enjoy your day, Eliza."

I watched him walk away, the air shifting in his absence, leaving a faint chill that had nothing to do with the weather outside. My fingers curled around the edge of the counter as I tried to shake off the unease that lingered.

He wasn't sorry. I knew him better than that.

I exhaled slowly and turned back to my espresso machine, willing my hands to steady.

I didn't want to tell Nate. Not yet. Not when things had just started to feel like they were finally falling into place.

But deep down, I knew Graham wasn't done. And I wasn't sure how much longer I could keep pretending I could handle him on my own.

I was wiping down the counter for the second time in five minutes when Cara popped through the back door like she owned the place. She had a to-go cup in one hand and her scarf askew.

"I need something with sugar and caffeine real bad," she breathlessly announced.

I wordlessly made her a mocha with whipped cream and slid a lemon bar across the counter.

She took a sip, then sighed like the drink had exorcised at least two personal demons. "Okay. I came to give you a debrief."

"On what?"

"Last night. After you left with Nate." She wiggled her brows. "Which, by the way, you *definitely* left with Nate. Don't try to deny it."

I tried not to blush and probably failed. "We had dinner."

"Mmhmm. Sure, you did." She smirked, then leaned

on the counter. "Anyway, I wanted to tell you what your oldest two sisters got up to."

"Oh my god."

"Oh yes," she said, sipping with relish. "Turns out, Graham tried to give a little speech to thank everyone for coming, brag about his imported truffle oil, the décor—I had no idea he was such an ass. I swear. He was always nice to me back in school. I had no idea that side of him existed. He was so condescending to you. What was up with that?"

"He's good at making people see what he wants them to."

Her expression shifted, guilt flickering in her eyes. "I should've seen the real him sooner," she murmured, tracing the rim of her cup. "I always thought Graham was harmless, you know? All charm and no bite. I hate that I missed the signs, and I'm sorry I wasn't there for you like I should have been."

Without thinking, I reached across the counter, squeezing her hand. "You have nothing to apologize for," I said softly. "You can't be there for someone if they don't tell you what's going on."

"Yeah, well, I'm here now, though, I promise. Anyway, Piper and Paige had no such illusions about him," Cara said, eyes dancing, "Piper started asking pointed questions in her bakery competition voice. About how exactly he sourced his flour, and if he had gluten-free options on his menu. Then Paige chimed in about how ironic it was that a man so full of himself was serving such small portions."

I choked on a laugh. "They didn't."

"They absolutely did. Lucy and I were trying to disappear into the wallpaper while Piper and Paige dismantled him with surgical precision. By the time dessert came out, Graham looked like he was trying to remember if he'd invited them or they'd invited themselves."

I laughed again, but it came out a little shaky.

Cara's smile softened. "Hey. You okay?"

I looked at her. Really looked. Cara wasn't just the sister who saw everything; she was the one who waited until you were ready to admit you needed her. She never pushed, never demanded confessions or explanations; instead, her presence was steady and patient, like a porch light left on for someone wandering home in the dark. In that moment, with her hand warm over mine and concern brushed across her features, I felt the pressure I'd been feeling since I got here ease.

I wrapped my arms around myself. "Graham came by this morning." I opened my mouth, searching for a way to explain, but the words tangled up. The truth felt heavy, like a stone pressing on my chest. "I didn't want anyone to look at me differently," I managed. "I thought if I kept quiet, it would all just fade away on its own. That's why I never said anything to anybody about him."

Her face darkened. "What did he say?"

"He apologized. Sort of." I hesitated. "But it felt fake. Like he was warning me more than anything."

Cara straightened. "He threatened you?"

"No, not directly. But he made it clear he knows people are talking. And he doesn't like being embarrassed." I hesitated. "And I think he blames me."

"Eliza—"

"He was awful when we dated," I said quietly. "Mean. Controlling. Always making me feel like I owed him. That I was lucky he chose me to be with." I bit my lip, anxiety twisting in my stomach. "I just—every time I think it's over, he finds a way to remind me it isn't." My voice was barely a whisper. "It's like he's always lurking in the background, waiting for me to slip up."

Cara's face crumpled for a second, then set. "I wish you had told us. I wish I had known. Oh, Eliza, I'm so sorry—"

My breath stuttered in my throat, the old memories scraping raw at the edges. I hadn't meant to say so much, hadn't planned on letting it spill out, but Cara's steady presence made it impossible to keep everything locked inside. The silence between us felt safe, almost protective, as if nothing Graham said or did could reach me here. For the briefest moment, I let myself lean into that comfort, wishing it could last.

"I didn't want to deal with the fallout," I admitted. "Or the pity. Or the I-told-you-so from my mother over dating an older man. And now I have a chance with Nate, and I'm scared that if Graham decides to be vindictive, he'll hurt the Pennywhistle. Or Nate. Or both."

Cara leaned across the counter and covered my hand with hers. "Then we don't let him."

I blinked. "What?"

"We don't let him scare you. Or hurt Nate. Or make you feel like you're alone in this." Her voice shook. "You're not." She squeezed my hand a little tighter, her eyes fierce with determination. "We stand together, Eliza. No matter what he tries, we'll protect you. You're not alone, please believe it." The words settled around me, heavy and reassuring, like a warm blanket against the chill of old fears.

I swallowed hard.

"You have us," she said firmly. "Piper and Paige are probably planning another takedown as we speak. And Lucy and I will do anything to help, too. We're not going anywhere. He can't hurt you now that you're home with your family. I promise. We're here, let us be. Okay? Please."

Something cracked open in my chest—something small and lonely and scared.

I squeezed her hand.

And for the first time in a long time, I believed I would be okay.

Cara didn't let go of my hand.

"I mean it," she said, her voice softer now. "You're not alone, Eliza. You never were. Even when you didn't tell us what was going on, we were here for you. We *are* here."

I looked down at our hands on the counter—hers warm and steady, mine pale and trembling.

"I thought maybe if I didn't say it out loud, it would

stay small. Contained." I shook my head. "But it wasn't. Not even close."

Cara's eyes shimmered. "Why him? Do you feel like talking about it?"

I let out a humorless breath. "He was polished. Confident. Everyone liked him. I think I wanted to believe he liked me the same way. He made everyone else feel—seen. Chosen. I wanted that." My voice wavered. "But then he made me feel like I had to earn everything. His approval. His attention. Even the right to break up with him."

Cara flinched. "That's not love."

"I know that now. It's why I left and came here. I had to get away. I have no idea what his game is now."

We sat with that for a minute. The hum of the espresso machine. The soft sound of a car driving off after I handed them their order. Sunlight shifted across the floor in golden stripes.

"Can I say something kind of sisterly and slightly unhinged?" Cara asked finally. She leaned in closer, her presence keeping me together. The quiet comfort between us felt stronger than words, filling the empty spaces I'd carried for so long. For the first time, the weight of what I'd been through didn't seem so impossible to bear.

"Always."

"I want to egg his car. Or slash his tires. Or write fake reviews about how his risotto tastes like vinegar and smells like feet."

A laugh burst out of me. "Risotto of Remorse."

"Exactly. Served with a side of 'this man peaked in high school.'"

I sniffled, then smiled. "Thank you."

She squeezed my hand again. "Also, you and Nate?"

I blushed.

"I saw the way he looked at you at the grand opening," she said with a teasing lilt. "Like he'd fight a bear for you. Or a restaurant snob. Same thing."

"He's a good man."

"You deserve good. You deserve the world."

Her words landed like a balm I didn't know I needed.

"Is Graham going to let this go? You knew him. What do you think?" I cleared my throat. "Do you think Piper and Paige were too much?"

Cara snorted. "I mean, they annihilated him. They were absolutely too much. But in the best way. You should've seen Paige when Graham tried to talk about wine pairings. She raised her hand like the restaurant was a classroom and asked if pretentiousness was a grape variety."

I laughed again, louder this time.

Cara grinned. "Then Piper faked a Yelp review out loud. It started with, 'I came for the steak, but I stayed for the misplaced arrogance.'"

"Oh my god."

"I've never been prouder to be a Darlington. It's gonna be fine."

I wiped my eyes, laughing and crying in equal measure. "I don't know what I did to deserve you guys."

Cara's smile softened again. "You're our baby sister. We love you. You were born. That's it. That's all it took."

A car pulled up to the drive-thru, and I composed myself, ready to greet the next customer.

Cara stood, brushing imaginary crumbs from her skirt. "You know where to find me if you need to disappear into a pile of used paperbacks and unsent therapy texts."

"I might take you up on that."

"Do. Anytime. We can alphabetize our trauma over hot mugs of tea." She hugged me, then brushed my hair back over my shoulder. "I'm going to take care of you, Eliza. Like I should have been doing all along. Don't you worry about a thing."

"What do you mean, take care of me?"

"It's not for you to worry about. I got you, okay?"

And I stood behind the counter, hands still trembling, but heart a little steadier. She was probably going to come back tomorrow with a stack of books to help me sort out my life.

I helped the waiting customer then stood behind the counter long after everyone had left, hands still trembling, heart steadier than it had been all day. I loved her for that—for the way she showed up, no questions asked, like it was the most natural thing in the world.

I would let my sisters love me, I decided. I would let them stand close. But I couldn't let them stand in the line of fire.

Graham didn't get to the top of Portland's restaurant scene by being careless or kind, and I knew better than to underestimate what he was capable of when he felt cornered. If this was going to end, it had to be because I faced him myself.

Outside, the Coffee Cabin lights hummed softly against the dark, and I drew in a breath, squaring my shoulders as I tried to figure out what to do.

Chapter 25
Nate

Nancy was holding down the front like a boss, dishing out sass and pie recommendations with equal flair. I leaned against the pass-through counter and watched her wrangle a table of teenagers with the patience of a saint and the dry humor of someone who had absolutely no time for nonsense.

"I'm stepping out for a bit," I told her.

She didn't look up. "Tell Eliza she should experiment with lavender lattes next time she's feeling fancy."

I didn't reply, mostly because I didn't trust myself to say anything that wouldn't give me away.

Because yes—I was going to see Eliza.

Yes—I'd been thinking about her since the moment I left her side.

And yes—I cared about her more than was probably wise at this point. But I wasn't walking away from her. Not even close. She was all I could think about.

The Coffee Cabin came into view just as a breeze

picked up. She was at the walk-up window, pulling shots, multitasking like it was an Olympic sport. From this distance, I could see that her shoulders were tight, her movements sharp and clipped. Not her usual rhythm.

She was holding it together.

But I could tell she was frayed at the edges.

I parked and walked up slowly, not wanting to startle her. When she turned, her face shifted instantly—something unreadable flickered behind her eyes. But she smiled at me anyway. Not the soft, teasing one I liked best. This one had a little too much effort tucked into the corners.

"Hey," I said, keeping my voice low.

"Hey," she replied, brushing a stray hair behind her ear.

"You okay?"

She hesitated.

I didn't rush her. I knew she'd tell me everything when she was ready. I knew Graham was stirring up feelings she thought she was over. It was only a matter of time before she let it go. Patience was the key.

Finally, she said, "I'm working on it." She let out a sigh. "Graham was here earlier. He got me shook up. I'm sorry."

I nodded and didn't push. Instead, I accepted the cup of coffee she handed me—perfectly made, just the way I liked it. No asking. No notes. She just knew. "Thanks. You always remember."

"Well, you always drink the same thing," she said, a

trace of a smile pulling at her lips. "I'd call it predictable, but I'm too polite."

"Wow," I said. "Dragging me in front of the espresso machine. Bold move."

She shrugged. "Your order is aggressively average. Black coffee, sprinkle of sugar. Boring." She looked at me, eyes crinkling at the corners as she grinned. "You're the opposite of your drink, you know."

I laughed under my breath, and something in her relaxed. The tension in her shoulders eased. A little life sparked behind her eyes.

She was trying so hard to hold it all together. I wished I could take some of the weight off her and carry it myself. I also wished I could just knock him around a bit and get him to forget about her, but I knew better. She'd hate that. I was about to ask if she wanted company later when a familiar black Range Rover slid into the drive-thru.

Graham.

I could've gone the rest of my life without seeing that guy's smug face again.

Eliza stiffened instantly. "What now?" she muttered.

He pulled up to the window like this was his show, and we were all just extras in it. His eyes flicked over me without even pausing, like I didn't matter.

"Eliza," he said, all smooth charm. "I don't like how I left things earlier."

She didn't rise to it. Just asked, "What can I get you?"

"Nothing. I stopped by to apologize—again." He said

it like we were all supposed to be grateful. "I think things got a little intense—both last night and this morning."

Eliza gave him a flat look. "That's one way to describe it."

He leaned out of his window, all casual familiarity. "You know how I can be. I don't mean it. I just speak my mind. Sometimes I get carried away."

Like that excused everything.

She gave a tight smile that didn't touch her eyes. "You said some pretty condescending things. You used to do it a lot."

He laughed—dismissive, low, a little too rehearsed. "You always were sensitive."

I bristled.

But I didn't move—yet. I promised myself I would only step in if his behavior went over the top. She was a grown woman. She could handle herself.

Then he looked at me. A glint of something sharp crossed his expression before he smiled at me. "Winters," he said, like the name tasted bad.

"Graham," I replied.

Silence stretched out between us.

He glanced between us again, taking in the space at the counter I hadn't backed away from.

"I hope there's no hard feelings," he said, all false sincerity. "This town's too small for drama, right?"

I stared him down. "Then maybe don't start any." I met his gaze steadily, refusing to let him see any hint of fear.

The air between us felt heavy, thick with things left

unsaid. For a moment, it seemed like he might say more, but he just shrugged, as if nothing about this mattered. Then he smiled like I'd told a joke.

Eliza's hand brushed mine, light as breath, grounding me, or maybe herself.

Graham finally drove his car through the drive-thru and rolled away.

Eliza's hands shook slightly as she picked up a rag and wiped down the counter for no reason at all.

"Sorry," she murmured. "You didn't need to be here for that."

"Yes, I did," I said quietly. "I wanted to be."

She looked at me, eyes rimmed with unshed frustration. Or exhaustion. Or both.

"I don't know what his game is," she whispered. "I can't figure out what he wants, other than to be number one, or whatever."

"I don't care what he wants. He won't get it, whatever it is," I told her. "But if he tries to hurt you, or make your life harder, I won't just stand by."

She blinked fast. "You don't have to protect me."

I met her gaze, steady and unwavering. "I know you can handle him," I said, voice low. "But I want you to know you're not alone in this, not now, not with me around."

Her breath hitched. She turned away slightly, like she didn't want me to see how much that meant. I stood there, watching her steady herself, knowing that I would come back again and again, for as long as it took.

She turned back, calmer now.

"I'm glad you stopped by," she said softly.

"I'll always come for you," I said.

And I meant it.

She huffed out a breath and rested her hands on the counter, bracing herself like she was holding up more than just her own weight.

"Do you think he'll try something?" she asked, her voice low and tight. "I don't know what to think anymore, and I hate it."

I didn't answer right away. Not because I didn't have thoughts—oh, I had plenty—but because she wasn't really asking for strategy. She was asking for reassurance.

"I think," I said carefully, "he's used to getting his way. And it's throwing him off that you're not staying quiet and letting him run the show."

She gave a dry laugh. "You mean like I used to?"

"I mean," I said, leaning in slightly, "that he's underestimating you. Which would be a mistake."

Her mouth twitched. "You really think that?"

I nodded. "I know it."

There was a pause. "I just..." She looked out past me. "I don't want him to mess with the Pennywhistle. Or you. Especially not because of me."

"That won't happen."

"You can't know that."

I reached across the counter, not quite touching her hand but close enough that she could see I meant it. "You've built something real in Honeybrook Hollow, Eliza. Nobody gets to take that from you—not him, not anyone." I watched her shoulders relax, and I knew my words were sinking in. "Whatever happens, we've got this. Together."

"Are you sure? I can't help but think—"

"I know myself," I said. "And I know I'm not afraid of him. But if that doesn't help—I also know my grandmother, and nobody messes with her. And your sisters were pretty fierce at the grand opening. Just saying."

Her eyes searched mine, like she was looking for a crack in the promise. She didn't find one.

I kept my voice low as I continued. "You're not responsible for what he does, Eliza. And I can handle it if he tries anything. So can the Pennywhistle. Its reputation is bigger than mine. I'm not worried."

Her brow furrowed. "He can be petty. And vindictive—"

"I could tell, I think he invited me to his grand opening knowing you'd be there and hoping he could make me jealous or something. I guess he didn't think we'd show up together."

She sighed. "Yeah, he likes to get his way. He doesn't want me back and I made it extremely clear when I left Portland that I never wanted to speak to him again—ever. I don't know why he keeps coming around."

"Maybe he doesn't want anyone else to have you. Some men are like that. Who knows? But, it doesn't matter. The Taste-Off is your chance to let him know, once and for all, that you're not the same person he messed with before. After you beat his ass, then he'll see. And if that doesn't make him back off, then I will. If I can beat Piper and Paige to it, that is."

She let that settle for a second. Then she reached for a rag again, wiped an already-clean spot on the counter. "You always this good at pep talks?"

"I've got a soft spot for gorgeous women with espresso stains on their aprons."

That pulled a laugh out of her. The real kind. Warm and surprised and unguarded.

"There it is," I said, smiling.

"There what is?"

"That smile. The one that makes me think I should ask for your number. Again."

She rolled her eyes, but it was fond. "You already have my number, Winters."

"Doesn't mean I don't want to earn it every day."

She looked down and shook her head, but her cheeks flushed, and that was victory enough.

"Even when I'm a wreck?" She lingered for a moment, her hand resting lightly on the counter between us. It felt like the world had narrowed to just the two of us, suspended in possibility. I caught the gentle tremor in her fingers before she tucked a strand of hair behind her ear, gathering herself. There was a sense of something unspoken, but the warmth radiating from her gaze said enough.

"Especially then." The quiet hung between us, gentle and full. I brushed my thumb over her knuckles, then lifted her hand to place a soft kiss on her wrist. "I'm falling for you, wreck or not," I said, voice soft but sure. For a moment, everything else faded—the hum of the town, the footsteps on the sidewalk, even the uncertainty that had lingered in her eyes. It felt like the start of something we hadn't dared hope for, fragile but real.

She gave me a long look. "You're really not going anywhere, are you?"

"Nope." I squeezed her hand gently, letting the silence stretch, hoping she felt the promise in my touch. "Not unless you tell me to," I answered, a half-smile tugging at my lips. The weight of the moment pressed in, and all I wanted was to be someone she could lean on, someone who stayed. With her, it felt simple, even when it wasn't.

"I'm trying to get myself back together. I don't like who I was when I was with him. Seeing him here brought it all back. I should have dealt with it when I came to town, but I buried my feelings instead and tried to forget I was ever with him."

"I'll wait. I'm here. Promise." I didn't say more. Didn't have to. Because I'd already made up my mind about her. "You're worth it, Eliza. But we have more important things to discuss."

"Like what?"

"When can I make you spaghetti again, that's what."

"Is that a euphemism for something?"

I laughed, the sound light and easy, cutting through the heaviness that still lingered between us. "Only if you want it to be," I teased, letting go of her hand but holding on to the warmth that remained. I glanced up at the clock mounted over the doorway. "I should get going—I have to get to work. I'll be around if you want company later, or a cherry pie milkshake."

She smiled at me, softer now. "Maybe I'll stop by after I close up here. Might need someone to make sure I don't get lost in my own thoughts."

"I'll save you a seat at the counter," I said, backing toward the door and giving her a final, lingering look. "Don't work too late."

She nodded, still smiling, but it didn't quite reach her eyes. I caught it then—the way her shoulders stayed a little tight, the way she watched the window like she was bracing for something.

I stepped into the cold with the warmth of Coffee Cabin trailing softly behind me. The sound of her laugh lingered, but so did a thread of unease I couldn't shake. Eliza was strong—stronger than she knew—but something was pressing on her, getting under her skin in a way jokes and spaghetti couldn't fix.

And as I walked toward my truck, I had the sinking feeling that Graham wasn't done trying to make himself part of her thoughts.

I didn't know how yet, but I knew one thing for certain: whatever he was doing to her, I wasn't going to let her face it alone.

Chapter 26
Nate

"Nate," Nancy called as I walked into the Pennywhistle. She didn't say more, but the look she gave me—chin tilted, eyes narrowed, lips tight—spoke volumes. Something was off. She leaned in slightly, her voice dropping to a whisper for the next part, as if sharing a secret only meant for me. "Health inspector's here. He's in the back."

"Thanks," I said, heading straight to the kitchen.

The kitchen smelled like it always did after the lunch rush—citrusy cleanser, coffee, and whatever spices had lingered from the afternoon special. No sour milk. No spoiled anything. Still, unease coiled in my chest.

The inspector was already crouched by the walk-in fridge, tapping at a thermometer probe and frowning at his tablet.

"Morning," I said. "Everything all right?"

He glanced up, all business. "Inspector Callahan. Routine inspection. Going through the town today."

I nodded. "Nate Winters. Owner."

He barely acknowledged that, too busy tapping on his screen.

After a beat, he said, "Your fridge is running warm on the lower shelves. Not technically in violation, but higher than we like. Could be a sign the compressor's struggling."

I bit the inside of my cheek. "It passed last time. It's old but reliable." This was my first inspection since taking over as owner, and the weight of that fact pressed on me—every detail suddenly felt more critical, more personal.

I felt a flush of frustration—half at the fridge, half at myself for not catching it sooner. The Pennywhistle was my responsibility now, and every little hiccup felt weighted with that. I glanced at the thermometer display, willing it to dip just a few degrees lower, knowing it wouldn't. Still, I took mental notes: call the repair guy, check the budget, hope for a miracle.

He shrugged. "Barely passed last time. This time you're getting a formal warning. I recommend repair or replacement before your next check. Don't want it dropping out of range completely."

He printed the notice, handed it to me like it was a parking ticket, and said, "Next stop's the new restaurant across the square. You know the one."

I did. And the timing felt like something crawling under my skin. I nodded tightly. "Thanks."

I watched him leave the kitchen, stiff-backed and methodical, clipboard swinging at his side. The paper in my hand felt heavier than it should have, a thin reminder that I was one surprise away from trouble.

Once he was gone, I stood there for a long minute, staring at the walk-in like I could will it into compliance. Then I headed to my office—a cozy back room that doubled as storage and my personal clutter zone. One little window, a chipped desk, my favorite mug full of pens, and a clock that always ran five minutes fast. Home sweet home.

Nancy knocked and popped her head in. "I'll watch the front. Go ahead and stress out in here."

"Appreciate it," I muttered.

She gave me a sympathetic smile and disappeared. I sank into my chair, rubbing my temples as the enormity of it all pressed in. The fridge was just one more thing stacked onto a list that never seemed to get shorter, and the uncertainty gnawed at me. I tried to focus, pulling a legal pad closer and jotting down priorities, but the numbers blurred together, and the margins filled with anxious doodles. Replacing the fridge was not on this month's budget. Not even close.

A knock sounded at the door again. Softer this time.

"Come in," I said.

Eliza stepped inside, two takeout cups in hand, shutting the door behind her. I could already smell the coffee —hers always had vanilla or cinnamon or something that made the air better just by existing.

"I heard what happened," she said softly.

"Nancy?"

"Yeah, she mentioned it when I got here."

I took the cup from her and motioned toward the chair beside my desk. She sat, curling one leg beneath her, somehow looking both put together and like she might unravel any second. I knew the feeling.

"It's just a fridge," I said, trying to minimize it for her sake.

But she didn't buy it.

"You're worried."

I nodded, swallowing a sip. "It's old, but we've always passed. It might need repairs or to be completely replaced. Either way, I didn't plan on this expense yet."

Eliza frowned, brows pulling together. "You think he had something to do with it?" she asked quietly. "I mean, not physical sabotage, that's not really his style. But he'd definitely bribe an inspector or even just call him to come here to see what comes out of it."

I didn't need her to clarify who *he* was.

"I don't know," I said. "I can't prove anything. Just bad timing."

She nodded, but her lips were tight. "It feels like him."

"Yeah." I brushed my fingers along her side. "I hate that you're carrying the weight of it."

She gave me a smile. "Maybe we should forget about Graham. Maybe I should pep talk you like you did for me." Her eyes sparkled, and that was all it took.

"Come here," I said again, softer this time.

She leaned in first—just a gentle kiss, warm and slow —but it deepened fast. Her fingers curled in my shirt, and my hand slid up her back, not to push, just to hold. Her breath was warm on my cheek, the close comfort of her presence making the rest of the world fall away. For a moment, nothing else seemed to matter—just the air between us and the promise in her eyes. I let myself get lost in it, in her, wanting to hold onto this fragile peace before reality crept back in.

The kiss turned hungry. Like something we both needed and didn't want to let go of.

She made a small sound against my mouth, and I pulled her closer before catching myself. Her hand lingered for a moment longer on my shoulder, her thumb tracing an absent pattern through the fabric before she let go. The silence was heavy, but it didn't feel uncomfortable—just full, like the space between us was charged with everything unsaid. Time seemed to slow down, stretching those few seconds into something that felt almost infinite.

We pulled apart slowly. I didn't want to let go, but something in the way she looked at me made my chest ache like she was pulling away.

Her voice was quiet. "I should go." She stood up and paced a little, running a hand through her hair. "I shouldn't have kissed you. You're dealing with all of this, and I just—threw myself at you."

"Hey." I stood too, catching her wrist gently before she could retreat. "You didn't throw anything. That kiss?" I held her gaze. "It was the best part of my day."

She looked up at me then, eyes too bright, like she was holding something back.

"Eliza..."

"I'm scared I'll make things hard for you," she said quickly, like she needed to get it out before I could stop her.

There it was. Not fear for herself—fear of being a burden. Of being the problem. I could see the walls going up, not out of self-preservation, but guilt. The kind that came from being made to feel responsible for other people's discomfort for too long.

"You won't," I said, stepping closer, lowering my voice. "You make everything feel easier. I promise."

She shook her head faintly, already reaching for her coffee like it was an exit strategy. "I'll see you later, Nate."

I nodded, even though every part of me wanted to ask her to stay. "I'll walk you out."

Outside, the air was sharp with a breezy chill, and I shoved my hands into my jacket pockets to keep from reaching for her again. I wished I'd said more. Wished I'd told her that if Graham was circling, if he was trying to make her doubt herself again, I wasn't going to let him win. Not this time. Not when I could already see what she couldn't yet—that she was strong, and capable, and still very much *herself* beneath the old wounds.

The Taste-Off wasn't just a competition. It was a chance. A way back into the kitchen on her own terms. A way to remember that her joy didn't belong to Graham— or to anyone who'd ever tried to shrink it.

She turned at her car door. "Text me if anything changes with the fridge?"

"Yeah," I said. "I will."

She hesitated, fingers curling around the handle. "Thanks for letting me stop by."

"Eliza..." I started, wanting to tell her all of it—that I wasn't afraid of hard things, that I believed in her more than she knew, that I wasn't going anywhere.

But she smiled, small and careful, and I let the moment rest where it was.

As she drove away, I stood there a second longer, resolve settling in my chest. Whatever Graham was playing at, I wasn't backing down. And neither was she— whether she knew it yet or not.

Outside, the air was sharp with chill, and I wished I'd said more. Wished I'd told her how much I wanted her to stay, even if just for a few more minutes.

She turned at her car door. "Text me if anything changes with the fridge?"

"Yeah. I will."

She hesitated. "Thanks for letting me stop by."

"Eliza..." I started, but stopped short. Instead, I just smiled. "Um, thanks for the coffee."

She gave a small, tight smile in return. Then she got in and drove off, taillights fading into the dark.

I stood there a moment longer than I needed to, jaw tight, heart unsettled. Because if that kiss was a goodbye... I wasn't ready. Not even close.

Chapter 27
Eliza

The morning air bit at my cheeks as I unlocked the Coffee Cabin. Cold, quiet, gray-blue sky stretching overhead like a sigh waiting to happen.

I'd barely slept.

Nate's kiss still lingered on my lips. So did the look in his eyes when I pulled away—like he didn't want to let me go but knew I needed the space. Which I did. And I didn't. Both things were true at the same time, and it was exhausting.

I had just gotten the espresso machine warming up when the knock came. Sharp, intentional. Not friendly.

I turned, and there he was.

Graham.

His reflection hit the glass before he did, tall and polished in some ridiculous designer jacket, his expression unreadable until he got closer.

My stomach knotted, and I felt my shoulders stiffen.

Why the hell is he here so early?

"Nice sweater," he said.

I didn't respond, forcing my voice to stay steady even as my pulse sped up.

He leaned one elbow casually on the counter, and I felt a flicker of panic at how close he was.

"Word gets around quick here, Eliza. You'd think you'd remember that."

I swallowed, aware of how exposed I felt behind the glass, all alone. My chest tightened, my grip on the counter almost painful, but I straightened my back, trying to make myself seem smaller and unthreatening, hoping he'd get the message without me having to say a word. "Word about what?"

"You. Me. Everything that was supposed to stay between us." His tone was low, pointed. "Remember?"

"Well, good morning to you, too." I forced a sugary smile.

He narrowed his eyes. "Cara knows we were together. Personally." His lips thinned. "You knew how this would make me look, and you told her anyway. She paid me a visit. I knew your sisters didn't like me; they made it obvious at my opening. I figured it was because I was your boss, and it didn't work out. I should have known you'd tell them everything."

Shit.

I thought Cara had run off to gather a stack of self-help, how to move past a toxic relationship books the other day, not to confront Graham.

Screw it. The cat was out of the bag now.

"Well, maybe if you didn't want people to think badly of you," I bit out, "you should quit doing bad things."

That made him flinch. It was small. But I saw it.

"You're still in the Taste-Off with Nate," he said, skipping past apology and straight into disapproval. "After everything."

"Yep," I said, popping the "p."

"You think that's wise?"

I shrugged, refusing to let his worry infect me. "People are always going to talk, Graham. It doesn't matter what I do or who I'm with—they'll find something to gossip about." I leaned on the window ledge, raising a brow. "Do I think cooking food with a good man in a town-wide event is going to ruin your pristine reputation somehow? I really don't care. Move on. I have." I had no idea where my bravado was coming from, but I was not about to fight the instinct.

He let out a slow, deliberate breath, as if weighing his next words. For a moment, I saw something flicker in his expression—regret, maybe, or something closer to vulnerability—but it vanished before I could name it. Instead, he straightened, steeling himself against any softness. His voice dropped. "You know it makes things harder."

"For who? You?" I held his gaze, refusing to let him see how his words unsettled me. There was a tension between us now, taut and barely hidden, a familiar ache that always seemed to resurface whenever old wounds were pressed. Still, I wouldn't let him have the satisfaction of seeing me falter.

"For both of us," he snapped. "The more attention we all get, the more people are going to start wondering what really happened between us."

"Nothing '*really happened*,' Graham. I'm not talking about it, isn't that the point?"

"You think being seen with Nate makes you look like the innocent party?" He hesitated, his jaw tight, before continuing. "You know how this town gets when rumors start. Doesn't matter what the truth is—people will twist it until it fits whatever story they want to tell."

My fingers curled against the window ledge, but I kept my tone even. "Then let them talk. I'm not living my life for anyone's approval anymore. And, don't forget, I don't have to pretend to be anything other than who I am. I am the innocent party."

"You're being irrational."

I laughed, short and sharp. "There it is. The old hits."

Graham ran a hand through his perfectly styled hair. "You need to think long term. The more noise there is around you, the more people are going to talk. You really want that kind of heat? On you? On Nate? I have things I can say too, if I choose."

My stomach twisted. And I hated that it did.

"There was an inspection at the Pennywhistle," I said, testing the words. "You wouldn't know anything about that, would you?"

He blinked, expression carefully neutral. "Why would I?"

"I don't know. Maybe you saw a chance to rattle some nerves. Throw a wrench in things."

"They inspected me, too. It was routine." He gave a soft, humorless laugh. "Besides, the place is ancient, Eliza. Do you really think I'd need to do anything to make it fail an inspection?"

"You didn't answer the question."

"I didn't report anything, if that's what you're asking," he said. "But if I had? It wouldn't be sabotage. It would be a concern."

I stared at him. "Concern for who?"

He smiled like he was doing me a favor. "You should really think about dropping out," he said finally. "If not for me, then for your own peace of mind. This whole thing's a distraction you don't need."

I clenched my jaw. "And what if I don't drop out?"

His expression chilled. "Then don't be surprised if people keep talking."

I let a small, cold smile spread across my face. "A big-city chef needing to manipulate and threaten the competition to win a small-town Taste-off... that's really sad, Graham."

He blinked, clearly not expecting that.

I felt a spark of satisfaction at seeing him flinch, but underneath it, my stomach twisted. He's going to hate that I just stood up to him and whatever gossip he spread could hurt Nate. Why the hell didn't I just keep my mouth shut?

I lifted my chin, keeping my voice calm and controlled. "You came back expecting to find me lonely and miserable, pining for you. That's not happening."

He opened his mouth, but I didn't let him speak I

could see it in the tight line of his jaw, the way his hands twitched, that this was all he had. I may have stood up to him, but I was still shaken, and I hated that he still had the power to make me feel this way.

He held my gaze for one more beat, then turned and walked off like he hadn't just lit a match and tossed it into dry grass.

I slammed the window shut behind him.

I braced my hands on the counter, heart pounding.

So much for a quiet morning.

The bell above the drive-thru window jingled, and I turned on instinct, forcing my expression into something neutral as I greeted the customer.

A familiar rumble pulled into the parking lot, and my pulse responded like it always did now—faster, fluttery.

Nate's truck.

The passenger door flung open before he'd even killed the engine. Tilly hopped out, full of energy in purple glitter sneakers and a sweatshirt with a dancing llama. Lois jumped down after her, tail already wagging like a flag in the wind, leash dangling from Nate's hand.

They were sunshine, both of them.

Tilly sprinted to the walk-up window and beamed. "Hi, Eliza! We came for a hot cocoa and marshmallows!"

Lois barked once, emphatically, as if seconding the motion.

I felt myself smile. Couldn't stop it.

"Well," I said, reaching for a bag, "you're in luck, I have pink ones just for you."

Nate came up behind her, wearing jeans and a

flannel rolled to the elbows. He looked like a lumberjack who moonlighted as a hot single diner dad.

"Hey," he said. His voice was soft, searching. "You good?"

My fingers tightened slightly around the paper bag.

"Just the usual morning rush," I said breezily.

He didn't buy it. Not fully. I could see it in the way his eyes lingered on mine—concern threaded through his easy smile.

But he didn't push.

For a moment, the world felt quiet, just the three of us under the awning while the drizzle painted silver streaks on the street.

I passed Tilly the marshmallows. "No charge for the Pre-K princess."

"I'm gonna save half for after dance class," she said solemnly.

"That's a solid choice."

Nate handed her a five anyway, gesturing to the tip jar. "Support small businesses."

She beamed at both of us, stuffed the money in the jar, then stuffed a marshmallow into her mouth.

I smiled at Nate, trying to let the warmth of his concern settle in my chest. For a second, I wished I could let myself lean into that comfort, just exist here without the shadow of everything else pressing in. He didn't leave right away.

"Everything okay?" he asked, quieter now. "You seem—"

"Yeah." I nodded a little too fast, too bright. "It's fine. Morning rush and all. Like I said."

He studied me. "You sure?"

No.

Graham's words still stuck to my skin like smoke. And standing here with Nate—steady, kind, sweet Nate —I felt the weight of all the ways things could go wrong.

Graham was angry. He'd been clear. He didn't want people talking about him. Didn't want people knowing about us.

What if he found a way to come after the Pennywhistle? What if he already had?

What if I ruined this for Nate?

What if he lost business?

What if Tilly got caught in the fallout? He'd come here to have more time with her. I couldn't put that at risk. What was I thinking, continuing to see him?

I swallowed and tucked a hair behind my ear. "I'm just tired. I didn't sleep much."

"Okay," he said, slowly. "If you're sure."

"I am."

He held my gaze another second, then nodded.

"We'll get out of your way," he said gently. "Tilly's already planning a post-dance class victory lap at the park."

"That's how champions are made."

He smiled, but there was still a question behind his eyes.

As he turned to go, Lois barked once, tongue lolling, tail swishing the air.

"You too, huh?" I said. "I'm fine."

She barked softly. Nate laughed and gave me a little wave.

"Dinner this weekend? Me, you, Tilly? We can find another favorite together."

I hesitated, searching his face for any sign that this was a mistake, but all I saw was the quiet encouragement I'd always relied on. For a moment, I wanted to say yes, to let myself believe that everything could be simple. But deep down, I knew it wasn't.

"I wish I could. I have a family dinner. Once a month. I can't back out."

He nodded in understanding, but I saw the flicker of disappointment on his face before he masked it with a reassuring smile. There was a momentary silence between us, filled only by the distant hum of a car engine and Lois's soft whine. I shifted my weight, wishing I could give more, but feeling the familiar pull of fear holding me back.

"Text me when you're home?"

"Yeah," I said, even though I wasn't sure what I'd say.

I watched as they drove off together—father, daughter, dog—and I watched them go with something sharp and aching blooming in my chest.

Not for the first time, I wondered what I was doing.

And who I might hurt if I didn't take a step back and think about it before I went any further.

Chapter 28
Eliza

By the time I got home from the Coffee Cabin, the sky had already started its slow slide into gray. The air smelled like it was going to snow, but my townhouse was warm and still—except for the watchful eyes of two cats perched on the kitchen counter like judgmental gargoyles. I scratched behind Remy's ears, nudged Linguini off the breadbox, and filled their bowls even though they weren't empty. I moved through the motions, not sure what else to do with myself. Everything inside me felt too loud. I filled the kettle and set it on the stove, watching the burner glow orange as if it held the answers I couldn't find. By the time the water boiled, I still hadn't decided what I was going to do. So I poured the tea anyway. The truth was, I was spiraling—and I didn't know how to stop.

Everything inside me felt like a tangled spool of yarn, and every time I tried to sort it out, I made it worse. I kept replaying Graham's words at the Coffee Cabin, the casual threat buried beneath the fake smile. I couldn't shake the feeling that I was dragging Nate into something bad just by existing in his orbit.

And Tilly. God. The thought of her getting hurt in any of this made my stomach clench. Not that Graham would do anything to her. But if Nate lost the Pennywhistle somehow or had to find another job—ugh. So much could happen. He was finally in a place where he could spend more time with her. I couldn't be the reason he lost it.

I sank onto the couch, my nerves shot, my eyes dry and burning. I didn't want to be alone—but I couldn't talk to my sisters. Not yet. They'd want to help, to fix things, to protect me. And that meant charging into battle when I was still trying to figure out if I even wanted to fight.

But I didn't want to lose Nate. The thought of hurting him was inconceivable. And that made everything worse.

I picked up my phone.

> Me: Can you come over? I have to talk to you.

His reply came less than a minute later.

> Nate: Be there in ten. I'll drop Tilly off at my grandparents' place.

For a moment, I stared at the screen, watching the little bubbles that meant he was still there, still on the other end of all this mess. The relief was sharp and sudden, cutting through the static in my head. I set the phone down and wrapped my arms around myself, trying to slow my breathing, counting heartbeats as if that could keep the panic at bay. I tried to focus on the familiar things—the cats winding around my ankles, the faint whistle of the kettle cooling, the muted sounds of Honeybrook Hollow behind double-paned glass. Still, every sound seemed too loud, every shadow too deep. But at least Nate was coming. Maybe that was enough for now.

I had to talk to him. I needed to explain why we had to stop seeing each other. Again. Damn it.

When he knocked, I opened the door and let him in without a word.

He stepped inside, his expression shifting from worried to soft the second he saw me.

"Hey," he said gently, not pushing, not asking me for anything, just being there when I needed him, which was more than I could ever want.

I let out a breath. "Hey."

We stood there in the soft quiet of my living room, the only sounds the hum of the fridge and Remy's light thump as he jumped off the windowsill. Nate opened his arms. I didn't hesitate.

I walked into his hug and stayed there, his body warm and solid against mine, his hand smoothing down my back like he could iron out the chaos inside me.

He kissed my hair. "You okay?"

"No," I whispered.

He didn't say anything. He just held me tighter.

I tipped my face up to his and found him already

looking at me, brown eyes full of something I couldn't name without breaking.

I pressed my cheek against his shoulder, letting myself breathe in the familiar scent of him, the blissful comfort that came with every gentle touch. For a few moments, wrapped in the safety of his embrace, the world outside faded to a blur, and I let myself believe that maybe, just for tonight, things could be simple. The quiet wrapped around us, softening the edges of everything I was too afraid to say.

When he kissed me, I didn't pull away.

I should have said his name. Should have told him everything that was clawing at my chest. But instead, I let the kiss answer for me—slow and searching, like we were both afraid to ask the question out loud. His hands framed my face, warm and careful, and I slid my arms around his neck, pressing closer because the truth was, I didn't want to lose him.

Not yet. Not ever.

Some part of me knew I was falling—too fast, too deep—and that scared me enough to make me reckless. I told myself I needed one more moment. One more memory of what it felt like to be held by him. To be wanted. To be safe.

So, I kissed him back.

We moved together like we'd done it a hundred times already, like our bodies knew a language our hearts were still trying to translate. By the time we reached my bedroom, words felt impossible. Clothes were shed between soft laughter and breathless pauses, his eyes never leaving mine, like he was checking in with me every second.

When he pulled back long enough to ask, "Eliza, are you sure?" I nodded, even as something inside me whispered that this wasn't just about wanting anymore.

It was about love.

Being with him was tenderness and heat and comfort all at once—his touch reverent, his mouth gentle, like he was memorizing me. I held onto him, to the way he said my name like it mattered, to the way my heart felt too full for my chest.

And afterward, when we lay tangled in the sheets, my head on his chest, his fingers tracing slow, soothing paths over my shoulder, reality crept back in.

The silence wasn't empty. It was heavy. Sacred.

And it was also full of everything I hadn't said.

Guilt settled in my stomach, sharp and unwelcome. I'd asked him here to talk. To warn him. To protect him. And instead, I'd let myself pretend—just for a little while —that none of it existed. Exactly what I'd done since I got into town. Bury my head in the sand and pretend that my problems weren't real.

I pushed up onto one elbow, staring at the familiar curve of his jaw, the rise and fall of his chest beneath my hand.

"I don't think we should do this," I whispered. "I shouldn't do this with you."

Nate went still beneath me. "What do you mean?"

I sat up, pulling the sheet around me like armor. My voice shook, but I forced the words out anyway. "Us. The

Taste-Off. All of it. I asked you here to talk, and I didn't. I just—" I swallowed. "I wanted one more moment with you before I did the right thing. I'm so selfish, and I'm sorry."

His eyes softened with understanding. "It's going to be okay," he whispered. I couldn't look away.

"I'm falling in love with you," I admitted, the truth burning as it left me. "And that's exactly why I can't be the reason you get hurt. Or Tilly. Or the Pennywhistle. I won't let Graham touch your life because of me. Even if it means walking away from what I want most."

My chest ached, every breath a fight.

Nate didn't move for a long second. He just looked at me, eyes searching my face like he was trying to memorize it and understand it at the same time.

Then he reached up and brushed his thumb over my cheek, so gentle it almost undid me.

"Eliza," he said quietly, "you don't get to decide what hurts me."

My breath hitched.

"I know you think you're protecting me," he went on, voice steady but thick with feeling. "And damn, I love you for that. But loving someone isn't about stepping out of the way so they don't get hit. For good people, it's about standing next to them when it comes. But for me, it means taking the blow."

Tears burned behind my eyes. "Nate—"

He sat up too, keeping the sheet around his waist, close enough that our knees touched. "I chose you. No matter what is going on, I will choose you. Whatever

Graham is trying to do, whatever mess he's stirring up—you won't face it without me. Not after this. Not after knowing what it feels like to hold you, and have you look at me like I matter."

"You matter," I whispered. "Too much and that's the problem. I'll do anything so you don't get hurt."

His mouth curved in a soft, sad smile. "But you matter too. And I'm not walking away from that because it's hard right now."

"But Nate—"

He took my hands in his, warm and sure. "If you need space, I'll give it to you. If you need time, I'll wait. But don't tell me this—us—was just a goodbye you needed to get through the night. Because it wasn't for me."

My chest ached so badly I thought it might split open.

"I don't want to lose you," I said. "But—"

"No buts. You won't lose me," he promised, like it was the simplest truth in the world. "Not unless you truly want me gone. And Eliza... I don't think that's what you want."

I shook my head, tears finally spilling. "No. It's not."

He pulled me into his arms again, pressing a kiss to my hair, holding me like he could keep us together, and keep the world out. "Then we'll figure it out," he murmured. "Together. Even if it's messy. Even if it scares us."

I clung to him, breathing him in, knowing I was standing on the edge of everything I'd ever wanted.

"I just need a minute, okay? Some space to figure out what I have to do."

He pulled away, worry deepening across his face. "Eliza..."

"I'm serious," I said quickly, before he could talk me out of it. "Graham isn't going to stop. I think he blames me for everything. He expected to come back here and be a big shot, and it's not going as expected. And I think—I think he's going to come after you and the Pennywhistle. I can't let that happen. I won't do that to you, Nate."

His voice was low and steady. "You think he's responsible for the inspection."

"I do." My throat tightened. "But I can't prove it. And if we go to the Taste-Off together, if we win or even come close, it's just going to make him angrier."

Nate reached for my hand, threading our fingers together. "You think stepping away will protect me."

"Yes."

"You think I wouldn't walk through fire for you?"

That stopped me cold. The sincerity in his voice. The way he looked at me was like I mattered more than anything else.

"I'm scared, Nate," I said, voice shaking. "Not just for you. For Tilly. For what he might do if he really wants to hurt me."

He exhaled, pressing a kiss to the back of my hand. "I hate that he has you this twisted up."

"I just... I need some space. I need to think."

Nate nodded slowly, but I could see the hurt flicker in his eyes.

"Okay," he said. "I'll give you space. But I'm not going anywhere. Not unless you tell me you don't want me."

"I don't want you to go away," I said quietly. "But I don't know how to do this right."

His smile was sad and soft. "We'll figure it out."

Tears pricked my eyes. I kissed his cheek, then stood up and gathered my robe.

"I'm going to make some tea."

I slipped into my robe and wandered into the kitchen. For a moment, I hovered in the soft spill of light from the stove, listening to the quiet house and my own frantic heartbeat. The silence between us stretched, not awkward, but heavy with everything we'd said. I wanted to tell him I was grateful. That his patience was the only thing keeping me from unraveling completely. But the words caught in my throat, tangled up with fear and longing.

Steam curled from my mug like a ghost I couldn't shake. I stood there holding it with both hands, barefoot on the cold kitchen tile, pretending the warmth was enough to steady me. It wasn't.

Behind me, I heard the soft rustle of blankets, then footsteps—slow, hesitant. Nate had gotten dressed in the dim light of my bedroom, and when he stepped into the doorway, he looked undone. Hair mussed, hoodie half-zipped, eyes soft with worry and something else. Something raw.

"Eliza," he said gently.

I couldn't look at him.

"I couldn't stay in your bed. Not without you there. I don't want this to end. I don't want a break or space or—damn it. I can't tell you what you need, and I won't try to force you to change your mind."

That almost broke me right there.

He walked farther into the kitchen, stopping when he was close enough to touch but far enough that I'd have to move toward him. It was such a Nate thing—an invitation without pressure. A door held open.

"Will you talk to me?" he asked softly.

I stared down at my tea. "I don't know if I can." My throat felt tight, my voice unfamiliar. "Everything feels too big. Too fast. Too much. And I'm so worried that Graham is going to—I don't know—do something to ruin it."

His brows pulled together with worry. "If this is about us, Eliza, we don't have to rush anything. I meant what I said. We can slow down. We can—"

"It's not that," I whispered.

"Then what is it?"

"I..." My breath shook. "I don't know how to do this."

He didn't move, didn't crowd me. But I could feel him, warm and patient and steady in the doorway.

"Eliza," he murmured, "talk to me."

So I tried.

"I'm scared," I said. "There. That's the ugly truth. I'm terrified. I came here and hid out. I didn't deal with any of my feelings, and now I'm in a whirlwind, and I don't know what to do."

He stepped closer, just one careful stride. "What scares you the most?" he asked.

"Graham," I whispered. "Of what he might do. What he could do. He's angry, and I know how he gets when he's angry. Manipulative. Cruel. And he's not subtle about who he blames for anything." My chest tightened painfully. "I think he'll go after you. And the diner. You could lose everything, and it would be my fault."

His breath caught. "Eliza—"

"If I stay in this competition with you, I'm putting a target on your back," I said, voice wobbling. "If I stay with you *at all*, I might be doing that."

His expression changed—not hurt, not angry. Devastated.

"You're not responsible for Graham's actions," he said, low and fierce. "He doesn't get to take things from you. Or from me."

"But he will try," I said. "I know he will."

Nate took another step. "Then let him try."

I shook my head. "I can't let you fight my battles. Or get caught in the crossfire of them."

"You think I can't handle him?"

"That's not it," I whispered. "I know you can. That's what scares me. You'll take the hit. You'll protect me. You'll stand between him and me even if it costs you something. And I can't—" My voice broke. "I can't be the reason anything happens to you or Tilly. You're finally in a place where you get to spend more time with her. The Pennywhistle is everything; it's your legacy. It's your livelihood. I won't ruin that. I can't."

Silence fell, heavy as the snowfall outside.

Nate swallowed, eyes locked on mine. "Eliza... I love you."

The words landed like a blow and a gift all at once. I sucked in a breath.

"I love you," he said again, voice rough. "I'm in this. I'm in you. I don't know when it happened, but it did, and I don't want to pretend it didn't to make things easier. You have to know. You're important to me, Eliza. You're everything."

I felt like I was being torn in two because I felt the same.

"I love you, too," I whispered, tears slipping down my cheeks. "And that's the problem. I love you too much to let you risk your daughter's future for me."

His face crumpled—just for a second. Just long enough for me to see the truth. The hope, the fear, the way he'd already handed me his heart without hesitation.

"Eliza," he said, stepping toward me. "Please."

"I can't be the reason something bad happens," I cried. "I can't." I set the mug down before I dropped it. "I need space. I need to think. And you—you need to be safe from me."

He shook his head almost violently. "The safest place I've ever been is next to you."

"Don't," I whispered, voice shaking. "Don't make this harder."

"I'm not trying to make it harder," he said, pain threading through every word. "I'm trying to make you understand. When you know from the bottom of your soul someone is meant for you, you fight for them."

I backed up until I hit the counter. Remy and Linguini circled my feet like they sensed the crack spreading down the middle of me.

"I need to be alone," I said. "Just for a little while. I need to figure out how to keep you safe. I need to figure out how to be strong enough to take care of you, like you do for me."

He stared at me as if the ground had shifted beneath him. "I don't need protecting."

"Maybe you don't. But Tilly does. You'll see that once you're not right here. When you're back home and with her, then you'll understand," I whispered. "That's why you're going to let me do this. Just for now. Please give me some space to figure this out. Please. It has to be me. I'm almost ashamed to tell you that if it weren't for Tilly, I'd probably let you protect me. And I want you to know—to believe—that if this works out for us that I'll protect her too. She deserves that."

His chest rose and fell, slow and tight.

"Okay," he said finally. "If you need space, I'll give it to you."

My heart felt like it was tearing. "Thank you."

He took a step back, then another, like each one cost him something. At the doorway, he paused.

"I'm not going anywhere," he murmured. "Even if you need distance. Even if you're scared, I'm not leaving you alone in this. Call me when you need me. Anytime. I mean it, Eliza. Promise me you'll call if you need me, so I can go."

I squeezed my eyes shut as tears spilled hot and relentlessly. "I promise."

When I opened my eyes, he wasn't in the doorway anymore, but the room still felt full of him—his warmth, his steadiness, his hope.

And the terrible fear that loving him might break us both.

I clicked the door shut, soft as a breath, and the silence that followed felt like something sacred and ruined all at once. I stood there for a second, motionless, as if stillness might somehow rewind time, might take back the words I couldn't unsay. Then, my legs gave out.

I sank to the floor, arms wrapped around myself, the wooden floor cold against my skin as sobs cracked free from my chest. Remy nudged against my knee, and Linguini curled close at my hip, but nothing could ease the ache clawing its way through me. I had never felt so hollow and so full of love at the same time. And it hurt. God, it hurt. Because I knew I hadn't walked away from Nate to protect myself.

I'd done it to protect him and his daughter. And it still felt like breaking both our hearts.

Chapter 29
Nate

Morning came anyway.

I made breakfast on autopilot—toast popping up a little too dark, eggs scrambled softer than usual, fruit cut into uneven pieces because I kept spacing out. Tilly sat at the counter in her pajamas, legs swinging, conducting a stuffed-animal meeting with very serious authority.

"Okay," she announced to the reindeer and the dog, who was very much asleep on the rug, "today is a school day, so no nonsense."

Lois snorted in her sleep.

"That means you," Tilly told her sternly.

I huffed a quiet laugh despite myself and slid a plate in front of her. "Eat before the meeting gets out of hand."

She eyed the eggs suspiciously. "These are normal eggs."

"Define normal."

"They're weren't loud," she said. "Are you sad?"

"No," I protested mildly. "Well, maybe a little bit. I'll be fine."

She patted my hand. "It's okay."

I closed my eyes for a second, smiling. "Thank you for your patience with me."

She took a bite, nodded approval, then leaned closer, lowering her voice like she was about to share a secret. "Daddy?"

"Yeah, sweetheart?"

"You're thinking loud, though."

I squinted. I'd almost forgotten how observant she was. "Am I?"

"Uh-huh." She pointed her fork at my forehead. "Your face gets all scrunchy. Like this." She demonstrated, crossing her eyes and scrunching her nose.

I laughed then, real and surprised. "That's not what I look like."

"That's *exactly* what you look like."

"Noted."

She studied me for another beat, then slid her plate closer to mine. "You can have my strawberries," she said solemnly. "They help with sad thoughts."

My throat tightened. "How do you know I have sad thoughts?"

She shrugged, utterly unbothered. "Sometimes people do. It's not a big deal. They go away."

I took one of the strawberries and bit into it. "You might be right."

"Also," she added, "if they don't go away, you can tell

me. Or Grandma. Or Lois. Lois is a good listener, but she does fall asleep."

Lois let out a long, dramatic sigh on cue.

Tilly nodded. "See?"

The drive to school was calmer, lighter. Tilly hummed along to the radio, making up lyrics about waffles and backpacks. When we pulled up, she hopped out, adjusted her jacket, then leaned back in through the open door.

"Daddy?"

"Yeah?"

"You did a good job today. Quiet eggs are good too."

My chest warmed in a way that felt dangerously close to tears. "Thanks, sweetheart."

She grinned. "You're welcome."

Then she ran off toward the building, waving once over her shoulder like she always did—confident, certain, completely unaware of how much she carried me with her.

I waited until she was inside before I drove away, the quiet returning—but softer now, buffered by strawberries, loud sad thoughts, and the steady reminder that even on hard days, I was someone's safe place.

I drove to the Pennywhistle on autopilot. Everything felt too quiet. Too tight in my chest. Like the part of me that had started to stretch toward something good was curling back in.

My grandma met me at the door with a wary glance and a full coffee pot in hand.

"Dining room is half full. I put the cinnamon rolls in

the warmer, and Nancy is handling refills. You okay, sweetheart?"

I gave her a tired smile. "I'm fine, Grandma. I've got it."

She squeezed my arm. "He's in booth four."

I didn't have to ask who *he* was. I spotted Graham the second I turned around—sprawled across the booth like he owned the place, stirring his coffee with deliberate slowness while eyeing the morning crowd like they were there for him.

My gut tightened. The Pennywhistle always felt like home. Until he walked in.

I slid behind the counter, poured myself a mug, and walked over to his booth.

"Coffee's good," he said, glancing up with that glossy, insincere smile. "Not as trendy as what you get across town at the Coffee Cabin, but it has that old-school charm."

I didn't answer. Just stood there until his grin faltered.

Finally, he set his cup down and leaned back. "Trouble in paradise?"

My jaw clenched. "You need something, Graham?"

He shrugged. "Breakfast. And maybe to offer a little friendly advice."

I didn't respond.

"You know, Eliza gets pouty when she doesn't get her way. Makes things complicated. It might be good to keep a little distance. I saw her pull up to the Coffee Cabin on my way here. She had that look about her. Familiar."

I set my coffee down carefully. "You done?"

"Not yet." He picked up his mug, like this was casual. Like he wasn't twisting knives under the table. "It's a small town. People remember what they hear. Just saying —being too close to her might not do your reputation any favors."

I leaned down, hands on the table.

"You don't get to talk about her," I said, my voice low. "You sure as hell don't get to warn me off like you're doing me a favor. Eliza is not a complication. She's the best part of my day—always. If you've got a problem with that, I suggest you take it somewhere else."

He blinked, but the smirk returned. "Guess I hit a nerve."

I stepped back. "Enjoy your breakfast. It'll be your last here."

"You're throwing me out?"

I smiled without warmth. "Call it customer selection."

Graham sat there like he wanted to say more, but then my grandma appeared at my side, crossed her arms, and raised one eyebrow like she'd been listening from the start.

He stood up, brushed imaginary crumbs off his sleeves, and smiled at her with politician polish. "Good morning," he said to her, startled.

"Get. Out." She didn't break her stare. Graham hesitated, searching for some angle, and apparently finding none he could work with.

The tension hung in the air—sharp, but fleeting.

With a stiff nod to both of us, he moved past, his smile melting away as soon as he thought no one was looking. He left with fake charm and a nod toward the counter.

She patted my shoulder. "You looked like you're about to punch him in his big dumb face."

"I'm fine," I lied.

"You're not," she said, gently. "But you're allowed to not be."

"He's an ass, Nate," Nancy said as she patted my shoulder. "Always has been. Soon enough, the half of town that didn't know it will find out. Don't you worry about that."

I looked around the diner—still half full, clinking spoons and murmured conversation. Conversations that seemed to agree with Nancy and my grandma.

"We've got it covered," Grandma gave my hand a squeeze.

"Grandma—"

"I'm serious. Take a walk. Go for a run. Take Lois. She's probably dying to get out of the house. Your grandpa loves walking her, but he can't run like he used to."

My lips twitched. "You just want me to stop brooding around the customers."

"That too."

I grabbed my jacket and keys. The cold air would help. Maybe.

She was right about one thing—I needed to get out of my own head before I did something stupid. Like, drive back to the Coffee Cabin and kiss Eliza again until she forgets why she ever pushed me away. Or go to Graham's restaurant and punch him in his smug face.

I went home to change into my workout gear, picked up Lois, and ran.

And tried not to think about how it felt like I was losing something I'd only just started to believe I could have.

Chapter 30
Eliza

A few days had passed since everything cracked open, and somehow that made it worse. Time gave my thoughts too much room to stretch and circle. Graham hadn't disappeared—he'd simply learned how to linger. A comment disguised as civility. A glance that suggested unfinished business. The familiar pressure of feeling smaller than I meant to be, quieter than I was.

That unsettled me most. Not knowing what he wanted—or even if he knew himself. With Graham, silence had always been the sharpest blade—he never yelled, never resorted to outright cruelty. Just enough implication of what simmered beneath his surface to keep me second-guessing my instincts, wondering if I was the problem. I hated that it still worked. I hated that after everything I'd been through with him, he could still reach inside me and flip that switch.

The scent of smoke from the barbecue hit me as I

rounded the back gate at my grandparents' place, sharp and comforting all at once. Laughter drifted across the yard, tangled with the crackle of the fire pit and the hiss of sausages hitting the grill. Paige's daughters were sitting by the fire pit, cider mugs in hand, poking at the flames with long sticks like it was their solemn responsibility to keep the fire alive.

The place carried the weight of a hundred ordinary memories I had only recently realized shaped the entirety of who I was. It was proof that I'd always had a place to land, even when I forgot it.

The Honeybrook Inn rose at the front of the lot, all welcoming windows and warm light, the trees lining the pathway to the main entrance already covered with frost. The Coffee Cabin sat closer to the road. Behind the house, the old barn stood solid and weathered, doors thrown open, string lights spilling out like stars caught on nails.

Grandma's three pugs tore through the grass like chaos incarnate, snorting and wheezing and absolutely convinced they were winning some invisible race. Someone laughed when one of them skidded sideways near the picnic table, and the sound forced me into the present and out of my head.

The Darlington Weenie Roast was in full swing— cozy and comforting, the way it always was, even with the cold biting at our noses. String lights crisscrossed the yard from the barn to the back porch. A flannel blanket was tossed over the picnic table like an afterthought. A pot of cider simmered near the back door, steam curling up into the night air.

I paused just inside the yard, hands tucked into my coat sleeves, letting it all wash over me. This place. These people. I'd spent so many years convincing myself I was the extra piece—the one who didn't quite fit in. And yet here I was, heart aching, because this was where I'd always wanted to be.

Graham had made me feel like I was a burden. Like needing people was a weakness. Like my feelings were something to manage quietly, so they didn't inconvenience him. But I knew it had started with my parents—it's why I let him get away with it.

Standing there now, watching my sisters laugh, watching my grandparents laughing at the grill, I felt the lie of that settling uneasily in my gut.

I didn't need to disappear to be strong. I didn't need to carry this alone to prove anything.

Cara found me first, like she always did. She didn't announce herself, just slipped in beside me near the cider pot and handed me a mug.

"You okay?" she asked quietly.

I nodded out of habit. Then shook my head. "No. But I'm here."

"That counts," she said, bumping her shoulder into mine. "Also—I need you to know something before you hear it from someone else." She took a breath. "I talked to Graham."

My stomach dipped. "I know. He told me."

"Okay. Yeah, so I confronted him," she said, calm and

unapologetic. "Not publicly. Not dramatically." She met my eyes. "I didn't like the way he was circling you. I didn't like the way he spoke about you. And I especially didn't like the way he assumed he still got to have opinions about your life."

"You didn't have to do that."

"I know," she said. "I wanted to. Honestly, I needed to."

Relief washed through me first—warm and unexpected—followed by something sharper that stung behind my eyes. Gratitude, maybe. And the strange, disorienting feeling of being defended without having to ask. I'd spent so long bracing for impact that I'd forgotten what it felt like to have someone step between me and the blow, no questions, no hesitation. I took a careful sip of cider, letting the heat settle, and wondered when I'd started believing I had to handle everything alone.

Piper and Lucy came out of the back door, hands wrapped around her mug. "Okay, yeah. We were listening to you two." Piper said, letting out a guilty laugh. "He reminds me of Dad," she said bluntly. "Not the obvious stuff. The quieter parts. Something about him rubbed me the wrong way whenever I'd see him around town. I knew I didn't like him, but I couldn't put my finger on it until the restaurant opening. He's arrogant. Everything is about him with no regard for anyone else. He doesn't care how what he says and does effects anyone. As long as he gets something out of it, who cares? Right? Just like Dad."

Piper's words sat heavy between us for a moment.

The comparison stung, but it made sense in a way that was hard to admit. I watched the steam curl from my mug, searching for words. "He always expected gratitude for the bare minimum," I said finally, my voice small. "And any boundary I had was an insult to him."

Cara nodded, her expression darkening as she listened, while Piper squeezed my hand in silent support and Lucy smiled softly.

Speaking the truth hit harder than I expected. "But it wasn't just him," I said slowly. "You're right about dad. But, for me, it really started with my mom," I admitted. "I learned really early that my feelings were something to keep tidy. I didn't want to be a burden. I barely even saw Dad at all."

"You'll never be a burden to us," Piper declared. "Never. I want to cry just thinking you feel this way."

"I don't even know what he wants from me now," I admitted, the words spilling out faster once they started. "That's the part that messes with my head. If he wanted me back, he'd say it. If he wanted me gone, he'd stay away. But instead it's this—hovering. Watching. Like he's waiting for me to mess up."

Lucy shifted closer, her voice softer than usual. "Men like that don't always want *you*, Eliza. Sometimes they want control. Or to know they still have access."

I swallowed. "Access to what, though? I don't work for him. I don't belong to him. I barely even talk to him."

Cara exhaled slowly. "You moved on. You're happy. You're visible again. That alone can feel like a threat to someone who's used to deciding the narrative."

Piper nodded. "Especially if he thought coming back to town would make him the hero—the success story. And instead, people are paying attention to *you*. Everybody loves the Coffee Cabin. I mean, the crowd it draws every morning proves it."

"And Nate took over the Pennywhistle," Lucy added. "It was already loved in this town, but now it has Hot Diner Dad running it. Graham probably hates that. Especially now that the two of you are in the Taste-Off together."

The idea settled uncomfortably in my chest. "So what—this is about his ego?"

"With guys like him?" Lucy's mouth curved into a sardonic grin. "It usually is."

"This would explain his issues with Nate." I rubbed my arms against the cold, suddenly tired. "I hate that I still try to figure him out. Like if I can understand his angle, I could protect myself."

Cara reached for my hand. "You don't have to figure him out. You just have to live your life and let us take care of you."

That was when Paige appeared at the edge of the yard, expression sharp with purpose, cheeks pink from the cold, jacket half-zipped as if she'd rushed over here. "Okay," she said, cutting straight through the moment. "I have news, and you're not going to like it—but you're going to feel vindicated."

We all turned to her.

"I talked to the health inspector," she continued. "He was just at the Tavern. He's a gossip; we chat every time he comes in. I didn't even have to try to get him talking. Graham pushed for that inspection at the Pennywhistle. Demanded it, actually. Hoped they'd find something big enough to shut Nate down for a bit."

I went still. My hands curled around the mug. "So I wasn't imagining it."

"No," Paige said gently. "You weren't."

For a moment, no one spoke. Then Piper swore softly. Cara's jaw tightened in a way I recognized—protective, furious, yet contained.

"I'm done letting him make me smaller," I said, surprised by how steady my voice sounded. "I don't care what he wants anymore."

"That's my girl," Paige said.

"Well," I said, forcing a small smile, "before I do anything dramatic or confrontational or life-altering. Can we please go eat? I'm starving, and Grandma's going to get suspicious if we don't join them."

Relief settled in—not because everything was fixed, but because I wasn't alone in it anymore. I knew what I needed to do next. But I didn't have to do it *right this second*.

We drifted back toward the long picnic tables where everyone had gathered—grandma and grandpa bundled in their coats, Paige's daughters shoulder to shoulder, laughing over something on a phone. Piper and Lucy's significant others, Ren and Spencer, were arguing cheerfully about the correct way to toast a bun. Hunter, Paige's ex-best friend and current boyfriend, was flipping hot dogs with the confidence of someone who had done this a thousand times and still enjoyed it. Grandma passed me a paper plate already loaded, as if there'd never been a question of whether I belonged here.

I sat between my sisters, warmth pressed on both sides of me, the fire popping and hissing nearby. Conversation rolled easily—small things, familiar things. Gossip about town. A joke about the Taste-Off. Grandma shooing one of the pugs away from the table with exaggerated sternness. I ate without thinking too hard about it, letting the noise and the laughter do their quiet work, letting myself be held up by the people who loved me even when I didn't quite know how to ask for it.

For the first time in days, my chest didn't feel tight. I felt relief. I felt loved. I felt like I could handle Graham and everything would be okay.

Later, when the fire burned low and the pugs had finally exhausted themselves, Grandma found me by the barn. She didn't ask questions. She just opened her arms.

I went into them like I'd been waiting all night.

"You don't have to be brave all the time," she murmured into my hair. "You just have to be honest. I know you talked to your sisters; I could see the looks on your faces when you were huddled together before dinner. I'm proud of you."

I nodded, throat thick. "I think I'm ready to let—"

"To let us love you?" She smiled, warm and knowing. "To finally believe you belong here?"

"Yeah. That." My answer caught in my throat, fragile and uncertain, but I managed a small laugh. "I think I am," I whispered, letting the words settle between us like a secret invitation. For the first time in ages, the ache inside me didn't feel so heavy; it felt more like hope—raw, tentative. Grandma squeezed me tight, her hands steady and sure, and I let her warmth settle me, just breathing in the quiet balm of her presence.

We stood like that for a while, the barn looming gentle and familiar behind us, dusk tangled in the trees. The world felt softer, just for a moment—a lull between storms, a promise that starting over was possible. I pulled back, wiping my eyes, and gave her a watery smile. "Thank you," I said, meaning every syllable.

"Don't thank me, honey. I love you. We all do."

"I love you. So much."

We held on to each other for another quiet minute, letting the hush between us say what words couldn't. In that embrace, the sharp edges of the past softened, and I realized that letting myself be seen was its own kind of bravery.

When I left to go home, the night felt different— clearer. Colder. Brighter. I walked to my car with my shoulders back, heart pounding not with fear, but resolve.

For the first time in a long while, I wasn't running from anything.

I was choosing myself.

Chapter 31
Eliza

The night air bit at my cheeks as I crossed the backyard toward my car. Above me, the sky was a spill of black velvet, pricked through with stars—bright, sharp, unflinching. The kind of sky that made you feel small in the best way. The kind that dared you to be brave.

In the silence of the car, I caught my own reflection in the window—a face I hardly recognized, determined and open. The radio played low, a soft hum keeping me in the present. Every breath felt like a promise. I would keep showing up, no matter how much my hands trembled. I was done hiding from myself.

The town lay mostly quiet, porch lights glowing soft and amber, streetlamps humming like sentinels there to light my way. I gripped the steering wheel too hard as I turned onto Sycamore Street, the rubber squealing in protest. Then I saw it—across from the library, impossible to miss.

Graham's restaurant blazed against the dark.

All glass and steel and intention. Light poured out of it, sharp, the windows framing diners like an advertisement. It gleamed the way money does—polished, expensive, a little cold. It wanted to be admired. It demanded it.

I parked crooked and didn't fix it. I got out and for a moment, I hovered at the curb, breath frosting in front of me, clutching my keys like a talisman. My feet refused to move, rooted by the weight of possibility and memory. But something stronger carried me forward—a stubborn, quiet certainty that tonight, things would change. My pulse thundered as I crossed the pavement and pulled open the door.

Inside, the foyer smelled like fresh-cut flowers. It was all marble floors, sculptural vases, and blooms arranged to look effortless but clearly costing more than my monthly electric bill. The hostess opened her mouth, took one look at my face, and thought better of it.

I didn't slow. I moved down the hallway with purpose—past the pristine open kitchen, where cooks stiffened when they recognized me; past the glowing wine wall curated to impress people. My boots struck the floor in hard, echoing clicks that announced my presence whether I wanted them to or not.

I wandered through the restaurant's gleaming back hallway, uncertain, searching for his office and hoping my feet would somehow lead me there. I didn't know exactly where it was, but determination propelled me forward, until instinct—or luck—guided me to the right door.

I didn't knock.

Graham shot to his feet as I barged in. "Eliza?"

"Don't," I said, shutting the door behind me with deliberate care. "Don't say my name like that. I'm talking. You're listening."

He hesitated, then sat back in his chair, schooling his expression into calm. Always calm. Always controlled. "This really isn't the time—"

"No," I cut in, stepping forward. "You don't get to decide timing anymore. You're always getting into my space. It's my turn."

His jaw tightened. "What is this about?"

"You know exactly what it's about." I planted my hands on his desk. "The health inspector. The Pennywhistle. You pushed for that inspection. You wanted something—anything—to stick."

His lips curved into a thin smile. "That's a serious accusation."

"You wanted Nate to fail," I said flatly. "Because you hate that people like him."

His eyes flashed. "This isn't about him."

"Oh, it absolutely is." My laugh was sharp, humorless. "You hate that he's loved without trying. That his place feels like home instead of a showroom. That the town didn't fall at your feet the second you walked back in."

"That diner is old," he snapped. "Outdated. People will move on."

"They won't," I said. "And that eats at you."

He stood abruptly. "You're projecting."

"Am I?" I straightened, meeting his gaze. "You came

back here expecting applause. Expecting to be the golden boy returning home. And instead, people are still lining up at the Pennywhistle."

"That man is a distraction," Graham shot back. "And so are you. I don't need this."

Something in me went very still. "You're jealous," I said quietly. "Of Nate."

His mouth twisted. "You think he's some hero? 'Diner Dad'? Please. He's small-town safe. Predictable. You always said you wanted more."

"I wanted respect," I said, my voice rising. "I wanted someone who didn't make me feel like I had to earn affection by being smaller, quieter, better behaved. I wanted to try things. I wanted to talk about my dreams. I wanted—I just wanted love. What's wrong with that?"

"You're emotional," he said coolly. "You always were."

I barked out a laugh. "Do not ever try that again. I'm not emotional—I'm done with dealing with you. What do you call someone who stoops this low out of jealousy and inadequacy? Someone who plots and schemes because he isn't getting the attention or validation he thinks he deserves? *You're* the emotional one in this scenario, and I'm sick of dealing with the fallout from your tantrums."

He folded his arms. "I didn't do anything illegal."

"Illegal isn't the bar," I shot back. "You don't need to break laws to hurt people. You need leverage. Pressure. The same tools you always used."

His eyes narrowed. "Careful."

"No. You be careful." I leaned closer. "You were my

boss. You were older. You made sure I felt chosen, indebted, and lucky. You made sure everything stayed secret because it benefited you. And when I pulled away, you punished me for it."

"You quit," he said. "You ran."

"I survived," I snapped. "And I don't owe you silence to protect your reputation."

For the first time, his composure cracked. "You think this town will side with you?"

"I don't care," I said. "Because I'm not afraid anymore."

He scoffed. "You spiral. You quit when things get hard—like my restaurant, like us, like *me*."

"Maybe I quit some things. You bully when you're losing control," I said. "We all have patterns."

Silence stretched between us, taut and dangerous.

"I don't need to listen to this—"

"If you come near Nate again," I said softly, "if you try to sabotage his business, if you so much as whisper my name with anything but respect—I will end you socially, professionally, and personally. I will make your life so miserable you'll be begging on your knees for me to leave you alone. And if I don't finish the job, my sisters will."

A flicker of unease crossed his face.

"There is room in this town for both of us," I continued. "But only if you shut up, stay in your lane, and leave me alone. You never owned me. You never will."

He looked away, jaw grinding.

"Say it," I demanded. "Say you'll back off."

"I thought," he muttered, "that you'd see the value in keeping things quiet."

"Quiet is how you kept control," I said. "That's over. I never intended to tell the town our history or start gossip. But I am entitled to share my life and my hurts with my family. You have no right to expect me to keep your dirty little secrets."

I turned and walked out, closing the door behind me with a soft, final click.

Outside, the sky stretched wide and fearless above me, stars burning like a promise.

I drew in a deep breath of cold air.

For the first time in years, I didn't feel like prey.

I felt like a woman who had finally discovered who she was—and wasn't willing to forget it.

I didn't drive anywhere fast. I let the town slide slowly past my windows as I headed home, Sycamore Street giving way to darker roads and familiar turns. My hands shook a little on the steering wheel now that the adrenaline had nowhere to go. My chest felt hollow and full at the same time—like I'd finally exhaled after holding my breath for years.

When I got home, the lights were off and the silence wrapped around me like permission to stop being brave for a minute.

Remy greeted me at the door with an indignant meow, tail flicking like he'd been personally offended by my absence. Linguini trailed behind him, blinking sleepily, already demanding a treat. I kicked off my shoes, shrugged out of my coat, and dropped to my knees on the rug, pressing my face into their fur.

"I did it," I whispered, voice cracking. "I really did it."

They purred like they believed in me. They butted their heads against my chin like they were proud of me.

I fed them, washed my hands, and moved through my small space slowly, carefully, like I'd turned into someone else. A woman who could stand up for herself and still be okay. Pride settled in my chest—quiet but all mine. I hadn't folded. I hadn't apologized. I hadn't made myself smaller to keep the peace.

I thought about Nate.

The way his eyes always searched my face. The way his hands were gentle, even when his voice was firm. The way he made space for me without asking me to disappear into it. I pulled my phone from my pocket, thumb hovering over his name.

Should I call him? Tell him everything? Ask him to forgive me for pulling away, for being scared, for not trusting that good things could last?

Or should I let him sleep? Let myself sleep. Show up at the Taste-Off tomorrow—clear-eyed, honest, ready.

My body answered for me before my heart could argue.

I changed into an old sweatshirt and crawled into bed, the sheets cool against my skin. Remy jumped up first, circling twice before settling against my chest like a watchful little guardian. Linguini followed more carefully, kneading the blanket before flopping against my hip with a sigh. I stroked their fur, slow and absentminded, letting the warmth and quiet sink all the way into my bones.

My eyes burned, not from tears this time, but from the deep, bone-heavy exhaustion that comes after you finally stop running. As sleep pulled me under, one thought stayed with me—steady and bright enough to hold onto.

Tomorrow, I would show up at the Taste-Off.

And maybe—if I was very lucky—Nate would be there, ready to meet me where I stood.

Chapter 32
Nate

The morning of the Taste-Off arrived like a sucker punch. I woke up before the sun, nerves tight in my chest, reaching instinctively for my phone on the nightstand.

No messages. No missed calls.

No Eliza.

I didn't blame her for pulling back. I just missed her.

I lay there longer than usual, staring at the ceiling while the house settled around me. The coffee maker clicked on in the kitchen, filling the quiet with a familiar hum, and I took that as my cue to move. I dressed on autopilot—jeans, Pennywhistle hoodie, boots—every motion threaded with the same looping thought. Would she come? Or was this the day I learned how to let her go without answers?

Coffee in hand, I stood at the window for a minute, watching the sky lighten over Honeybrook Hollow. The town was already stirring, as if it knew today was important. I told myself I'd be fine either way. I told myself the Taste-Off was about the food, the diner, and showing up for the community.

I told myself a lot of things that I didn't believe.

Then, I went to wake Tilly.

By the time she was dressed and eating toast at the counter, I was back in motion—focused, practical, steady enough to almost fool myself. I loaded the last of the supplies into the truck—chafing dishes, utensils, the cooler with ingredients I'd triple-checked—when Tilly drifted close, hugging her jacket around herself even though it wasn't cold. She watched me as if she were memorizing the day.

"Good luck, Daddy," she said quietly, like luck worked better if you didn't shout it.

I smiled and crouched in front of her. "Thanks, sweetheart. That means a lot."

She nodded, then tipped her head, studying my face. "Is Eliza still coming to cook with you?"

"I don't know, but I hope so," I said, honestly, because she deserved the truth.

Tilly considered this, then said matter-of-factly, "I hope so, too. I like her. You smile a whole lot when she's around." She paused, then added, as if sealing the argument, "And the spaghetti was better when she helped you cook it. I bet the chicken pot pies will be better if she helps, too."

That hit me right in the chest.

"Hard to argue with that." I ruffled her hair, feeling her faith in me settle something restless inside. "But I'll do my best no matter what, okay?" I said, trying for reas-surance as much for myself as for her.

She grinned and nodded like she believed it was already true. For a brief, calm moment, I let myself imagine Eliza at my side in the booth—her laughter among the clatter, her hands steadying mine when doubts crept in. It made the day feel less daunting, the unknowns a little softer around the edges.

I'd built a whole life around showing up for the people I loved—and right now, I didn't know if she was still going to show up for me. I tried to ignore how much it hurt because I understood where she was coming from.

Before Tilly could respond, my grandparents pulled into the driveway. Grandma climbed out with her familiar brisk warmth, Grandpa already calling Lois's name. She trotted over happily, leash held in her mouth, while Tilly bounced into Grandma's arms.

"We'll meet you there," Grandma said, squeezing my shoulder, her voice gentle but certain. "You focus on cooking. We'll take care of our Tilly. Lois too. No worries, Nate. You got this."

"Focus on kicking that Graham's butt," Grandpa muttered as he hooked Lois to her leash, then handed it to Tilly.

I hugged Tilly, longer than necessary, kissed the top of her head, and watched her take Lois's leash like it was a very important job. As they climbed into the car, she waved at me through the window, all confidence and trust.

I finished loading up my truck, then shut the door,

resting my hands on the steering wheel for a second to let myself breathe before heading toward the park—toward the Taste-Off, the crowd, and the woman I was still quietly hoping would choose to meet me there.

I told myself to keep moving, to focus on the list in my head—tables, burners, the cooler in the back—but the space she left followed me out the door.

Cara had texted earlier, casual on the surface, careful underneath. *I'll be there. I can jump in if she can't.* I appreciated it more than I could say, even as my chest tightened around the word *if*. I didn't want a backup. I wanted Eliza. I wanted her to choose this, to choose us, without feeling like she was walking into a storm. So, I drove toward the park with my jaw set and my heart wide open, quietly hoping she'd be there.

The park looked transformed.

White tents lined the green grass, as if lifted straight out of a movie set with their canvas tops snapping lightly in the breeze. Strings of café lights crisscrossed overhead, already glowing faintly even though the sun was still high, as if the town couldn't help itself—it wanted this to feel special. Booth signs fluttered, chalkboards leaned against table legs, and volunteers dressed in Honeybrook Hollow sweatshirts moved with clipboards and purpose, pointing people where to go, laughing as they did it.

The air smelled like butter and sugar and onions, hitting hot pans. Savory drifting into sweet. Sweet drifting back into savory. The kind of smell that makes you hungry even if your stomach is already tight with nerves.

I parked near the edge of the grass and hauled my supplies from the truck, nodding to familiar faces as I went. People called my name—asked how the Pennywhistle was doing, joked about judges being bribed with extra portions, and wished me luck as if it mattered to them, too. Maybe it did. The Pennywhistle wasn't just my place. It was theirs. I knew when I arrived here that the Pennywhistle belonged to the town as much as to me.

Our booth sat near the center, close enough to the stage that I could see the microphone and the banner stretched behind it in cheerful, charming letters:

Honeybrook Hollow
Taste-Off

Cara was already there, sleeves rolled up, hands on her hips like she was ready to kick Graham's butt just as much as I was. She flashed me a look that said *See? You're not alone.* I smiled back, and we started unpacking, setting out cutting boards, lining up knives, and checking the burners.

I kept glancing up. Toward the paths. Toward the crowd thickening at the edges of the park.

Toward the place where Eliza might appear.

I tried to focus on the tasks at hand—chopping the vegetables, setting up for the roux, the timing that mattered if you wanted everything to come out right. This kind of cooking usually calmed me. Today it didn't. The noise pressed in, the laughter scraped against my nerves, and every second dragged as my eyes kept drifting to the place where Eliza should've been standing. I stood there in the middle of it all—the lights, the noise, the town I'd chosen—and waited, hoping with everything I had left that Eliza would still choose me too.

"Alright," Cara said briskly, stepping in beside me and tying on an apron. "Until she gets here, I'm your emotional support sister-slash-sous-chef. Give me a knife and tell me what to chop, or send me over to Graham's booth..." She flashed me an evil smile.

I huffed a quiet laugh. "I've got this. You don't have to—"

"I know," she cut in gently, already reaching for a carrot to chop. "I want to."

She was already elbow-deep in responsibility, which was impressive considering she'd insisted she was "just moral support." She had a clipboard now. I hadn't given her one. I didn't know where it came from.

"Smile," she said, nudging me with her hip. "You look like you're about to defend a case instead of serve pot pies."

"I used to do that professionally," I muttered.

She grinned. "Relax. People like you. Also, Tilly just told three strangers you're the best cook in the state, so expectations are reasonable."

I glanced toward the crowd instinctively.

No Eliza.

Our table looked good; everything was now in its place, like the Pennywhistle had stretched itself outdoors for the night.

Cara started chopping carrots with efficient confidence. "She'll come," she said softly, not looking at me. "Eliza doesn't miss things that matter. And this matters. I know she'll be here."

I nodded, even though my chest ached with the effort of holding onto that belief.

Across the park, Graham's booth gleamed. It was sleek and polished, all matching signage and curated aesthetics. He'd entered both categories—Sweet and Savory—and his staff moved around him in quiet, synchronized steps. He looked perfectly at ease, like this was exactly the stage he'd expected.

Then the speakers crackled.

"Well, hello, Honeybrook Hollow!" Mabel's voice carried across the park, bright and delighted, and the crowd cheered like she was a celebrity—which, in this town, she absolutely was.

"If everyone could start making their way closer to the stage," Mabel continued, "we're about to begin our annual Taste-Off! Three categories, three chances to argue with your neighbors about food, and absolutely no throwing forks—yes, Joyce, that means you. Get ready! Judges vote for Sweet and Savory, but the crowd picks the overall favorite!"

Applause and laughter rippled through the park.

Cara and I got to work.

I diced onions while she chopped carrots and celery, the rhythm familiar, putting me at ease. Olive oil warmed in the pan. Garlic hit heat and bloomed instantly, the smell wrapping around us like an old song. She nudged the salt toward me.

"You're doing great," she said quietly as she slid chicken into one of the pans.

"What if she doesn't—?"

"She will," Cara said. "I know it."

The Taste-Off buzzed around us—music, laughter, the clink of sample cups and forks. Piper's bakery booth was already swarmed with people watching her work. It was all pink banners and sugar-dusted chaos and Piper doing exactly what she did best. Across the green, Graham's setup gleamed. Crisp linens. Plates arranged like art.

He caught my eye and nodded once. Confident. Assured.

He expected to win.

I turned back to my table, telling myself I didn't care, telling myself I wasn't watching for signs of Eliza every thirty seconds.

The crowd shifted.

A murmur ran through the park, attention tugged toward the entrance. I looked up without meaning to.

Eliza stood right inside the lights.

No apron yet. Coat open. Pretty coral red dress. Boots. Her hair was loose around her shoulders. She was beautiful, and I hoped she was still mine. Our eyes met, and for one suspended second, everything else fell away—the noise, the booths, the competition.

She walked straight toward me.

"I'm here," she said, breathless, stepping into my space. "I'm so sorry I'm late."

I didn't answer. I just pulled her gently aside and into my arms.

"You okay?" I asked quietly, searching her face.

Her eyes shone. "I will be. If you can forgive me."

"There's nothing to forgive," I answered immediately.

Her breath caught—not sharp, not panicked. Relieved. Like something heavy had finally been set down.

"Nate," she whispered.

I leaned in, slow enough to give her time to pull away, close enough that she could feel the choice in it.

She didn't hesitate.

Her hands fisted lightly in the front of my apron as my mouth met hers—soft at first, familiar and careful, like we were both making sure this was real. Then she kissed me back, deeper this time, surer, and the noise of the park faded into nothing.

The cheers, the music, the clatter of dishes—all of it disappeared until there was only her, warm and steady, and finally in my arms.

When we pulled apart, her forehead rested against my chest, her smile small and certain.

"Okay," she said quietly. "Now I'm ready."

I smiled, thumb brushing her jaw.

"I'm not."

She barely had time to look up before I leaned in again—no hesitation this time, no careful pause. I kissed her again like a decision had already been made, and we were just living inside it now.

Her hands slid into my hair, and she laughed softly

against my mouth, the sound warm and full. The park might as well have vanished. The booths, the lights, the crowd—all of it faded until there was only this. Us. Right where we were supposed to be.

When I pulled back, just barely, I bent low and rested my forehead against hers.

"Now," I murmured, "I am."

Her breath was uneven, forehead resting against mine. She shook her head, lips trembling. "We'll talk about everything later?"

"Later," I agreed, brushing my nose against hers. "After this."

Her shoulders relaxed as if she'd been holding herself rigid. She nodded once, steady on her feet now, then turned back toward the booth.

And just like that, we were in it. Together.

Cara appeared at Eliza's shoulder, her eyes bright, a knowing smile on her face. "You've got this," she said softly. "Both of you." She squeezed Eliza's arm, gave me a quick nod, then slipped away into the crowd. "I'm going to find Grandma before she starts telling strangers our life stories."

Cooking with Eliza felt like exhaling. Like my lungs finally remembered what they were for. She took over the pastry without asking, and I handed her the rolling pin. She smiled at me—small, happy, beautiful—and something warm settled deep in my chest. We moved around each other easily, hands brushing, bodies learning the space, the rhythm of us finding our way back.

I glanced up once and caught Graham watching from

across the park. Our eyes met. For a second, his jaw tightened, a scowl cutting across his face—then he looked away, sharp and bitter, as if he couldn't stand to see us together.

I didn't care. He had no power over her anymore.

All I saw was Eliza, right where she belonged—beside me. That's all that mattered.

We slid the mini pot pies into the ovens together, careful and synchronized, as if we'd been doing this for years instead of minutes. Little white ramekins lined up in rows, each filled with golden chicken, soft vegetables, and gravy rich enough to make you believe a meal could change your life. Eliza had brushed the pastry lids with egg wash, her movements precise and confident, her focus settling into that calm, capable place I loved seeing her in. The ovens hummed to life, heat blooming around us, the air already smelling of butter, thyme, and comfort.

When the first batch came out, the crusts were puffed and bronzed, their edges flaking just enough to make a mess of the parchment. Steam curled up as we cracked them open, releasing that deep, savory scent that made people slow as they passed. Heads turned. A small line formed without anyone announcing it.

Judges came through first, clipboards tucked under their arms, trying to look neutral and failing. Eliza set the ramekins down with quiet pride, explaining the dish without overselling it—classic, cozy, simple. One judge closed his eyes after the first bite. Another nodded, scribbling quickly. A third went back for a second forkful, as if she hadn't meant to, but couldn't help herself.

Then came everyone else. Locals, kids on tiptoe, couples sharing bites, someone murmuring, *"This tastes like Sunday dinner when I was a kid..."* Eliza caught my eye then, her mouth curving into a soft, stunned smile, as if she couldn't quite believe what she was seeing—or that she'd let herself hope for it.

I watched her glow in the middle of it all, steady hands, bright eyes, finally taking up the space she deserved. And as tray after tray emptied and the line kept growing, I knew—no matter how the votes shook out— we'd already won something important.

The afternoon thickened with anticipation. Judges moved from booth to booth, clipboards tucked to their chests. Volunteers refilled water pitchers and reminded people how to vote. The air carried layers of scent—warm pastry, sugar, roasting meat—until the whole park felt wrapped in comfort. Eliza brushed her hands together and leaned in close enough that her shoulder bumped mine, grounding me. I smiled down at her, and she smiled back, nervous and brave all at once.

A swell of cheers rolled across the park, and Cara appeared at our booth, grinning, a small paper tray in her hands. "You have to try this," she said, already laughing. "Piper went full overachiever."

Eliza took the cupcake first—vanilla bean cake, impossibly light, filled with spiced pear compote and topped with a swirl of browned-butter cream cheese frosting and a delicate shard of caramel. She froze mid-bite. "Oh," she said softly. "She absolutely murdered this."

"Right?" Cara said. "There's edible gold leaf on top. Gold leaf. I watched someone whisper to it before eating."

Another cheer went up near the stage, louder this time, and when Mabel announced Piper as the Sweet category winner, the park erupted. Eliza clapped hard, laughing, pride lighting her from the inside out. "Of course, she won," she said, like the result had been inevitable all along. "She can't help herself."

I spotted my grandparents near the edge of the crowd —Grandpa nodding like he knew we were going to win, Grandma already dabbing at her eyes as she waved at me. Tilly bounced between them, while Lois sat at their feet, tail thumping, clearly convinced a pot pie was within reach.

Eliza's fingers slid into mine then, tentative but sure. I squeezed back, my chest tight with feeling, with hope, with her.

When the announcement for Savory came, I barely processed it at first.

"Savory Category Winner *and* the Crowd Favorite— Pennywhistle Pantry!"

Eliza gasped. I pulled her into me without thinking, her laugh muffled against my chest. She looked up at me, eyes bright and disbelieving.

"We did it," she whispered.

"No," I said softly. "You did. You being here with me made all the difference."

For a second, everything went fuzzy. Applause blurred into sound without edges, and then Tilly was there—sprinting across the grass with zero regard for personal space or dignity, her curls flying, her sneakers flashing.

"We WON!" she shouted, slamming into Eliza's legs and wrapping her arms around her like this outcome had been inevitable. "I *told* you the pot pies would be better when you cooked together!"

Eliza laughed, the sound breaking loose and bright, and dropped to her knees to hug her back. "You did, huh?"

Tilly nodded fiercely. "And you make my dad happy," she added, as if that settled the matter entirely.

I felt my throat close around something big and unmanageable as Eliza pressed a kiss into Tilly's hair and whispered, "He makes me happy, too. And so do you."

Behind her, Grandma clapped her hands together, eyes shining. Grandpa whistled—loud, unapologetic—and Lois circled us like a furry victory parade, tail wagging so hard her whole body got involved.

"That's your diner," Grandpa said proudly, gripping my shoulder. "And *that's* how you do it. Proud of you, Nate. So proud."

Grandma hugged Eliza next, long and tight. "I knew you had it in you," she murmured. "Both of you."

Then the crowd shifted again, and suddenly Eliza's sisters were there—Piper first, already reaching for Eliza like she'd been holding this hug in all day. Paige followed close behind, fierce and glowing, Lucy beaming like she'd just witnessed the ending of her favorite book, Cara quiet but grinning from ear to ear, eyes soft and knowing.

"You did it," Piper said, voice thick with pride. "I knew you would."

Paige smirked at me. "Not bad, Diner Dad."

Lucy squeezed Eliza's hands. "That was magic."

Cara met Eliza's eyes and nodded once, like this was exactly the version of her she'd always believed in.

I stood there, surrounded by family—hers, mine, the kind you choose and the kind that shows up anyway—and realized something settled and certain in my chest.

This wasn't just a win.

This was us, exactly where we were meant to be.

I caught sight of Graham.

He stood at the edge of the park near his booth, jaw tight, hands shoved into his pockets. No entourage. No audience. Just a man watching something he thought he owned slip completely out of his reach. A few minutes later, he turned and walked away—quietly, unnoticed, already irrelevant.

I didn't watch him go.

All I saw was Eliza—smiling, radiant, leaning into my side like that was where she'd always been meant to stand.

As the crowd slowly dispersed, the park settled back into itself—string lights shimmering in the dusk, volunteers stacking trays, laughter softening into the hum of a good day ending. Her head tipped against my shoulder.

"We should probably... I don't know. Clean up?" she said after a beat, nodding toward the ribbon still draped over our booth.

"Eventually," I said. "I'm enjoying this part."

She smiled up at me, slow and sure. "Me too."

Tilly took my hand on one side and Eliza's on the other, swinging between us as we walked back toward my grandparents. Lois padded along behind, content and watchful. It felt—completely, beautifully—like a picture someone might frame. Or a memory I'd reach for years from now and feel in my chest.

Eliza squeezed my fingers. The night didn't need fireworks or speeches or promises said out loud. It had already given us proof of what happens when you stop letting fear make your decisions.

She leaned closer, her voice barely there. "I love you," she whispered, like it was something sacred.

The words landed deep—quiet and absolute. I bent my head until my forehead brushed hers.

"I love you too," I murmured back. "Always."

As we left the park together, I glanced back once.

The booth lights were going dark. The space Graham had taken up was empty. Whatever power he'd thought he had here was gone, dissolved into the night like it had never mattered.

Ahead of us was the cleanup, the drive home, and plans. Plans for the evening, tomorrow, and into the future. And Eliza—right beside me, exactly where she belonged. I closed my hand around hers and didn't let go.

Chapter 33
Eliza

The last box slid into the truck bed with a soft thump, and I turned to find Nate already watching me. His smile was soft—the kind that didn't need a punchline to feel like joy. My heart was still racing from the win, the music, the laughing, the way Tilly had bounced in place when our names were called. I couldn't stop smiling even if I wanted to.

We'd cleaned our booth in record time, thanks to my sisters, both sets of grandparents hovering nearby to help, and Piper's efficient, mildly bossy energy as she darted back and forth between our booth and hers. The glow from the stage lights still shimmered across the park lawn, catching the strands of lights in the trees and the delicate glitter of night as it began to settle in.

Lois wagged her tail at the truck, already curled into her spot in the backseat like she was waiting for us to get our act together.

"You ready?" Nate asked, brushing his hands on his

jeans as he looked between me and the truck like we were his two favorite things.

I nodded, feeling the weight of the night settle around my shoulders—but not in a heavy way. More like a blanket, soft and certain.

Tilly climbed into the back with Lois, chattering about the votes and how she'd told her grandma they were totally going to win. "And then Lucy brought Larry the llama, and I think he voted too, even though llamas probably like to eat grass more than pot pie," she said as she buckled in, petting Lois behind the ears.

We pulled away from the park, the warm murmur of the crowd trailing behind us. Outside the window, Honeybrook Hollow glowed like a dream.

I exhaled. "This town, man. It's ridiculous how perfect it looks tonight."

"It does that on purpose," Nate said, glancing at me. "Wants you to fall in love with it."

"I already did," I murmured. "A long time ago."

His eyes softened. "Me too."

Tilly leaned forward between the seats. "Hey. Are we celebrating at our house? Like with games, or a movie? Can Lois pick the movie again? She liked the one with the talking animals."

I laughed. "She fell asleep ten minutes in."

"She was *thinking*," Tilly insisted.

Nate chuckled, then turned down the radio and tapped the steering wheel gently.

"Actually, sweetheart," he said. "We wanted to tell you something."

She perked up, immediately suspicious and interested. "What is it?"

Nate looked at me. I nodded, heart pounding for reasons that had nothing to do with pot pies and small-town cooking competitions.

"We love each other," Nate said simply. "Eliza and me. We're together now."

Tilly's eyes went wide and shiny. "For *real?*"

I swallowed. "For real. Only if that's okay with you."

She let out a delighted squeal and reached forward to hug me over the seat. "You're like boyfriend and girlfriend now, right? Like, you'll come over and make spaghetti again and smell like coffee and hug Lois and—"

"Yes," I said, tears slipping down before I could stop them. "If you want me to."

"I *do,*" she whispered, beaming. "*This* is the sparkliest day ever, Daddy!"

My heart cracked wide open.

Nate reached over and took my hand.

Nate's house glowed softly when we pulled into the driveway—porch light on, windows golden, as if it had been waiting for us to come home.

Lois bounded inside ahead of us, flopped immediately onto her dog bed, and gave a satisfied snort. Tilly ran to change into pajamas and came back out holding a blanket, dragging it behind her like a cape.

"Can we do pancakes in the morning?" she asked sleepily.

"You bet," Nate said, lifting her into a hug. "With

chocolate chips and whipped cream and maybe a few sprinkles for winning."

"Even though I didn't cook?"

"You were our mascot," I said. "You get pancakes forever."

She gave a happy sigh and kissed Nate on the cheek, then did the same to me. "I'm really glad you're here," she whispered.

"I am too," I whispered back.

Later, when she was tucked into bed and the house was quiet, Nate and I curled up on the couch. The quilt was wrapped around us, Lois snoring softly nearby, and the soft rhythm of the night hummed in the background—crickets, trees shifting in the breeze, the breath of something steady and safe.

"I've never felt this," I said finally. "Not ever."

Nate brushed his thumb over my knuckles. "Me either."

"It doesn't feel like falling," I whispered. "It feels like standing still for the first time."

His smile curved into something that felt like forever.

And in that quiet, full moment, I let myself believe it.

Chapter 34
Nate

Three months later

The stars came out early, soft and steady over Honeybrook Hollow like they were waiting for us.

I parked the truck on the hilltop that overlooked the town, a place Tilly called the "twinkle spot" when she came with me once to watch the fireworks in July. Eliza had never seen it. It felt right to do this here—something just for us.

The bed of the truck was packed with every blanket I owned, a mess of quilts and pillows that probably looked like a fort or a sleepover gone rogue.

Tilly and Lois were headed to the Honeybrook Inn for a giant sleepover with Eliza's sisters, Paige's daughters, my grandmother, and theirs. Mabel was calling it a welcome-to-the-family party. We were also invited to the next weenie roast, and I couldn't wait to see what that was all about.

Graham's restaurant was still hanging on, though it was not the smashing success he'd been expecting. From what I heard, he'd lowered his prices, increased his serving sizes, and dialed down his pretentious bull crap in an attempt to fit back into town. The jury was still out on how long he'd last.

The Pennywhistle, on the other hand, was thriving. Friday nights had become something of an event, thanks to a rotating series of specials Eliza planned and cooked herself—comfort-forward, thoughtful dishes that felt like they belonged to this town. People came in asking for *her* food by name, lingering longer, laughing louder, treating the place like exactly what it was meant to be.

The Coffee Cabin was flourishing too. Eliza had expanded the space and added a real kitchen, turning it into more than just a stop for coffee. Her breakfast menu had Honeybrook Hollow lining up early, eager for whatever she was creating that day. Watching her step fully into that role—confident, capable, joyful—felt like witnessing something bloom right in front of all of us.

Back to the moment at hand...

The town sparkled from the stars above and the town below—string lights at The Honeybrook Inn, the soft glow from the Coffee Cabin, the quiet flicker of porches and streetlamps.

She turned to me as we lay back on the pile of blankets, her head on my chest, our fingers tangled between us. "This is amazing," she whispered.

I kissed the top of her head. "Thought it was time you saw where I go when I need to breathe."

"I love it here," she said quietly. "I love you."

God, I would never get used to the way those words landed in my chest.

"I love you too." I sat up a little, shifted to reach behind me, my heart thudding. I'd carried the ring in my coat pocket for weeks, waiting for the right night, the right breath, the right stars. "Eliza."

She sat up too, her dark eyes blinking, her hair a little wild from the wind.

"I built a life here hoping I'd find someone who felt like home." My voice shook, but I didn't care. "Then I met you and realized I didn't have to keep looking."

She stared at me, already teary. "Nate..."

I pulled out the ring box and flipped it open. The band was simple and elegant—rose gold with a bezel-set diamond and *"Meant for you"* engraved inside.

"Yes," she whispered as she read the words on the band. The sound breaking me wide open.

"I want forever," I said. "I want all your moods and your mornings and your coffee and your fire. I want you with Tilly and Lois, your cats, spaghetti, late nights, and everything in between. I don't care about anything else. Just you."

She was crying, laughing and crying.

I cupped her cheek, my thumb sweeping under her eye. "Will you marry me, Eliza? No more waiting. No more almost. I want forever with you."

Her breath hitched. Tears spilled, bright and beautiful. "Yes," she whispered, like she was afraid the word might break if she said it too loud. Then she smiled, radiant and sure. "Yes. God, yes."

I pulled the ring from the box with shaking fingers and slid it onto her finger. It fit like it had been waiting for her all along.

She stared at it, then at me, and made this soft, broken sound that wrecked me.

I kissed her then—slow at first, like I was savoring the truth of it, the taste of her, the feel of her hands fisting in my jacket. Then deeper, harder, like every second we'd held back was finally catching up with us. She climbed into my lap, curling against me, and I held her there like I might never let go.

We laughed breathlessly between kisses, foreheads pressed together, noses brushing, the cold night forgotten as warmth built between us. Blankets shifted, the truck bed creaked softly, and the world narrowed to the two of us and the stars burning bright overhead.

And there, wrapped in blankets and moonlight and the steady beat of each other's hearts, we loved each other —slow, reverent, aching with all the feeling we'd been carrying. The kind of love that isn't just heat, but home. The kind that says stay.

When we finally lay tangled together, breath evening out, she rested her hand—ring gleaming—over my heart.

"You're my home," she whispered.

I kissed her hair, her temple, her mouth, over and over, like I couldn't get enough. "And you're mine. Always."

Above us, the stars kept watch. Around us, the night held still.

And I knew, without a doubt, I'd never stop loving her. Love doesn't always come easy. But when it's meant for you, it finds you. And it never lets go.

Epilogue

Nate

If there's one thing I've learned since taking over the Pennywhistle Pantry, it's that nothing truly important in this town happens without two things: coffee and meddling grandmothers.

I was wiping down the front counter after the lunch rush—Nancy had already kicked me out of the kitchen for helping—when the bell over the door chimed, and Grandma walked in with Mabel at her side, both of them bundled in scarves and looking far too pleased with themselves.

That was my first clue.

They slid into a booth like they owned it. Which, to be fair, as Honeybrook Hollow royalty, they sort of did.

"Time for lunch," Grandma announced. "We're starving."

Nancy appeared like she'd been summoned by destiny. "The usual?"

"Yes, please," Mabel answered.

I poured coffee and brought it over, setting the mugs down carefully. "So," I said, already suspicious. "What's the occasion?"

They exchanged a look. A long one.

The kind that should come with a warning label.

"Well," Mabel said, stirring cream into her coffee, "we thought it might be time for a little confession. Eliza knows some, you do too. But it's time to lay it all out there."

My shoulders tensed. "I don't like the sound of that."

"Oh, hush," Grandma said. "You love a good story."

"Actually, I do not," I said flatly. "This one feels like it's going to be a big one."

Mabel leaned forward, eyes sparkling. "Do you remember, Nate, how you *just happened* to come through the Coffee Cabin every morning when you moved to town?"

"Yes," I said slowly. "I remember falling in love with Eliza over a takeout cup and an outdoor counter."

"And do you remember," Grandma added, "how Eliza *just happened* to be working those mornings all by herself?"

"I made sure she was alone," Mabel said. "And I very graciously kept myself out of the way. Which, for the record, was not easy."

My stomach dropped as I stared at them. "You didn't."

They both smiled.

They actually *smiled* and they were smug.

"I may have told her I had a little cold," Mabel said smugly. "I needed my rest, isn't that right?"

"Absolutely, you did." Grandma winked. "And let's not forget about the cocoa," she added. "I told Tilly to ask for it. Told her it was the best cocoa in the entire world, and it was made by the prettiest Christmas coffee elf who ever lived. Children can be very persuasive when given the right motivation."

"You used my kid," I said, horrified.

"She was delighted to help," Grandma said proudly. "She loves Eliza, just like I knew she would."

"I love Eliza," Mabel said. "Very much. And she needed someone good. Someone kind. Someone who would make her feel like she deserves to feel."

"And you," Grandma said, softening, "needed someone who would choose you, *and* Tilly. We knew the two of you were perfect for each other."

I opened my mouth. Closed it again.

"You're unbelievable," I said finally.

"And yet," Mabel said, lifting her mug, "here you are, happy as you could possibly be..."

Before I could respond, the bell over the door chimed again.

I didn't have to turn around to know it was her.

But I did anyway.

Eliza stood just inside the diner, sunlight catching in her hair, one hand tucked into the pocket of my jacket—

my jacket. I loved seeing her in things that were mine. I just loved her.

She smiled when she saw me, that easy, knowing smile that still knocked the breath out of me. "There you are," she said. "I was looking for my fiancé."

My heart did the thing it always did now—stumbled, then settled.

"Fiancé," Grandma repeated brightly. "Don't you love the sound of that?"

Yes, in fact, I did.

Eliza slid into the booth beside Mabel, leaning in to kiss her cheek. "What are you two up to?"

"Confessing," I muttered as I slid in across from her.

Her eyebrows shot up. "Oh no."

Mabel patted her hand. "We were just explaining how very patient we were with the two of you."

Eliza looked between them, then at me. "Patient?"

I sighed. "They orchestrated our entire meeting."

She blinked once in shock. Then she laughed. Really laughed—head tipping back, hand coming to rest on my arm.

"Oh, I know they did," she said. "I knew you didn't just accidentally show up every morning like a lost little puppy."

"I resent that," I said. "Dogs are very dignified."

She grinned at me. "You absolutely are not."

Grandma beamed. "See? Perfect match."

Eliza squeezed my hand under the table. "Well," she said, eyes warm, "I guess I should thank you both."

"We accept baked goods," Mabel said immediately.

"And now that you're cooking again, something fancy will do."

"And wedding invitations," Grandma added. "Front row."

"Deal," Eliza said.

I looked at her—really looked at her—here in the diner that had raised me, surrounded by the women who'd loved us into being brave enough to choose each other.

"Worth it," I said quietly. "All of it."

Eliza smiled at me like she knew exactly what I meant and agreed wholeheartedly.

And for once, Honeybrook Hollow had nothing left to add. It had already given us everything.

Yours to Keep
Cara

Paper & Pine was quiet in that late-afternoon way I loved —sunlight slanting through the front windows, the scent of tea and shortbread lingering in the air. Eliza sat at the small table near the front, one ankle tucked under her chair, stirring her tea like she wasn't thinking about anything at all. She had a soft, settled look about her now, and I found myself smiling at it—quietly glad she was happy.

I was behind the counter when *he* walked past the window.

He was on his phone, head tipped slightly as he listened, and then he laughed—low and easy, the kind that carried even through the glass. It was gone almost as soon as it came, swallowed by the street, but it landed anyway. Right in the center of my chest, like it used to. Familiar, even though everything about our lives had changed.

He didn't slow. Didn't look in. He just kept walking down Sycamore Street with that unbothered confidence he carried everywhere—including behind the bar at the Twilight Tavern. I told myself it didn't matter, that I only noticed him because he was familiar.

Except my hand stilled on the counter anyway. I didn't look away until he was completely out of sight.

Eliza didn't follow my gaze right away. She noticed me noticing. Then she turned, eyes flicking to the window just in time to catch Jasper's reflection disappearing from the glass.

She lifted a brow. "Huh."

I looked back at her. "What?"

"Paige's bartender," she said mildly. "You watched him walk down the street like you were afraid he might vanish. In fact, you watch him *every* time we're in the bar the exact same way, don't you?"

I opened my mouth to deny it.

Closed it again.

Heat crept up my neck, equal parts annoyance and something else I knew I was in total denial of and would absolutely *not* be talking about.

"He's around a lot," I said. "You know, in town. No big deal."

"Mmhm," Eliza murmured, deeply unconvinced. She took another sip of tea. "If you say so."

Jasper was already gone, the street outside empty again. Still, that laugh lingered in my head, warm and unexpected, and my pulse took its time settling—as if I had heard something I wasn't ready to forget.

Eliza smiled into her mug.

That smile said she'd seen everything.

And worse—she was going to remember.

Yours to Keep is coming July 14th!

About the Author

Nora Everly is a lifelong bookworm. She started reading the good stuff once she grew tall enough to sneak the romance novels off the top of her mother's bookshelf and it has been non-stop ever since.
Once upon a time she was a substitute teacher and an educational assistant. Now she's a writer and stay at home mom to two small humans and one fat cat.
Nora lives in the Pacific Northwest with her family and her overactive imagination.

Find her at noraeverly.com

Also by Nora Everly

The Sweetbriar Mountain Series:

In My Heart

Heart Words

From the Heart

Heart to Heart

Change of Heart

Cross Your Heart

Sweetbriar Holiday Stories:

Holiday Hearts

Conversation Hearts

Honeybrook Hollow:

Next to You

Make You Mine

By Your Side

Meant for You

Yours to Keep

The Cozy Creek Collection:

Fall at Once

Autumn Grove

Once We Fall

Fall for Me

Oh Brother!

Crime and Periodicals

Carpentry and Cocktails

Hotshot and Hospitality

Architecture and Artistry

Teachers' Lounge

Passing Notes

Star Crossed Lovers:

(*As Piper Everly, co-written with Piper Sheldon*):

<u>Midnight Clear</u>

Get exclusive sneak peeks of upcoming releases through Nora's newsletter and Facebook group, The Everly Afters.

www.ingramcontent.com/pod-product-compliance
Lightning Source LLC
Chambersburg PA
CBHW011845300726
48970CB00009B/2657